ERIC AND THE TWINS

by

PETER JAMES CHILD

Benbow Publications

Copyright 2013 by Peter James Child

Peter James Child has asserted his right under the Copyright, Designs and Patents Act, 1988 to be identified as the author of this book.

All rights reserved. No part of this publication may be reproduced, stored in a retrieval system, or transmitted in any form or by any means, electronic, mechanical photocopying, recording or otherwise without the prior permission of the copyright holder.

Published in 2013 by Benbow Publications

British Library
Cataloguing in Publication Data.

ISBN : 978-1-908760-03-6

Printed by Lightning Source UK Ltd
Chapter House, Pitfield
Kiln Farm
Milton Keynes
MK11 3LW

First Edition

OTHER TITLES BY THE AUTHOR

ERIC THE ROMANTIC
ERIC AND THE DIVORCEE

THE MICHEL RONAY SERIES

MARSEILLE TAXI
AUGUST IN GRAMBOIS
CHRISTMAS IN MARSEILLE
CATASTROPHE IN LE TOUQUET
RETURN TO MARSEILLE

THE INSPECTOR HADLEY SERIES

THE TAVISTOCK SQUARE MURDERS
THE GOLD BULLION MURDERS
THE TOWER OF LONDON MURDERS
THE AMERICAN MURDERS
THE DIAMOND MURDERS
THE ROYAL RUSSIAN MURDERS
THE SATAN MURDERS
THE MEDICAL MURDERS
THE WESTMINSTER MURDERS
THE GIGOLO MURDERS
THE HOLY GRAIL MURDERS
THE DIPLOMAT MURDERS
THE MACABRE MURDERS

NON FICTION

NOTES FOR GOOD DRIVERS
NOTES FOR COMPANY DRIVERS
VEHICLE PAINTER'S NOTES
VEHICLE FINE FINISHING
VEHICLE FABRICATIONS IN GRP

ACKNOWLEDGEMENTS

Once again I wish to acknowledge all the help and assistance given to me by Sue Gresham, who edited the book, and to thank Wendy Tobitt for yet another splendid cover presentation. Without these patient and very talented ladies this book would not have been possible and I owe them a great deal.

Peter James Child.

INTRODUCTION

The birth of twins is always a double blessing... provided that they remain close as they grow up, but problems can arise when sibling rivalry turns into hate. Fortunately the appearance of a handsome stranger guides Kate and Samantha to a new understanding despite many problems that they encounter due to their behaviour towards one another. However, the stranger becomes a source of rivalry as they both fall in love with him and unfortunately he is unable to reciprocate as he is on a mission to guide them to happiness...

Characters and events portrayed in this book are fictional.

CHAPTER 1

ONCE I STARTED HATING HER... I JUST COULDN'T STOP!

Well, it is all dear Mother's bloody silly fault! As far back as I can remember it was always Samantha this and Samantha that... never Kate... poor old me... and Dad was next to useless when it came to backing me up. I guess when we were young he was scared of upsetting Mother, then having to suffer one of her tantrums... but, he made up for it when we were seventeen. After meeting Sophie, a new secretary at his office, he suddenly left home, walking out one wet Friday night and moving in with her. They were married after an acrimonious divorce from dear Mother, she was so angry and would you believe, she still goes on about it six years later?

I like Sophie because she's easy to get along with and is a real laugh when out shopping... retail therapy or bagging the bargains as she calls it. She spends as much as she can on all her plastic... right up to the limit on every card, or the 'hilt'... she says she always likes things right up to the hilt. She's a bit of a sex bomb and still dresses fashionably young, I think that is why Dad went off with her soon after they met. It was no surprise to me, although it came as a shock to dear Mother and Samantha. I realised that their marriage had gone stale, as so many do, they hardly talked between tantrums and I never thought Mother was very interested in 'erotic activity' or 'horizontal line dancing' as Sophie calls it.

Men can be relied on to keep to a wife provided she gives him what he wants most of the time... no headaches or other excuses for not pandering to his demands, or every peculiar sexual fantasy... schoolgirls in short skirts and nurses in even shorter white uniforms, with stockings and suspenders... you know exactly what I mean! While I am sure that all well adjusted women only really want a romantic candlelit dinner with a handsome, interesting and mature man who listens... and preferably has money.

However, I think I am getting ahead of myself and should

explain. Samantha is my twin sister, just ten minutes older than me and she has always been Mother's favourite. It is hard for me to say when I first became aware of my desperate hateful feelings towards Samantha but I guess it all really came to a head with David Butler and I can remember everything as if it were yesterday. After several boyfriends, who were spotty and groped incessantly, David was a refreshing change. I met him when I was nineteen after I had just passed my driving test. He was the young car salesman at Bracknell Motors where I bought my first little car, a Fiesta… well, actually, Dad bought it for me. I was very happy and could not stop talking about my car to anyone who listened. Mother was vaguely interested but Samantha was positively bored, she had passed her test and bought a car six months previously with a deposit from Mother, which was supposed to be a loan, but I had my doubts if she ever paid it back.

My best friend Emma, who is in sales and marketing at Delacor Paints where we both work, was very pleased for me. I told Roger, who is a lab assistant with me in vehicle finishes, and he said his sister bought a Fiesta and it was always breaking down… something to do with the electrics… he was such a miserable plonker!

David phoned me on the Wednesday evening following my collection of the car and asked if everything was alright with the Fiesta. I said it was, so far, then he asked if he could pop round and just check the owner's service book, which I knew was just an excuse to see me. I said 'yes' of course and he arrived about half an hour later. I watched him drive up and after he rang the bell I hurried to open the door. Mother asked who it was, so I told her and noticed that Samantha pricked up her ears and put down the latest celebrity 'goss' magazine she was reading. David was all smiles and said he hoped hadn't disturbed me, so I just smiled back and said 'no'… thinking, 'you can disturb me any time you like, baby blue eyes.' We went out to the car and he fumbled in the glove compartment for the service book and after glancing through it he said, 'the next service is due at seventy thousand miles, Miss Harris.'

'Is it really?' I asked in what I hoped was an interested tone.

'Yes... and I should have told you that when you collected the car.'

'Oh dear.'

'I am sorry.'

'Never mind... but now you've told me, I'll make certain I book it in for a service when it gets close to seventy thousand.'

'Yes, please do, Miss Harris... because I wouldn't want you to break down or anything.'

'Neither would I... especially at night.'

'No... of course not.'

'So was there anything else you wanted to talk to me about?' I asked while giving him a short flutter of my eyelashes as I gazed up into his face. He hesitated for a moment and I thought, 'well go on then... ask me out.'

He blushed slightly and half whispered, 'I know this is a bit sudden... but I was wondering if you'd like to come out for a drink or something... whenever you're free that is.'

'Yes... why not?' I replied as I fluttered the eyelashes again and his face beamed.

'Oh, that's fantastic... how about this Friday?'

'Yes.'

'Great... I'll pick you up at eight... is that OK?'

'Yes it is,' I replied as Samantha walked out of the house and poked her nose in.

'Is there something wrong with your car already?' she asked... as if she cared.

'No... its fine, thanks.'

She glanced at me and said in her 'knowing' tone, 'well I just wondered, Kate... old second hand cars do have problems you know.'

Before I could say anything, she looked at David and said, 'I bought a Volkswagen Golf recently... I think they're so reliable... don't you?'

'Yes, I'm sure they are,' he replied.

'This is my twin sister, Samantha.'

David nodded and said, 'I can see that... you're identical...except for the colour of your hair.'

'Kate dyes hers.'

I ignored her catty remark about my Sun kissed blonde highlights and said, 'so, David, I'll see you on Friday then.'

'Yes… yes, I'll be here at eight.'

'Bye then.'

'Bye,' he smiled, turned away and walked down the path to his car. As he drove away I gave him a little wave and Samantha said, 'well, he looks more than a bit dishy for a car salesman.'

'Yes, he does,' I replied before I went back into the house. Samantha caught me up and as she closed the front door, said, 'well now… aren't you the lucky one?'

'It makes a nice change,' I replied before I went into the lounge and slumped down on the settee.

'What does?' asked Mother as she turned away from the television and glanced at me.

'Kate has got herself a date with the salesman who sold her the Fiesta,' said Samantha.

'Oh, really, that's nice,' said dear Mother in a disinterested tone before she resumed watching the television.

I sighed and thought, 'no change there then.'

I told Emma about my date with David the next day and she was excited as I was. The poor girl had just been dumped by some twit who was never really interested in a long term commitment. She asked me to find out if David had a brother or good friend so we could perhaps make up a foursome. Emma is always optimistic and full of hope… that's why I like her so much. I promised I would call her on Saturday morning and let her know how it all went… and if David had a suitable brother or friend.

I hurried back from work on the Friday and went immediately into fast shower and make up mode. I was uncertain what to wear but after slipping on my frilly undies and 'push up bra'(I thought David should see everything available… and I did have quite nice, firm boobs back in those days), I chose my little black dress.

David arrived dead on eight and after a casual call to Mother from the hall, 'bye… don't wait up!' I swept out of the house. There was a reply which I vaguely heard, but it was little more than a grunt, 'bye.'

David was all smiles, said 'hello,' and opened the door for me so I could slip into his Mondeo. We drove towards Ascot and he stopped at the Two Brewers pub just outside the town.

'Is this your local?' I asked.

'Yes... I hope you like it.'

'I'm sure I will,' I replied and I did.

David found a table in the corner of the busy pub and bought me a Bacardi and Coke while he had just a half of Lager. We sat and talked for some time and I found him interesting, charming and very amusing. I do like people who make me laugh and he did with his comments about life in general and awkward customers in particular. When I told him I worked in the vehicle paint lab at Delacor, he was impressed.

'Then you'll know more about cars than I do,' he said with a smile. 'Now, let me get you another drink and you can tell me all about yourself,' he said. I nodded, smiled as he stood up and thought, 'I do like to be waited on and listened to by a charming man... instead of being constantly 'groped'... what a refreshing change!'

As we sipped our drinks, I told him all about my work and when I mentioned Emma and her recent unhappy 'dumping' he smiled and said, 'it's just happened to my cousin, Alan, he was engaged but she broke it off about a month ago... he's been feeling sorry for himself so perhaps we could arrange to go all go out one evening and cheer them up.'

'Oh, that would be lovely.'

'Good... I'll tell Alan his luck has changed'

'And I'll let Emma know... she will be pleased.'

'That's all fixed then... a special blind date for them.'

We talked for what seemed only a short time before David glanced at his watch and said, 'it's almost eleven, Kate and I have to be at work in the morning, Saturday is our busy day you know, so I think we'd better go... if you don't mind.'

'Of course not,' I smiled.

When he stopped the car outside my house in Ascot Drive, he said, 'this has been a lovely evening, Kate... so let's do it again...'

'Yes why not?'

'Would you like to come out for dinner next Saturday night?'

Without a moment's hesitation, I replied, 'yes, David, that would be very nice.'

He smiled, leaned across and kissed me gently on my lips and whispered, 'good.'

I slipped out of the car and waved him goodbye, I felt as if I floated up the path to the front door, feeling very happy and charmed by this lovely man... so there is a God after all!

The next morning I phoned Emma and she was so excited about meeting Alan that she could not stop asking questions about him. I honestly didn't know the answers but said I'd find out more when I saw David on our dinner date next Saturday. The following week we were both wishing our lives away while talking about David and Alan when we met in the canteen at lunchtimes.

Saturday eventually arrived and other than a few unwanted comments from Samantha and remarks from Mother about David, the day passed relatively quickly without too much argument. I spent time getting ready and chose my little red dress for my dinner date. I looked quite presentable by eight and finished off by dabbing Givenchy L'intense in all the right places before hurrying down to wait for him to arrive.

David drove up and I hurried out to his warm Mondeo. He said 'hello' then gave me a little kiss before he swept me away to the Castle Hotel in Windsor.

'The food here is superb... so I hope you enjoy it,' he said as he parked the car amongst the Jaguars and Mercedes in the crowded car park.

'I'm sure I will,' I replied with a smile before he got out and opened the door for me.

At the entrance to the restaurant in the plush hotel, David gave his name to the Maitre d' and we were shown to a cosy table for two in the corner with a 'reserved' notice, which the waiter hurriedly removed as he handed us the menus.

After a long discussion on what I wanted to eat, I eventually decided to start with smoked salmon followed by Tournedos

Rossini… which David highly recommended. He had the same and ordered a bottle of Burgundy to accompany our meal. I began to feel a little lightheaded and dreamy after a few sips of the wine and blushed when David said I looked absolutely fabulous.

'I do try my best,' I whispered while gazing into his twinkling blue eyes.

'And it shows,' he whispered back before touching my hand, which I had casually placed on the table. I wondered if I was in love yet… time would tell.

After the meal we drove leisurely to Bracknell and I felt all warm and comfy in the car. I thought I could go on forever just driving along with David and was sorry when he stopped the car outside my house. He didn't speak but just kissed me passionately and I knew he felt the same as me. When our lips parted he whispered, 'I want to go on seeing you forever Kate.'

'Do you really?'

'Yes…'

'Oh, David,' I whispered before we kissed again.

Suddenly there was a tapping on my window and I turned to see Samantha staring in at me. I wound the window down and before I could say anything she said, 'glad you're back… Mother has just had a blazing row with Dad on the phone and she is having one of her turns again… so you'd better come in.'

Trust Samantha to spoil the moment. Feeling angry inside but trying not to show it, I turned to David and said, 'I'm so, sorry…'

'Don't worry, Kate, we've had a lovely evening… now you see to your Mother and I'll phone you tomorrow morning,' he replied with a smile.

I kissed him quickly and said ,'goodbye,' before I slipped out of the car, gave him a little wave and followed Samantha into the house to see the latest state of dear Mother.

It was not serious and I had a feeling that it was a bit of a put up job. When the tantrum finally came to the end it seemed that Dad had asked reasonably if dear Mother would consider buying his half of the house. She stated forcibly that would only happen over her dead body! I sighed, nodded and made no comment then went up to bed feeling thoroughly fed up.

David phoned the next morning and we made plans to go out again on Friday. From then on we just became closer and closer. One wonderful night about a month later I knew I needed him and we made love for the first time, in my bedroom, when Mother and Samantha were out for the evening. He was gentle and very loving and afterwards, I felt as if I was in heaven.

I had met his parents by then and had Sunday lunch twice with them. Also, we'd arranged a foursome with Emma and Alan at the Two Brewers, we had some good times together.

Three months later David proposed and, of course, I accepted. He bought me a crossover ring with four sparkling diamonds and when I showed it to Mother and Samantha the look on their faces was of pure jealousy. I had a nasty feeling then that everything would end in bloody disaster… and it did.

It was all a whirlwind from the announcement of our engagement, punctuated by silly objections from Mother and much help from David's parents, before finally plans were made for us to marry in the September. Samantha and my birthday's were on the 16th and everything was set for our marriage on the 23rd. Samantha insisted that we had a birthday party, which was her way of ensuring she was the centre of attraction just before my wedding… my big day. Mother sided with her and said it would be good for us… but I doubted that.

Well just about all of Samantha's friends came and she played up to them as usual, I was left behind in the excitement, although I had David and of course Emma and Alan. The party was going quite well and everybody was asking me about the wedding and where we were going on honeymoon. I was happy to tell them that David had booked a luxury hotel overlooking the sea at Mellieha Bay in Malta. I was told more than once I was a lucky girl to have caught David and I agreed… that is until I noticed that he and Samantha were missing. I made my excuses to Alan and Emma and went in search of my future husband. They were nowhere to be found in the house so I went quickly out to the garage with my suspicious mind working overtime. When I opened the garage door I saw David at the front of Samantha's Golf. He looked up instantly with horror and as made my way towards the front of the car I saw that Samantha was spread-eagled on the bonnet of her bloody Volkswagen, skirt pulled up and legs wide open.

'Oh fucking hell!' exclaimed David and I thought, 'you're dead right… you're fucking my sister and I'm going to give you hell!' before I screamed, 'how could you, David? How bloody could you?' He went red in the face as he struggled to zip up his trousers while Samantha slid off the bonnet in a nonchalant fashion before pulling her skirt down.

She glared at me and said, 'he's always fancied me more than you, Kate… so get over it.' Then she pushed passed and made her way out of the garage and back to the party. By now tears were streaming down my face and I felt as if I were going to faint. David stammered his reasons and begged for forgiveness.

'It's all a terrible mistake… I'm so sorry, Kate… I don't know what came over me… it'll never happen again I promise you… I really mean it… I really do,' he wailed as he put his arm around me which I shrugged off and marched out of the garage into the front garden. He followed me and tried to put his arm round me again then said, 'listen, Kate…'

'Just leave me alone!' I shouted as I pulled away. He lifted up his arms in a hopeless gesture and went back inside the house leaving me to sob on my own. I felt as if my world had just collapsed all because of David's stupidity and my jealous sister. My mind struggled with a cascade of confused thoughts… how could I forgive David? Should I marry him? Would he really be faithful to me for the rest of our lives? Oh dear God… what is the answer to all this?

I stood in the garden for about twenty minutes trying to cope with what had happened before I could face the party again and tell Emma.

When I found her in the kitchen sipping a glass of wine she said, 'Kate, you look awful… has something happened?'

I nodded and replied, 'let's go somewhere quiet.'

Emma followed me upstairs to my bedroom where I told her what David and my sister were up to in the garage.

She gasped and said, 'no… I can hardly believe it.'

'It's true... he was having her on the bonnet of her car.'
'My God,' she said indignantly as I burst into tears.
'Oh, Kate... I'm so sorry... what are you going to do?'

I just shook my head and whispered, 'I don't know... I really don't know.'

'Well give yourself time to think about it...'

'Time... I'm supposed to get bloody married to him next Saturday!' I screamed in desperation. 'How can I trust him now.'

Emma sighed and said, 'I know how you feel... it was the same for me when I found out that my Bob was having it off with a girl at work.'

'Men...why do they do it to us?' I wailed.

'God knows,' she whispered as she shook her head.

We sat in silence for awhile then Emma asked, 'so Kate, are you going to marry him?'

'I don't know.'

'Well you'll have to make your mind up soon.'

'I know.'

'Well, best leave it 'til tomorrow... you'll be able to decide after you've had a good night's sleep....'

'You don't think I will be able to bloody well sleep do you?' I interrupted angrily. Sometimes Emma does say stupid things without thinking.

'I suppose not,' she replied sheepishly.

'Emma, just leave me for a bit... I want to be alone now.'

'Alright, I do understand.'

She left my room and I started to cry once again... what was I to do? Suddenly it all became crystal clear... I would not marry David, that would be his punishment, and I would stay clear of all men from now on because they only hurt you. I decided to join something worthwhile, like Oxfam or Save the Children and go to some far flung place in Africa to help poor women and their children. Yes, I would be a martyr from now on and that would be good, it would clear my mind of David and everything to do with Samantha and her wicked, jealous ways.

I said nothing more the night of the party and managed to put on a brave face when I went downstairs to join the birthday celebrations. Samantha just smirked at me every time we accidentally met, before darting quickly into other rooms to talk to her friends. Emma kept asking me if I was alright so I just smiled and replied, 'I'm fine,' but she didn't believe me. David came and asked sheepishly if we could talk but I replied, 'there's nothing to talk about,' while still smouldering deep inside. He was plainly confused by this and just shrugged his shoulders and went off somewhere to find another drink. It is surprising how love and respect for someone you care about can so quickly be replaced by hateful loathing because of their betrayal.

I thought I would never get over David's brief affair with Samantha, but I did, after I told him a few days later that the wedding was definitely off as far as I was concerned. I told him to make the announcement to everyone and he could say that I had changed my mind unless he wanted to broadcast the real reason... that he was a lying, unfaithful bastard and I caught him and Samantha in the act, in the garage of all places, the night of the party. He looked totally bemused... did he really think I'd marry him after what he had done?

Everything to do with the wedding had to be cancelled at the last minute and it was costing David and his parents a fortune... but I didn't care because it was his fault. I don't know whether he told them the real reason but as I was never to see them again I must say I was not bothered. Dear Mother was quite unmoved by the whole affair and when she eventually asked me why I had changed my mind I told her straight.

'I found David in the garage screwing my sister on the bonnet of her bloody car!'

Mother's jaw dropped in surprise and she struggled to say something but I got in first and said, 'it was my birthday party and a week before my wedding so ask yourself... what kind of woman does that to her sister?'

Mother shook her head and replied, 'I don't know but I blame David entirely for this... I was always bit unsure of him... after all he's a car salesman and you know what they are like.' I was speechless and just shook my head in utter disbelief and went up to my room to write letters to Oxfam and Save the Children. I posted them on the way to work before I told Emma what I was planning to do and she looked horrified, asking, 'you're going to work in Africa?'

'Yes why not?'

'But you hate snakes and creepy crawlies… and spiders and things.'

'I know but I'll manage somehow.'

'You're going to leave your job here?'

'I am.'

'And what will you do in Africa?'

'Help poor people.'

'You must be mad, Kate… and believe me, you'll find someone to love again…'

'I don't want to.'

'Kate, you're making a big mistake because of one stupid man and your awful sister.'

'Possibly… but that's the way it is, Emma.'

I knew I had to wait for a reply from Oxfam or Save the Children before I gave in my notice to leave Delacor Paints. I was certain they would snap me up and I would be on the first available flight out to somewhere hot and dusty where I was desperately needed. I planned to announce my new career abroad as a life saving martyr to dear Mother and Samantha when I had a date to leave the country.

The first letter to arrive was from Oxfam and I tore it open. It was a grave disappointment to me as it said, very nicely, that they had all the field staff they needed for Africa at present but they would keep my name on file just in case there was an opportunity in the future. A week later a similar letter arrived form Save the Children. I thought, 'what do these people want I wonder?' Surely someone who is willing to go and help the poor and needy in Africa is a God send?

While I was deciding on who next to offer my services, Samantha delivered an unexpected bombshell… she announced primly at dinner one evening that David had asked her to marry him… and she had accepted! I glared hatefully at Samantha as Mother congratulated her before I threw my fork into the spaghetti and stormed out. As I hurried up to my room with tears streaming, I thought, 'God, is there no end to this torture?'

I called Emma straight away with the news, I could hear the

disbelief in her voice as she gasped, 'for goodness sake! What are you going to do, Kate?'

'What can I do?'

'Nothing I suppose.' There was a long pause before I said, 'but believe me, Emma, I will have my revenge one day... and it will be soon.' But it wasn't soon and just before Christmas that year, Samantha broke off the engagement. She didn't give any real reason so I thought the whole thing was a just an opportunity to upset me by flexing her sexual powers. David was distraught and I did feel slightly sorry for him... but only a little sorry because I knew it would soon pass.

I was unable to find any organisation that would whisk me off to Africa in the near future and so I put my plans for my life saving crusade on the back burner for the moment. Emma was relieved and to a certain extent so was I.

Life at home continued in an uneasy mode with me planning revenge of some kind, until the following March when Samantha said she was looking for a new job. She announced that she was bored with her present management position... I called it a 'property pusher'... in Jackson's Estate Agents. So I wondered 'what next for Miss Tormentor... the She Devil?'

I did not have to wait long because shortly afterwards she applied to Phipps and Bracewell for a job they advertised in the local Press, and they employed her. They were solicitors to the well heeled in Ascot dealing with messy divorces and apparently they thought she was Miss Wonderful giving her a position as a junior clerk. Samantha was full of it and I had to endure stories about the personal tragedy of their high living clients night after night. That is until she brought Steven home one evening. He also worked at Phipps and Bracewell, Samantha said he was a junior solicitor but I doubted that, he looked more like a clerk to me. From the very beginning Dear Mother was all over him, making silly remarks about how clever he was to understand the divorce law, which was so complicated nowadays... and she should know!

Sometime later Samantha went to party at Steven's place to celebrate something or other and there she met Miranda for the first time. Samantha knew that Miranda was Steven's sister and an air hostess working for United Atlantic, flying to America from Heathrow, she came back from the party full of it as usual. How glamorous it was, all the important show biz people Miranda met and so on... Mother lapped it up but I was bored listening to it all. A few weeks late a miracle happened... Samantha announced that she was going to be an air hostess working for United Atlantic. It was all Miranda's idea and although my dear sister had not attended any interviews or anything she was absolutely convinced she would get the job and soon be on her way across the Atlantic with all the wonderful celebrities travelling first class. I wondered and held my breath because if she actually got the job she would be out of the way most of the time and that would only leave dear Mother for me to contend with. Believe it or not, United Atlantic employed her and she started training at Heathrow... the power of positive thinking! She was given a very smart uniform, lots of goodies, like swish leather travelling and overnight bags along with several pairs of shoes. I thought, 'the devil certainly takes care of his own.'

Within a few weeks of starting her new career as a high flying hostess, Samantha was invited by another hostess she flew with to share her flat near Heathrow. I was in heaven at the wonderful news... the She Devil would now be out of the house permanently! Dear Mother was not too happy, saying, 'I hope you'll find time to come and see us occasionally, Samantha.'

'Of course I will... and whatever you do, don't worry about me,' replied Samantha... as if I would.

On the following Saturday, Samantha loaded everything she had into her Volkswagen Golf, waved to dear Mother, who had a tear or two, and drove off to her friend's flat near Heathrow. I gave an enormous sigh and went back into the house feeling relaxed with a broad grin on my face. Now I could get on with my life without anymore interference from the She Devil... or so I thought.

Life jogged along as it does and other than a few arguments with dear Mother, some unnecessary comments from Samantha about my weight when she decided to visit us and a bit of a bust up with silly Roger at work, nothing much happened. I decided that I would definitely not volunteer for any work helping African women and their children, which was a relief to Emma who had recently been dumped by Alan for no good reason. You see what I mean about men?

One Monday afternoon Mr Butler, head of the vehicle finishing lab and my top boss, arrived with the sales manager, Jonathan Caldwell, and a very good looking young man who was introduced to us all.

Caldwell said in his posh voice, 'I'd like you to meet Robert Moore, he's just joined the division as a technical representative and he will be working with you in future.' I thought, 'well he can work with me any time,' until I remembered that after David I had given up on all men forever. Nevertheless, Robert had a captivating smile and when he shook my hand I melted just a little bit.

'And what do you do?' he asked in soft velvet tones as my toes curled.

I blushed slightly and replied, 'I check the colour match of each batch of paint against the master panel.'

'Then you're a very important person,' he said and I blushed again as Roger spoilt the moment by piping up, 'and I have to check them after Kate has finished... just to make sure she hasn't made a mistake.'

'Well I'm sure she doesn't make many,' replied Robert with a smile as Caldwell whisked him away to meet some of the others.

'Thanks Roger,' I mumbled as Robert, Caldwell and Mr Butler moved on.

On Friday morning the phone rang in the lab and Roger answered it. I glanced at him and noticed a puzzled look on his face as he put the receiver down on the desk.

'It's for you,' he said blankly.

'For me?'

'Yes.'

'But nobody calls me here.'

'Well it's you he wants to talk to... I think it's that new salesman... what's his name.'

'What does he want I wonder?' I asked as I put down the colour panel I was checking, took off my gloves and made my way over to the untidy desk.

'Hello.'

'Is that you Kate?'

'Yes, who's speaking please?' I asked but I had recognised the soft velvet voice of Robert Moore.

'It's Robert... Robert Moore, your new tech representative, we met on Monday.'

'Oh, hello.'

'Hello there, how are you today?' he asked and I thought, 'I wonder what's coming next?' as I replied, 'I'm fine, thanks.'

'Good... now I was wondering if we could meet up sometime, have a drink perhaps?'

'I don't think that would be a good idea.'

'Oh, why is that?'

'It's a long story...'

'Then tell me about it over a drink,' he interrupted.

I hesitated, thought for a moment and asked myself, 'why not?' before replying, 'yes... yes, alright.'

'So, how about tonight?... straight after work.'

I thought, 'he's a fast mover,' and replied, 'okay... I finish here at 5.30... so pick me up outside the staff entrance.'

'I'll be there, bye.'

'Bye.'

Robert was waiting with a big smile when I emerged from the staff entrance and whisked me away in his company car to The Partridge. As we drove along he said, 'thanks for coming out with me... I know it was a bit sudden but I had to see you.'

'Really? Why?'

'Because I thought you looked a little sad when I met you on Monday and nobody as lovely as you should be sad,' he replied with a smile.

I thought, 'yes, he certainly is a charming fast mover, but he's wasting his time with me if he thinks he'll get his leg over! I remember David's betrayal all too vividly,' but I replied, 'I'm not sad… just overworked and underpaid.'

'Oh dear,' he whispered as we pulled into the pub car park.

He bought the drinks at the busy bar and we found a table in the corner to sit.

'Cheers,' he said and I replied before sipping my white wine. He smiled and said, 'so… tell me all about yourself, Kate.'

'Nothing much to tell,' I replied.

'I don't believe you.'

'It's true.'

'Well let's start with Delacor Paints… how long have you worked there?'

'It seems like forever… but it's about three years now.'

'Do you like your job in the lab?' he asked.

'It's alright I suppose,' I replied in a disinterested tone as my mind began to wander and I thought, 'he seems quite keen the way he is looking at me, so perhaps I'll give him the run around and then dump him when I feel like it.'

'Perhaps you'd like to be in sales or something,' he said which brought me back to reality so I smiled and replied, 'possibly… but tell me about yourself.' Knowing that all men ever want to do is talk about is themselves I knew I was on to a sure thing so he just smiled and kept talking. He only stopped to drink his lager before carrying on relentlessly. I just smiled in the right places but was quite bored with it all so I glanced at my watch and said, 'I must go home now… my Mother will wonder where I am.'

'Yes of course, I'll drop you off.'

I guided him to my house where he pulled up outside and said, 'I've enjoyed this evening, Kate… can we do it again?'

'Yes why not?'

Good… how about next Friday? I'm in for a sales meeting so I could meet you again when you finish.'

'Yes, okay.'

'Perhaps we can have a bite to eat after our drinks.'

'That'll be good.'

He leaned across, gave me a little peck on my cheek and said in a whisper, 'until next Friday then.' I nodded, climbed out the car and waved as he drove away. I thought, 'I'll just see how this goes but I won't keep him too long… unless I change my mind.'

The week flew by and other than telling Emma about Robert I kept quiet about him. When I was getting ready for work on Friday morning I told dear Mother that I would be back late.

'Going out with someone?' she asked.

'Yes.'

'And where did you meet him?'

'At work… he's a new tech rep on the department.'

'Well you must ask him back, Kate, so I can meet him,' she said with a smile and I was immediately suspicious. Women can never completely trust their Mothers.

After drinks at The Partridge, Robert took me to a little Italian restaurant where we had Lasagne followed by ice cream. The meal was only so-so and I made a note to give it a miss if ever he suggested we went there again. Arriving back at my house I foolishly invited him in for a coffee and warned him about dear Mother.

'I should like to meet her, Kate,' he said as climbed out of the car and I thought, 'you may regret it, baby.'

As I opened the front door horrors upon horrors overwhelmed me as I heard Samantha's voice cackling away with dear Mother. I didn't know what to do… I was in a tizzy but said, 'it sounds like my sister is here.'

'You didn't tell me you had a sister,' said Robert as I led the way into the lounge.

They both glanced up and I saw the look in Samantha's eyes as she fixed her gaze on Robert and quickly undressed him.

'Ah Kate… is this your young man from work?' asked Mother with a silly grin.

'Yes… this is Robert… and this is my Mother and sister, Samantha.'

'Please to meet you I'm sure,' he said before he turned to me and said, 'you didn't tell me you had a twin sister, Kate.'

'That's because she's ashamed of me,' piped up the She Devil.

'I can't believe that,' said Robert with a smile.

'It's true,' persisted Satan's sister with a grin.

'Would you like some coffee, Robert?' asked dear Mother attempting to gloss over the unpleasantness.

'Please.'

'I'll go and make it then,' she said with a smile.

'Come and sit down,' said Samantha, adding, 'and tell us all about yourself.'

I thought, 'oh dear God… is this déjà vu all over again?'

Robert sat close to Samantha on the settee and had the look of a startled rabbit in the glare of headlights. I thought, 'hurry up and blink or you'll go blind,' as the She Devil mesmerised him.

During the next hour or so I hardly got a word in edgeways and by the time Robert left I felt exhausted and angry.

After I had said 'goodbye' to him with a little kiss and waved as he drove away I returned to the lounge to give Samantha a piece of my mind when dear Mother said, 'he seems quite nice.'

'Yes… and he's all mine,' I said firmly.

'You're welcome to him. Kate… now I must go, Mum… early flight to New York in the morning,' said Samantha as she stood up and flounced towards the door.

'Yes of course, dear,' replied dear Mother as she followed the chosen one out.

I went to bed still seething and fell into a troubled sleep.

Well it all happened quite quickly after that. Robert stopped seeing me, making lame excuses like so much work on his area to cope with and… you've guessed it… started meeting the She Devil when she was back in the country. When Mother hesitantly told me what was going on, I just fell to pieces… would I ever be free of my bloody sister?

CHAPTER 2

KATE IS VERY LOW ON PERSONALITY... AND SHE BLAMES ME FOR IT!

My sister Kate has always been a pain... ever since I can remember. Mother has preferred me because I just get on with life instead of moaning about it all the time. I am sure you'll agree that there's nothing worse than a grisly kid! And Kate certainly did more than her fair share of grizzling. It got much worse when Dad went off with Sophie, his 'other woman' from work. It was a shock to us all when it happened, Mother was distraught over the whole sordid business and it ended in an acrimonious divorce. From then on Kate and I grew further apart until we could barely say a word to each other without it ending up in a bloody great argument. What makes her so... I don't know... so downright silly all the time over everything?

It came to a head with David. He obviously preferred me to Kate from the very start and with glances and little smiles I knew he was after me so I was surprised when Kate said they were engaged. I knew that David's heart wasn't in it and when we organised a birthday party a week before they were due to get married I had him in the garage. Unfortunately Kate found us just as he was about to do what I wanted, he tried to zip up his trouser, but she saw him. I just left them to it and told Kate that he always preferred me and she would have to get over it, but she didn't and cancelled the wedding... as if I cared. David was cut up about it but I soon changed his outlook on life when I made myself available and we had some fantastic sex at his place when his parents were out. When we announced our engagement Kate was all put out and she thought I had planned it all just to hurt her but that wasn't so. I quite liked David and he was a good screw with some imagination, which I do like in a man... don't you? Anyway, I decided that after all, he was not the man I wanted to spend the rest of life with. I needed to expand my horizons so after I dumped him I looked around for another job, somewhere interesting where I would meet new people... my kind of people. I was fed up with my job at Jackson's the estate agents so when I saw an advert for a clerk in a solicitor's office I applied and got the job at Phipps and Bracewell in Ascot. They were a very upmarket law firm dealing with matrimonial affairs and I was fascinated by the cases that they dealt with. You wouldn't believe what some of the wealthy get up to! There was one old chap who seduced all his secretary's in the back of his Rolls Royce and stuffed their knickers down the back of the seat... so his wife said, after their chauffeur found them and told her. That was a case to remember... the wife divorced him and got the house, their holiday flat in Portugal and the Rolls Royce as it all belonged to his business and for tax avoidance reasons she was the sole owner of everything!

I met Steven at the office, he was studying to be an articled clerk while working, and we hit it off immediately. We started going out occasionally and he invited me one Saturday night to what turned out to be a dreary party but where I met his sister, Miranda. She was absolutely unbelievable... very smart, very casual and very sophisticated... my kind of person and to top it all she was an air hostess flying with United Atlantic Airline to New York and Boston. I mean... how good is that? After she told me about all the show biz people and seriously rich millionaires she had met on the flights and how she got invited back to their parties, I thought, 'I could do this.' Miranda must have read my mind because she said that I'd be a natural hostess and United were busy recruiting at the moment so I asked her to get me an application form. I was confident I would soon be flying across the Atlantic with show biz celebrities travelling in first class and drinking Champagne. The very thought of it got me really going... a life of luxury with no Kate to argue with.

Within two weeks I was invited to attend an interview at United's office at Heathrow, where the chief recruiting officer for cabin staff, Miss Barnes, and her assistant, Mrs Tonbridge, asked me all the relevant questions. Afterwards I felt quite confident about my performance and within another week a letter arrived saying I had been accepted for training as an air hostess. I gave in my notice at Phipps and Bracewell, much to their surprise and disappointment. Three weeks later I started the course at Heathrow with six other girls. It was great fun and we had lots of laughs when the various trainers had their backs turned. I met Tania Wells on the course and right from the start we were like sisters... if only Kate had been the same as Tania. I think some of the other girls on the course were jealous of our friendship but I didn't care about them. Tania had a flat near Heathrow that was owned by her Father, he was a property developer, and Tania invited me to move in with her so we could share the rent and other things... like a suitable place to bring show biz men and millionaires... if we had a fancy.

While this was all happening for me and my life was changing for the better, Kate brought Robert home one night, he was a representative where she worked. I had only popped in to see Mother when Kate arrived with Robert. Well I liked the look of him from the beginning and it wasn't long before he phoned me. We started going out, which suited me just for the moment as I had my eyes on the future and more interesting horizons.

I must tell you about my first flight to New York. It was so exciting and quite magical. Tania and I were scheduled to be with the Chief Steward, Ricky Naismith, for training during the flight, but it was in fact just watching Ricky and the girls do their thing and pick up as many tips as we could. I helped Jasmine serving food while Tania helped Jane serve drinks in first class. The flight time was just over six hours but it seemed to go in a flash before Captain Mac McKenzie came on the address system and announced we would be landing at Kennedy Airport in thirty minutes and thanked the passengers for flying with United Atlantic Airlines. After we had landed safely and all the passengers had disembarked we tidied up the galley then checked the overhead lockers for any hand luggage that had been left. Ricky Naismith said he would take care of us at the hotel where we were staying before we returned to Heathrow the next day, but I said that as it was the first time I had been to America I wanted to see New York. Tania agreed as it was also her first visit. Ricky sighed and said he would show us around after we had booked in at the hotel, freshened up a little and had something to eat. As we were about to follow Ricky and the other cabin staff off the aircraft, Captain Mac appeared by the exit door with John Nicholson, the first officer and co-pilot. It was the first time I had seen them standing up as I only caught a glimpse of them seated in the cockpit when we were quickly introduced before the flight. They were both quite tall and good looking with Mac having black wavy hair tinged with grey at the temples, a deep tan and soft brown eyes. He smiled at me and asked, 'so did you enjoy your first flight?'

'Oh yes, thank you, Captain.'

'Good... and how about you?' he asked Tania.

She hesitated nervously before replying, 'yes... yes, it was fine.'

'I'm pleased to hear it, perhaps you can tell me more when we all have a drink at the bar in the hotel,' he replied with a smile before he stepped out of the aircraft and hurried along the walkway. John Nicholson gave me a wink and followed the Captain while my heart fluttered a little. John was so good looking with fair wavy hair, blue eyes and a deep tan... why are pilot's so handsome? I sighed and glanced at Tania who just smiled before we left the aircraft together.

Arriving at the hotel we were allocated our room, which was basic but comfortable, and we began to get ready for the evening with some excitement. After a drink with Mac, and hopefully John, at the bar... I wanted to see everything... Times Square, Manhattan, the Bronx... just everything. Tania looked good in a little black dress but I felt I was much more alluring in my blue number. We checked each other out before going down to the bar where Mac, John and Ricky were already drinking. John noticed us first and said, 'Captain, look what's just landed!' Mac turned, stared at us as we approached, smiled and whispered, 'well everything is just getting better by the minute on this trip.'

'Oh yes,' added Ricky.

'So what can I get you ladies?' asked John with a big smile.

'I'll have a scotch on the rocks,' I replied.

'Now that's my kind of drinking partner,' said Mac with a nod which pleased me.

'And I'll have the same, please,' said Tania.

'Wow! We could be in for a night to remember,' said Mac.

'Let's hope so,' I said as John beckoned the barman and ordered our drinks.

'Well for your first flight to New York you're certainly getting off to a flying start in the big apple,' said Mac.

'I intended to,' I replied as the drinks were placed on the bar before John handed them to us.

'So... here's looking at you,' said Mac as he raised his glass.

'Cheers,' I replied before taking a good sip of my scotch and adding afterwards, 'now that hit the spot.' I glanced at Tania and noticed she had gone a little red faced. I guessed that drinking scotch with ice was not what she was used to so I smiled and thought, 'never mind... stick with me and you'll soon get into it.'

'So tell me... what have you young bright things got planned for the rest of the evening?' asked Mac with a smile.

'Well we must have something to eat first, and then Ricky is going to show us the town,' I replied.

John smiled and said, 'not his little sleazy night spots... I hope.'

'Possibly just one or two,' said Ricky with a grin.

'That sounds like fun,' I said before taking another sip.

'If it's fun you're looking for... I have a much better idea than wandering around the town,' said Mac.

'Tempt us then,' I said with a grin not knowing what he had in mind... but guessed.

'A good friend of mine always has a little party at his apartment every Friday night,' replied Mac with a smile

'And tonight's the night,' I added.

'It certainly is.'

'So tell us about this friend of yours,' Tania said.

'Well, he's a very wealthy publisher called William T. Hurst, he has an apartment overlooking Central Park and has lots of interesting characters as acquaintances,' replied Mac.

'Not friends?' I asked.

'No, only a few very special people are friends of his,' replied Mac.

'Like you, Captain?' I asked with a smile before I finished

my scotch.

'Absolutely... would you like to meet him?'

'Only if I can be one of his friends,' I said, Mac grinned and replied, 'I'm sure I can arrange that for you.'

I mean to say... a party with a wealthy publisher on my very first night in New York must be good and who knows who I might meet if I don't fancy him?

'Right... let's eat, then we'll all go over to see William,' said Mac.

We were shown to a table in the centre of the spacious, busy restaurant and when I sat down beside John I noticed a very good looking man sitting alone at a nearby table. I glanced at him then looked again after I had sat down. He had blonde wavy hair, twinkling blue eyes, a deep tan and was broad shouldered. He gave me a slight smile before I turned away to concentrate on the others who were busy chatting and listening to Mac's recommendations for the meal.

After a delicious, tender steak, with a side salad covered with several dressings, followed by soft ice cream, I was full and ready to taste the high life. As I got up from the table I glanced at the handsome stranger and he smiled at me again, which gave me a buzz.

We left the hotel and all crowded into a yellow taxi which whisked us off through the busy traffic to the apartment of William T. Hurst... Mac told us on the journey that he liked to be called 'Wills'... Americans are so informal, even when you haven't met them yet. When we arrived outside the apartment block the doorman opened the doors for us and saluted Mac. As we gathered by the lift, Mac said, 'Wills has the penthouse suite.' I thought, 'this just gets better and better,' I glanced at Tania, who was all smiles. After a breath taking ride up in the lift we stepped out into a plush corridor and at the end was an imposing wood panelled door. Mac rang the bell and we waited. The door was flung open by a tall dark haired woman with too much makeup on and dressed in an of the shoulder red dress. I didn't like the look of her from the start and it was made worse when she smiled and said in a surprised tone, 'Mac... how are you my darling?' before lunging forward and giving him a kiss on his cheek.

'Hello, Fiona... how are you?'

'I'm good... I'm good... I see you've brought John and Ricky... how nice... and some sweet things,' she said as she glanced at me and Tania, adding, 'do come in... he'll be so glad to see you.' My toes curled up when she called us 'sweet things' then relaxed before we followed Mac into the luxurious penthouse suite, I couldn't believe how fabulous it was... just like a Hollywood movie set. Suddenly a tall, casually dressed, good looking man with a mop of dark hair appeared out of the circle of drinkers, who had been listening to his every word, and hurried over to Mac saying, 'hell... this is a great surprise, Mac.'

'A good one I hope,' replied Mac.

'Of course... now who are these little lovelies?'

'This is Samantha and Tania... two new members of my crew,' replied Mac.

'Well aren't you the lucky bastard!' said Wills.

Mac nodded and said with a smile, 'this is Mr William T. Hurst... who I told you about.'

'And only believe the good bits for Christ's sake,' said Wills with a grin as Fiona appeared and casually draped herself around him.

'Come on honey, let's not forget our other guests,' Fiona said in an impatient tone.

'Okay, okay,' replied Wills before he turned around and said, 'listen up everybody... this is Mac, my favourite airline pilot and his crew from England.'

There was a murmured chorus of 'oohs' before Wills added, 'so come and make them welcome.' The first out of the crowd was a strange, pale faced youngish woman with severely cut, jet black hair who looked at me and said, 'hi, I'm Kristal Day.'

'Hello,' I replied, wondering why she had picked me out.

Wills smiled and said, 'Kristal is my newest author with so much talent she'll be pumping out best sellers for years to come.'

'That's nice, 'I replied with a smile... I mean what else could I say?

'My first book did okay,' said Kristal in a nonchalant tone.

'It was more than okay, honey… we've sold hundreds of thousands already and it's now heading for its first million!' exclaimed Wills with a smile.

'What is it called?' I asked.

'Erotic torture for women,' replied Kristal with a curious smirk.

'Really?'

'Uh, uh… really.'

'So what's it about?' I asked naively and Wills laughed out loud while Mac and John smirked.

Kristal looked mad as hell before she replied, 'it's all about men getting what they all deserve!'

'I hope you don't include us,' said Mac.

'Maybe,' she replied.

'No, Kristal doesn't mean that,' said Wills anxiously glancing at her.

Kristal glared at him and said, 'I might'… then turning to me said, 'Wills is almost a good publisher these days but a lousy host… so, honey, let's get you a drink and you can tell me all about being a hostess, whatever that entails.'

'Thanks,' I replied realising that I was going to be questioned by a man hating lesbian. I was looking forward to spending some quality time with Wills from the moment I met him… well handsome millionaires are so very attractive… don't you agree? As he was quite enamoured with Kristal, I thought the best way to humour Wills was to show interest in this peculiar woman who was destined to pump out best sellers for him. I planned to catch him later but after she poured me a large scotch on the rocks at the sumptuous bar, I could not get rid of Kristal and her insane questioning about the men in my life was getting boring. I thought, 'she's using my experiences to write the sequel to 'Erotic torture for women' which I guessed would be entitled, 'The final orgasm'. I could see the Dollar signs in her eyes as I tried to answer her daft questions… and it was the only time I wished that Kate was with me… she would have been able to fill in all the sordid details about men and their deceptions for this quirky lesbian, with no trouble.

Eventually Mac came to my rescue and said, 'Sam, come and meet Rafael, he's quite an interesting character.'

'I'd love to,' I replied with a relieved smile and gave a nod to Kristal. As I followed Mac, I glanced over at Wills and noticed that Fiona was still hanging on for grim death while a young blonde with very large boobs in a short, too tight blue dress was making eyes at him while he spoke to her... I know the signs.

I whispered to Mac, 'is Wills married to Fiona?'

'No.'

'Is he married?'

'Occasionally,' replied Mac with a grin and I laughed then asked, 'anyone at present?'

'I don't think so... why... do you fancy your chances?' he asked with a smile. I gave a slight shrug as my mind wondered what it would be like to be married to a handsome millionaire, shop every day on Fifth Avenue and live in this penthouse suite... I decide it would be just heaven!

Tania was already talking to Rafael when I arrived with Mac.

'Rafael, meet the other new young lovely in my crew... Samantha.'

I looked at the short, stocky, grey haired man wearing glasses, smiled and said, 'call me Sam... everybody does.'

'Hi there, Sam.'

'Mac tells me that you're interesting.'

'Well, thanks for that... but I don't know why,' replied Rafael with a smile.

'Yes you do... tell them about your predictions,' said Mac.

'Alright, but I must say that they don't all come true,' said Rafael.

'Well most of them do,' said Mac and Rafael gave him an appreciative look. This interested me and I sipped my scotch on the rocks before asking, 'so I guess you're writing a book?'

'Yup... Wills has been very generous with an advance and he thinks we'll sell a million or so,' replied Rafael.

'Well if you can predict the future you must know exactly how many,' I said with a grin.

'I wish.'

Tania asked, 'so do you write your predictions down then put them in a sealed envelope and get someone to open them when something happens?'

'You're almost right...but Wills wants to do it live on the TV networks... which could be a great sales promotion for the book... when I've finished it that is,' he replied.

'And when will that be?' asked Tania.

'Well, if I don't get any more interruptions... in about two month's time for the first draft,' he replied.

'Then what?'

'The editor will start going through it with her big blue pencil!'

'It sounds as if you think you'll be asked to re-write most of it,' said Tania.

'Lottie Franks, Wills editor in chief, is a stickler... so I guess I'll be re-writing lots of it,' he replied with a sigh.

'So tell us about your latest prediction and when it will come true,' I said.

'Ah well, there hangs a long story,' he replied.

'So start near the end,' I said.

'But if you can't... we've got all night,' said Tania with a smile and Rafael grinned.

'Okay... but I must say you Brits are mighty persistent!'

'And we always manage to persuade people to do what we want in the end,' I said as I fluttered my eyelashes at him.

'With our charm!' added Tania and Mac grinned.

'Right... '

Rafael then started telling us a long winded story about a Spanish Conquistador in gold plated armour that would be discovered next year by a Native American in the Black Hills of Dakota... as he droned on I almost lost the will to live and so glanced across at Wills. He caught my eye and smiled back as the big bustier was trying to attract his attention while Fiona still looked suitably glum. Suddenly Wills broke away from the blue bombshell and Fiona, and made his way across to us. As he arrived Rafael finished his story and Tania said, 'how interesting,' while I smiled at possibly the new man in my life.

'So, are you being entertained and amazed by my prophet?' asked Wills.

'Oh yes, Wills, it's all fascinating,' I replied and Tania nodded.

'Good... and I'm sure when we organise a prime time programme on the TV networks about his predictions, the sales of Rafael's book will go through the roof,' Wills said with a smile.

'I'm sure it will be a great success because everyone wants to know the future,' I said, as I wondered what my future would be.

'Now that's what I like to hear, honey,' said Wills and my heart fluttered slightly when he called me 'honey'.

'I'm glad we're on the same wave length,' I said.

'Sam... I think we just might be... now, come and look at the view across the Park,' said Wills with a sweep of his hand towards the open picture window.

Mac glanced at us and said, 'go on... it's spectacular.'

'Are you coming?' asked Tania.

'No thanks... you know I'm afraid of heights,' replied Mac and we laughed before we followed Wills across to the window then stepped out onto the paved patio that surrounded the suite and gazed across the Park at the lights of New York. Mac was right... it was truly spectacular. The city had such life and vibrancy that you could feel and almost taste from this high point. I was truly amazed and was just about to make a comment when Wills said, 'I love this place... its God's little acre and it's so nice to share it with people I like.'

'So do we come into that category?' I asked with a smile.

'You certainly do.'

'Well that's good to know,' said Tania.

Wills sighed and casually put his arms around us as we stood either side of him and the feel of his warm hand on my back sent little shivers down my spine. He gently moved his hand up and down and said, 'just look at all that real estate... and the money it represents.'

'It's amazing,' I said before glancing at him. He sensed my glance and turned then gently kissed me on my cheek.

'You're not supposed to do that,' I whispered.

'I do lots of things I'm not supposed to but I do them because I just want to... and I wanted to kiss you to show my appreciation of what you said about Rafael's new book.'

'And I think Rafael's book sounds really fantastic too,' said Tania with a smile so Wills laughed then kissed her and I was slightly jealous.

We stood for some while looking at the view before Fiona

came out and said, 'honey, you'd better come in and circulate.'

'Why?' he asked as he glanced round at her.

'Some of your friends are getting restless... especially Kristal... you know what I mean?'

Wills sighed, nodded and said, 'excuse me ladies... I'll catch you later.' I glanced at Tania and raised my eyebrows as he went inside with Fiona.

'I think he fancies you, Sam.'

'Possibly,' I replied before I gazed out across the Park with my mind in a whirl of excited expectations. Was it possible that he would really become involved and committed to me... or did he only see me as English 'totty' he could shag occasionally and leave me when he felt like it? Time would tell.

We left the view and went inside to get more drinks and see what was happening. As we made our way across to the lavish bar, Mac appeared and said, 'I think it's time we went.'

'But we've only just got here,' I replied.

'Listen to me, I'm the Captain and I know from experience that you will feel dead on your feet during the flight back to Heathrow tomorrow if you don't get some sleep now.'

I pulled a face and glanced at Tania who looked similarly unhappy.

'Right then, Captain,' I said.

We said 'goodbye' to everyone and when Wills knew we were leaving he broke away from Kristal, who was having an intense conversation with him, came over to the door and asked, 'so when are you back in New York, Mac?'

'Same time next week,' replied Mac.

'Well make sure you drop by and bring your crew with you.'

'Right... we'll see you then,' said Mac with a smile and we followed him out. I glanced back at Wills and he blew me a kiss then winked... I smiled and my heart fluttered.

On the journey back to the hotel in the taxi, John made some comments about Wills having an eye for new friends... especially female ones.

'He's always been the same ever since I first met him,' said Mac.

'They're like lost lambs in a slaughter house,' added Ricky with a grin.

'Yes... and the outcome is always disappointment followed by tantrums,' said Mac as he looked at me.

'Well I'm not disappointed...' I began but John interrupted and said, 'yet!'

'And I don't have tantrums!' I said loudly before I turned away and looked out of the window.

'Good... but just be careful, Sam, that you don't get swept away by it all,' said Mac and I did not reply but just gazed out at the bright lights.

We took the lift to the third floor, said 'goodnight' to them in the corridor and made our way to our room. As I fell onto my bed I said, 'I don't feel like going to sleep yet.'

'Well I do... I'm just about totally knackered,' replied Tania with a sigh.

'Right... I'll tell you what... you go to bed while I go down to the bar.'

'Don't be silly... you know what Mac said and you'll regret it tomorrow,' said Tania as she started to unzip her dress.

'I might... but I'm not ready to give in yet,' I replied before I got up, looked in the mirror, touched up my hair and put on some lip gloss.

'You're bloody mad, Sam,' said Tania as I made for the door.

'Probably.'

I needed to have one last drink and think about what had happened this evening. I had met a wonderful millionaire publisher called William T. Hurst... I wondered what the 'T' stood for... but put that to the back of my mind... I would ask him next time we met. His lifestyle would suite me down to the ground and I wondered how I could replace Fiona... the only known obstacle to my possible new life with Wills. After all, in this life it is who you know and millionaires are in my very top list of people I should know.

The bar was still quite busy with smart looking, but over dressed women, and cigar smoking men who laughed too loudly. I spotted an empty bar stool at the far end and made for it. I perched myself up on the black leather padded chrome stool and looked at the handsome young barman for attention. He quickly noticed me and asked, 'so what can I get you, ma'am?'

'Scotch on the rocks please.'

'Coming right up,' he replied with a smile before putting some ice cubes in a tumbler and turning to the optics. He drained down the scotch and placed it in front of me on the black glass topped bar.

'Are you staying here, ma'am?'

'I am.'

'Shall I put this on your room?'

'Please... it's 304.'

'Okay,' he said with a smile as the man sitting on the next stool turned and said, 'hello, Samantha.'

I gasped in surprise as I looked at his handsome tanned face and twinkling blue eyes. It was the man I noticed earlier when we were having dinner in the restaurant.

'How do you know my name?' I asked firmly but not too firmly as I thought, 'well, my first night in New York has certainly taken another turn for the better'. I wondered if this handsome stranger was a millionaire, as the City appeared to be full of them.

Smiling he replied in a clipped tone, 'I know a lot about you.'

'So do you work for United?' I asked with a quick flutter of my eyelashes as my brain went into overdrive thinking he might be a pilot or someone in the crew I had missed on the flight out... silly me!

'No I don't work for them.'

'Well you're obviously not an American,' I said with a smile.

'No, I'm a Norwegian.'

'How nice... so what do they call you in Norway?'

'Eric.'

'Just Eric?'

'You don't want to know the rest, I promise you,' he replied with a grin as I sipped my scotch.

'And why is that?'

'It would frighten you, Samantha.'

'Really?'

'Yes...'

'And what about your wife... how does she cope with just being called Mrs Eric?' I asked, hoping to get the right answer.

'I'm not married,' he replied with a smile and I thought, 'oh yes... the right answer and you will do nicely as my drinking companion. There is nothing so attractive to a girl than when a handsome man tells you he is not married... providing he's not lying of course.'

'So, Eric... tell me all you know about me and I'll try not to look surprised,' I said in what I hoped was a sophisticated tone. He laughed and replied, 'I will next time... when you know me a little better.'

'Is there going to be a next time?'

'Oh yes... I will be with you for some time to come,' he replied and I thought, 'now this is getting interesting' then asked, 'really... how so?'

'I will meet you on occasions...'

'Only if I agree, Eric,' I interrupted and he laughed.

'I'm sure I can persuade you to say 'yes', Samantha.'

'Maybe,' I replied before sipping my scotch while thinking, 'oh yes indeed.'

I decided to start asking him questions... well, when you get picked up in a bar it's only natural you want to know all about the man and if he's married and rich... I already knew about the married bit.

'So, Eric, are you in New York to do some high flying business?'

'No... I'm just here looking after you,' he replied.

'Why?'

'Because I've been told to,' he replied and added, 'and your sister Kate.' Now that threw me... and I gulped the last drop of my scotch as I tried to figure out what this handsome man was up to. Was he a weird Trans Atlantic Scandinavian stalker I wondered?

'How do you know my sister?' I asked in a serious tone as this Norwegian was now beginning to get under my skin.

'This is not the place to discuss this, Samantha... '

'So where is?' I interrupted... thinking he would say his room.

'The hotel has a roof garden... it will be quiet up there and we can talk,' he replied. For a moment I didn't know what to do... I thought he could be a serial killer or he might actually be some romantic guy who knew Kate... but I needed to know one way or the other. He could either strangle me and throw me off the roof or kiss me until I was breathless... I decided to risk it and take a brave chance on romance as his twinkling blue eyes looked into my very soul and mesmerised me.

'Let's go then, Eric,' I said as I slipped off the bar stool. He smiled then stood up and I was amazed how tall he was and noticed all the women looking at him as we left the bar.

He did not speak until we were in the lift and heading up at speed to the roof garden. He looked at me, smiled and said, 'a long time ago in my village we had a winter festival to honour the Gods of fertility so we used to find the most beautiful maiden and call her our Snow Princess then we let her choose a man.'

'How nice.'

'And I'm sure you would be our Snow Princess if you were living there at that time.'

I was beginning to think I had made the right decision to go up to the roof garden with this gorgeous, romantic man and asked, 'so where is this village of yours?'

'Near Trondheim, it's called Storvigga,' he replied.

'And what happens to this Snow Princess in Storvigga?'

'After she had been chosen by the villagers, young women would go to her hut and bathe her then rub warm perfumed oil into her naked body before they dressed her in a long, white soft fur coat which was fastened by gold chains around her waist,' he replied. I really liked the sound of this and my imagination ran riot with the thought of being rubbed all over with warm perfumed oil before I asked, 'and then what?'

'She was led into the great hall where she was able to choose an unmarried man to be with her and make love in front of the fire on a bed of furs.'

I felt a little shiver of pleasure as I asked, 'so when they had finished... did he have to marry her?'

'Only if she said she was satisfied by him.'

My mind boggled and asked, 'and what if he didn't satisfy

her?'

'She was able to choose another man.'

'And how long did this go on for?' I asked while my mind boggled again.

'Until she has had three men that night, then she had to choose one of them to marry or she would anger the Gods who would punish her,' he replied. I thought, 'lucky, lucky girl,' as the lift stopped, the bell pinged and my dreamy thoughts of being naked with this man on a fur bed in front of a roaring fire came to an abrupt end.

Eric led me out into the deserted roof garden and guided me towards the rail marking the boundary before the surrounding paved area below. I shivered slightly although the night was still comparatively warm... but I put it down to excitement. Eric noticed this and slipped off his jacket then placed it around my shoulders before he put his hand in the middle of my back... which was very comforting.

'What a view,' I said as I gazed out once again on the bright lights of New York... which was fast becoming my favourite place on Earth.

'It is, Samantha... now let's sit over there and talk,' he said, gesturing towards a white wrought iron two seat garden chair with large cushions. After we sat down I tried to snuggle up to him but he moved back a little so I asked, 'is there anything wrong with me?'

'No... nothing... absolutely nothing... but I find you very attractive and must tell you that I can't get romantically involved with you,' he replied.

'And why is that, Eric?' I asked in a disappointed tone.

'Because I've been sent to guide you onto a path of happiness, Samantha... and nothing else, I'm afraid.'

'Well if you're afraid of a little romance then I'm very disappointed because it would make me very happy to be on any path with you,' I said, thinking, 'trust me to get a man who was either gay or a liar!'

There were a few moments of silence and I gazed out at the New York skyline and thought, 'how come I get picked up by this man who knows Kate?' before he said, 'I've something important to tell you, Samantha... and you mustn't be frightened.'

I looked at him and replied firmly, 'I'm not frightened, Eric... so you go right ahead!'

'Thank you... now you are in danger...'

'Who from?' I interrupted as I quickly thought of all the people who hated me... Kate was at the top of the list.

'Yourself,' he replied.

'Me?'

'Yes... I'm afraid so.'

'And how do you work that out?'

'You're travelling down a path which will lead you to much unhappiness and disappointment...'

'Who the devil are you to tell me what to do with my life?' I interrupted.

'Because I'm your guardian angel...'

'Well, whoever you are... I think you're raving bloody mad!' I shouted and stood up, looked him in the eye then said, 'men!' before I flounced off towards the entrance to the hotel.

CHAPTER 3

NOW IT'S TIME THAT SAMANTHA MUST FEEL SOME PAIN…. TA-DAH!

After I discovered that my 'maniser' sister (I'm sure you will agree that she is the female equivalent to a man described as a 'womaniser') was having it off with Robert, I decided that I would strike back. I mean to say, how much do the little people have to put up with?

Now when planning revenge you must have an accomplice and of course Emma would be mine… I just needed to tell her. I would bounce my big ideas off her before starting the social destruction of Samantha… which was so long overdue. I was busy thinking how I could make her pay for all the trouble she had caused me since we were children when Mother dear announced, as she was cooking dinner on Friday evening, that she had a new man in her life. This was a surprise, but I was pleased because I knew it would take Mother's obsession with Samantha off her mind, leaving me free to plan my revenge on Satan's sister without any undue suspicion or interference from her.

I smiled and said, 'how wonderful, what's his name?'

Mother gave a little coy smirk and replied, 'he's called George… George Bradshaw… he's a widower… and he's very nice.'

'I'm sure… so where did you meet him?' I asked.

'At the Am Dram meeting… on Wednesday night,' she replied with a smile.

Mother had recently joined the local amateur dramatic society to have an outside artistic interest, but I think it was so she could find a suitable middle aged man for some company, but who hopefully did not have any interest in sex, a comb over, a woolly cardigan or spoke in a loud voice and fancied himself. The 'Bracknell Players' met every Wednesday to discuss which masterpiece to perform next, after their moderate success with 'The Importance of being Ernest.' They intended to lift another literary treasure from the pages of some great author or playwright, which they felt was certain to amaze their audiences. Apparently the widower first appeared last week and was immediately drawn to Mother... can't think why.

'So when am I going to meet him?'

'He's coming over for lunch on Sunday.'

'Oh, lovely.'

'And hopefully Samantha will drop over if she is not flying off somewhere after she gets back from her first flight to New York,' said Mother and I groaned inwardly on hearing that unwelcome news. I was about to tell her to make sure that Samantha did not entice George into the garage but thought better of it... then I wondered if I should say something. Older men can get silly and lose their composure when a young female thing makes eyes at them... and I was sure that George would be no exception. The garage was the chosen place where the sexual predator practised her dark arts... the widower would be as helpless as a new born baby when confronted by the devil's handmaiden with her skirt pulled up and her knickers round her ankles. I decided to make a comment out of fairness, or perhaps to start a little niggle in Mother's mind, so I said in an offhand manner, 'well, I just hope George can resist Samantha when he meets her.'

'What ever do you mean?' she asked with a surprised look.

'You know what I mean... she makes a bee line for anything in trousers which she thinks is remotely interesting... and George sounds interesting,' I replied. Mother glared at me and I knew I had struck a chord.

'You Kate, have a wrong opinion of your sister...'

'Wrong opinion? Huh! You bloody well know she ruined my chance of happiness with David and then Robert... you always see her through rose tinted glasses while I see her for what she really is... a scheming, man hungry sex-pot who doesn't care who she hurts!' I interrupted.

'Well, let me remind you, Kate, it was entirely your decision and not Samantha's that you chose not to marry David...'

'I couldn't after I had caught them at it in the garage!'

'But it was still your decision...'

'Would you have married Dad if you had caught him with

Sophie?' I asked and she shook her head then started to cry. I had definitely overdone it again... why, oh why, do I do this?

'Oh, I'm sorry, dear... I didn't mean to hurt you...'

'But you did, Kate... you really did,' she interrupted so I sighed, shrugged and went into the lounge and slumped down on the settee.

I thought, 'bugger Samantha... just bugger her... she is the cause of so much upset.'

We said very little over dinner and I went up to my room to read my book, while Mother parked herself in front of the television for the evening. Saturday came and went and the only thing that pleased Mother dear was the late night phone call from the devil's handmaiden to say she was back and how much she enjoyed the flight to New York. She would come over for Sunday lunch to tell us all about it... I was not happy.

George arrived at just after twelve on Sunday and was all smiles as he presented Mother with a bottle of red wine from Sainsbury's before she introduced us.

'So you're Kate...'

'I am,' I replied, wondering, 'why do daft people say that when they have just been told who you are?'

'And you'll meet Samantha when she arrives any minute now... she's just got back from New York you know,' beamed Mother.

'Oh, how wonderful,' replied George.

'Yes, isn't it? Now do sit down, George, and make yourself at home.'

I looked at this middle aged man and was thankful he did not have a comb over... he was practically bald except for some straggly grey hair around his shiny dome which hung over his ears. He was wearing a buttoned up beige cardigan over a green shirt with a dark blue bow tie and light brown corduroy trousers. It looked like a circus clown had dressed him as his side kick! I wanted to ask him, 'do you always go out looking like that?' but decided not to.

'Lunch will be ready soon,' said Mother in a soothing voice.

'Good... I've been really looking forward to this, June, so

thank you for inviting me,' said George with a smile.

Mother smirked and replied, 'you're very welcome, George... I don't suppose you get many home cooked meals these days... now that you're on your own.'

'No... mores the pity,' he sighed and gazed at her longingly. I wanted to tell him that however many times he came to Sunday lunch with a bottle of cheap plonk, a leg over with Mother dear was right out of the question! But I suppose that all old desperate men live in hope that they are still attractive to women.

'Now... would you like something to drink, George?'

'Please.'

'A sherry perhaps... or shall we open this?' asked Mother, holding up the bottle.

'I really don't mind, June, dear... you decide,' he replied with a smile.

I thought, 'June dear... and he only met her on Wednesday... a fast worker... but no matter how smooth you are, George, Mother is not interested in horizontal line dancing!'

'Well, let's give this a go shall we?' said Mother as she looked at the label then hurried from the room. There followed a few moments of silence before he said, 'I suppose you're looking forward to seeing your sister?'

I almost choked as I replied as enthusiastically as I could, 'yes, it will be good to see her and hear all about her adventures in New York.'

'Have you ever been over there?'

'No I haven't... but hopefully I'll make it someday.'

'Perhaps your sister can get you a cheap fare.'

'Yes... I'll have to ask her,' I replied... as if I would.

'I've never been to America... I'm more a European traveller you know... France, Spain, Portugal... that sort of thing,' he said.

'Oh really.'

'Yes, my late wife and I had many very enjoyable holidays over on the Continent... except one dreadful time when we were both stung by jelly fish off the coast of Spain.'

'Oh dear,' I said hoping I was not going to have to live through George's long explanation of the incident and what happened next... I was not emotionally ready for that at the moment as I was too strung up anticipating the arrival of the devil's sister.

Mother came to my rescue when she entered with three glasses of red wine on a tray and said, 'there you are, George.'

'Thanks, June, it looks lovely... it's so very red.'

I thought, 'what a plonker' as I took mine and said, 'thanks.'

'Well, cheers everyone,' said Mother.

'Cheers... and here's to you June, for all your hard work preparing the lovely lunch we are about to have,' said George with a smile as Mother blushed slightly. I'll give him his due... he keeps on trying but it will all be in vain... perhaps I should tell him.

I had just taken my first sip of wine when I heard the front door open and close followed by Samantha's voice calling out, 'I'm home!'

'We're in here, dear,' said Mother excitedly as she put her glass down on the coffee table and stood up for the entrance of the Queen of Sheba. George followed suit while I remained seated and continued to drink my wine in big gulps... I needed fortifying.

'Hello, my darling,' Mother gushed as she embraced the favourite one.

'Hi, Mum... Sis.'

'Hi,' I replied and gave a nod.

'Now did you have a good trip?' asked Mother.

'Yes, it was fabulous!' she replied and I thought, 'well with the She Devil's luck it couldn't be anything else could it?'

'That's just wonderful dear... I knew it would be good... now I'd like you to meet my friend George... we met at Am Dram.'

Samantha gave him a straight up and down look as she said, 'hello, I'm pleased to meet you.'

'And I'm absolutely delighted to meet you, Samantha... I've heard so much about you,' said the widower with a smile, and I thought, 'I bloody well bet you have!'

'Not all bad I hope,' said the She Devil with a grin as she glanced at me.

'No, not at all,' replied George hurriedly then added, 'I can't believe that you and Kate look so alike... it's quite uncanny.'

'Yes... isn't it,' said Sister Sam as she parked herself on the settee next to me. I recoiled slightly while George looked at each of us in turn and whispered, 'it's quite extraordinary.'

Mother beamed and asked, 'wine for you dear, or would you like something else?'

'No, wine will be okay.'

'I'll get you a glass then. And don't say anything about your trip until I'm back,' said Mother as she hurried from the room.

'Okay.'

'So, Samantha... how was New York?' asked George with a smile.

'I'll tell you all about it in a minute when Mum gets back,' she replied.

'Yes, yes, of course... silly of me to be so impatient... but I've never been to America and I'm very curious.'

'Yes, I'm sure.'

'I've travelled quite extensively on the Continent you know... France, Spain, Portugal... those sorts of places,' said George and I thought, 'here we go... the jelly fish saga is about to begin!' but Mother saved us and arrived back with the wine and handed it to her favourite child.

'There... now let's say cheers again,' she said and we did.

After Mother finished her wine she smiled and said, 'lunch will be ready soon... so while we are waiting, tell us about your trip, dear.'

And she did... we heard all about Captain Mac McKenzie, John, his handsome co-pilot, Wills Hurst the publishing millionaire and the party at his swanky penthouse apartment overlooking Central Park. As the Devil's Sister droned on, I watched Mother dear and George... their faces were absolute picture's... they were like small, wide-eyed children listening to the most wonderful fairy story ever told by their favourite Auntie.

When Samantha had finished her first opening gambit she said there was more to follow, Mother said that we should stop for lunch.

George sat in Dad's place at the top of the dining room table and

I sat opposite Samantha... neither of which pleased me. Mother dished up while George complimented her on her fantastic cooking... although he had not tasted it yet. The roast beef was tender, the Yorkshire pudding very crispy and the vegetables delicious ... I must admit that she is a good cook. We had apple pie and custard for dessert and then coffee in the drawing room where George warbled on about Mother's wonderful cooking skills and how he missed his wife. I did feel a little sorry for the old chap as I knew he was trying his very best to get his feet under the table but I knew Mother dear was only interested in a friendship... nothing more.

The Devil's Handmaiden needed no prompting from Mother to continue with her American adventure and went into great detail about the curious people she had met at Wills party. Kristal Day sounded fascinating but peculiar to me while she thought Rafael was creepy.

'I have to agree with you, Samantha, some of the American tourists I've met on the Continent leave a lot to be desired,' said George looking at Mother for some sort of agreement which was not forthcoming.

The She Monster ignored his remark and continued, 'so when we got back to the hotel, Tania went to bed, but I went down to the bar to have one last drink and would you believe... I met a Norwegian guy who said he knew you Kate.'

'Me?' I asked in wide eyed astonishment.

'Yes.'

'I don't know any Norwegians,' I replied as my mind went into overdrive thinking if it was somebody who had visited the lab recently.

'Well he said he knew you.'

'What's his name?' I asked in a bemused tone.

'Eric.'

'Just Eric?'

'Yes.'

'I don't know anybody called Eric.'

On hearing that, the She Devil looked smug and said, 'well I didn't think so... he was quite a sophisticated, good looking guy... and not somebody who would be interested in you.'

'Thanks a bunch,' I replied.

George looked perplexed before he said, 'I think that's a little unfair of you, Samantha.'

Sister Sam glared at him and replied, 'you don't know Kate like I do…and if you did, you wouldn't say that.'

There was a stunned silence for a moment then Mother asked, 'would anyone like some more coffee?'

I shook my head, excused myself and went up to my bedroom, closed the door, fell on the bed and cried at the injustice of it all. After some moments, I dried my tears and thought, 'it would be nice if a good looking guy called Eric really knew me… I wonder who he is… or did Satan's Handmaiden just make him up to embarrass me?' I wouldn't put it past her!

I went down a few minutes later to hear her talking about her next trip which was across to Boston on Tuesday morning.

George smiled and said, 'ah, home of the Boston tea party.' Mother nodded while Sister Sam looked perplexed and replied, 'I don't do politics.'

I plucked up courage and asked, 'so tell me more about this Eric.'

'Nothing much more to tell, he spoke to me and said he knew you,' she replied in an offhand tone.

'So how did he know you?'

She looked puzzled for a moment and replied, 'I think he was on the flight out and heard me talking to Tania when she was serving him drinks,' but somehow I didn't believe a word of it.

'Didn't you ask him how he knew me?'

'No… you didn't come up in our conversation,' she replied.

'So you had a conversation with this Eric at the bar then?' I asked in a curious tone.

'Yes…'

'And what did he say, dear?' asked Mother.

'Nothing much… we just chatted about the flight and then went up to the roof garden to see the view,' she replied.

'That sounds very romantic, dear.'

'Yes it was.'

'Then what happened?' asked Mother in an interested tone.

'We looked at the view for a while, which is absolutely fantastic, then I left him and went to my room,' she replied, but I thought there was more to it than that. My sister would never pass up the chance to snare a good looking guy! She's such a bloody liar!

'Well I'm sure you did the right thing, Samantha, foreigners who pick up young women in hotel bars can never be trusted,' said George glancing at Mother for her approval but none came. Poor old George… he was trying so hard… bless him.

I'd had enough by now and it was obvious that Satan's Sister was not going to tell me anymore about this good looking Norwegian so I decided to go out for some fresh air.

I made my excuses and left them to it, knowing that Samantha would be the centre of attention until she decided to leave.

I slipped on my comfy old coat and made my way in the warm afternoon sunshine to the nearby park to think. What could I do to bring my sister to her knees… and keep her there? Nothing came to me as I wandered along the road and turned into the park. As I gazed about, it brought back many happy memories when Dad used to bring us here as little tots to play on the slides and swings. Samantha was quite sweet back then and I wondered what changed her? The answer was Mother dear… some parents don't know what they are doing to their children… they are just blind to reality of their faults and without any common sense.

I made my way aimlessly towards the slides and swings and hardly noticed the young mums and dads with their children, who were dancing about as they do. Suddenly I saw two sweaty, old joggers gasping for breath and running towards me along the path. I smiled as they passed by, thinking, 'one day I'll be old and wrinkly like them, so I better make hay while the sun shines, before it's too late!' I glanced round to find somewhere to sit and think about the destruction of Satan's Handmaiden. There was an empty park bench near the play area under an old tree, which we used to run around when we were children, chasing each other until we were dizzy. As I made my way towards it a very tall man suddenly appeared from out of nowhere and beat me to it, sitting down at one end. I had to make up my mind whether I wanted to share it with a stranger or find another place to sit, but thought, 'I'm sure he won't disturb my thinking... so why not?' As I got close, he looked up and smiled at me and I thought, 'well he's a good looking guy and no mistake.' I just nodded and sat at the other end of the bench and gazed at the tiny children on the swings being pushed back and forth by their smiling parents.

I was thinking how I could embarrass Sister Sam, just a little at first, then step up the campaign until she was absolutely terrified of me and what I would do next... there is nothing like keeping your enemy on edge all the time before you destroy them.

Suddenly a clipped, soothing voice interrupted my thoughts, saying, 'it's a lovely afternoon isn't it?'

I turned, looked at the stranger and he smiled at me... it was a lovely warm smile... the kind a gentle lover would give to his beloved. His blue eyes twinkled and I felt captivated by some unseen magic in his tanned face... I just managed to nod slightly and murmur, 'yes it is,' before I looked away and thought, 'wow! Is this happening for real?'

'May we talk for a while?' he asked and I glanced at him again.

'What about?'

'You,' he replied as he gave me his devastating smile again... I wish he wouldn't do that... it's very unnerving for a woman looking for true love and not daring to hope.

'Me?' I asked in wide eyed astonishment. 'Do I know you?'

'No... but you will,' he replied and I thought 'now this could get very interesting.'

'Oh, really?'

'Yes, Kate... my name is Eric...'

'Oh, my good God!' I interrupted in shock as my lips began to quiver.

'Please don't be afraid of me,' he said calmly and suddenly I wasn't... but how did he know my name? It seemed that the Devil's Handmaiden had been telling the truth... which was a first!

'So who are you?' I asked cautiously.

'I'm someone who wants to help you.'

'And why would you want to do that?'

'Because you're very important to me,' he replied with that smile again and I thought 'important to him... am I going crazy or what?'

'So tell me why I'm important?' I asked this gorgeous man with my heart now full of hope.

'Well, it's a long story... but the essential truth is that, although we all have free will, some of us need a little guidance to ensure we follow our true path to happiness and at the moment, I'm afraid that you are not on the right path,' he replied, which was a slight disappointment to me.

'Are you something to do with the Salvation Army?' I asked.

'No, Kate... but I do admire their work.'

'Is that so?'

'Yes... now let's talk about you and your sister, Samantha,' he said and I thought, 'trust the Devil's Handmaiden to show up when I was just enjoying myself and forgetting all about her.'

'Must we talk about her?'

'Yes... I'm afraid so,' he replied.

I sighed and asked, 'before we do... tell me how you know her?'

'I've been instructed to watch over both of you and I've been doing that for some time now,' he replied.

'So who told you to spy on us?' I asked indignantly.

He smiled and replied, 'it's not spying Kate... it's caring for you both.'

'Well I can tell you that my sister certainly does not need your care... or anybody else's... she can more than look after herself!'

'You may think that, but you are very wrong.'

'Am I?... well I don't think so!'

He raised his eyebrows and glanced away from me for a few seconds then turned back and said, 'I was told this was going to be very difficult...'

'Who told you that?' I interrupted... well a girl's got to know these things hasn't she?

'Never mind for the moment... but from now on, I want you

to listen to me and let me guide you…'

'Does this mean we'll be going out together?' I interrupted with a hopeful smile.

'Possibly…'

'What do you mean, 'possibly'?' I asked in alarm.

He sighed and replied, 'I'm trying to persuade you and Samantha from going down the wrong path, it will lead you to such unhappiness, bitterness and turmoil that you'll regret it for the rest of your lives.'

'Does that mean you'll be taking her out as well?' I asked angrily as I sensed the Devil's Handmaiden was going to end up with the good looking guy while I was left standing alone at the altar again! Why does this keep happening to me?

'Yes… it's my duty to see you both,' he replied and I thought, 'that bloody well does it! I'm not playing that game again… he's welcome to Satan's Sister and I'll plan her path to destruction on my own!

I stood up, glared at him and said, 'well Eric… if that's your real name… you can count me out of this little game!' before I walked off towards the gate to the park.

I walked briskly along the path and sadly thought, 'I just feel like some innocent little butterfly that has flown into a spider's web and there are two spiders after me… Satan's Sister and this man Eric… however can I get free of their sticky web of deceit?'

When I arrived home, Sister Sam had left… thank heavens… so it only meant I had to deal with Mother dear and her thespian friend.

Mother glanced up at me and said, 'you've just missed Samantha.'

'Oh pity.' I said unconvincingly

'Yes, she's gone home to get some rest until she flies out to Boston on Tuesday.'

'I'm sure it must be very tiring travelling all the time and having to go to parties where ever you arrive,' I said sarcastically before I slumped down on the settee. Mother glared at me and said, 'that was uncalled for, Kate.'

'Well, it's how I feel about her.'

'Oh dear, oh dear,' said George with a shake of his head.

Mother looked at him and said, 'they've always been the same George... and I think Kate takes after her Father while Samantha takes after me.'

'It's such a shame when sisters don't get on... they should be so close, especially when they are twins,' said George. Mother sighed, nodded and asked, 'do you have any sisters, George?'

'No... just a younger brother.'

'Lucky you,' I said with a grin which he did not seem to appreciate.

I was taken aback when he continued, 'he was a Captain in the army and was killed on duty in Northern Ireland.'

'Oh, I'm so sorry,' I whispered.

He smiled and replied, 'you weren't to know, Kate... I think of him every day and thank heaven that he was my brother... we were always close, and when he was on leave we had many happy days together, with our wives.'

'Memories are such a comfort, especially when you get older,' said Mother.

'They are indeed, June,' George said in a whisper and I felt quite upset... I had put my foot in it once again. Perhaps I did need some guidance from Eric... but whatever he said I would still bring Sister Sam to her knees!

George spoke about many things and his travels and I was finding him quite interesting to listen to as the time passed. First appearances can be deceptive, which was certainly the case as far as George was concerned... at least in my eyes. Mother dear seemed to be enraptured by him and I realised that they suited one another and he would certainly be a good companion for her.

He left us in the early evening after some tea and Mother's home baked cakes. When he had gone I said, 'he seems very nice, I hope you invite him over again.'

'Yes, I will do.'

At work on the Monday I didn't waste any time when I met Emma for lunch in the canteen and told her all about Sister

Sam's 'fabulous' trip to New York.

'And she met a millionaire at his penthouse party... how fantastic!' said Emma.

'Well don't sound so pleased about it!'

'I'm not, but you must admit its bloody good for her first night there,' replied Emma with a smile.

'You sound as if you're on her side,' I said with a touch of bitterness.

'I'm always on your side, Kate, you know that.'

'Good, now I plan to do things to her that will make her squirm and beg for mercy,' I said firmly.

Emma looked at me for a moment and asked, 'is that really a good idea, Kate?'

'Yes it is ...and why not?'

'Well...'

'She's hurt me more times than I can remember... she's just a tart with no conscience whatever!'

'I know, but...'

'There's no 'but' about it, Emma she's for the big emotional chop... and its going to be done my way!'

She sighed and said, 'if you say so, Kate, but you could be wrong...'

'I'm never wrong when it comes to Satan's Sister!' I exclaimed loudly and noticed several office staff at the next table glance disapprovingly at me.

'Well I think you could be on a very slippery path...'

'Don't you start talking to me about paths as well as...,' I interrupted before I stopped short. She looked quizzically at me and asked, 'so who else is telling you that?'

'It doesn't matter,' I replied.

'Yes, it does Kate... I'm your best friend remember... so tell me.'

I thought, 'now I've put my foot in it again and will have to tell her about Eric.'

So I took a deep breath and replied, 'well while she was in New York, she met a Norwegian guy in the hotel bar, they started chatting and he said he knew me...'

'Knew you?'

'Yes...'

'But you've never been to New York,' she interrupted.

'No I haven't, but would you believe that when I went for a walk in the park yesterday... he only turned up.'

'How fantastic... what's he like?'

'Well to look at... he's absolutely gorgeous... but I think he's a bit peculiar,' I replied.

'Why?'

'Well he kept talking about how he was here to guide me and put me on the right path to my happiness... it was really all a load of bollocks.'

'Well, I don't think so, Kate... I wish some good looking guy would help me!'

'Oh I don't know... you might regret it and...'

'I doubt it... so what's his name?' she interrupted.

'Eric.'

'Eric who?'

'I don't know.'

'And are you going to see him again?'

'Apparently so.'

'What does that mean?'

'He said he'd take me out... and Sister Sam!'

'What... both of you?'

'That's what he said.'

'Well I think you're right... he does sound a bit peculiar... perhaps you should introduce him to me and he could take me out instead of you two... it would stop you squabbling over him,' she said with a smile.

'I doubt it.'

'Well you never know, Kate.'

I sighed and thought, 'she's not in any sensible mood to talk about my ideas for Satan's Sister so I'll leave it for the moment.'

'Let's go out for a drink tonight... I need cheering up on a Monday,' I said.

'Why not?... how about that little pub... you know the one... we passed it last week when we were going to the pictures and you said we should try it sometime,' she said with a smile.

'Right... I'll pick you up about eight.'

The afternoon dragged by in the lab with Roger behaving like an absolute plonker as usual. He does annoy me so much when he keeps checking everything I do all the time... and nit picking... can't I be trusted with anything these days?

Mother was not in a good mood when I arrived home and I wondered why but didn't bother to ask. I was sure she would tell me over dinner... and she did.

She looked at me when she had finished eating her egg and chips... we always have that on Monday... and said, 'Samantha may be thinking of living in New York you know.'

I thought, 'fantastic... I can't wait for her to be thousands of miles away!' She then went on, 'after you left us and went out for your walk on Sunday... which I thought was quite rude of you... and I think George did too... Samantha talked about New York and said she might fancy living there for awhile.'

I smiled and said, 'oh good.'

'It's not good at all... I mean, when would we ever see her?'

'I really don't know,' I replied... as if I cared what the Devil's Handmaiden did or where she lived.

'You don't sound very bothered about it.'

'I'm not.'

'You're just like your bloody Father... he never cared!' she said angrily.

I sighed and said calmly as I stood up from the table, 'I'm going out... don't wait up.'

I collected Emma just after eight and was surprised to see her wearing her little black dress and all made up and reeking of her favourite perfume. When we got into the car I said, 'you're a bit over the top tonight, Em... we're only going for a drink you know.'

'Yes I realise that... but you never know who we might meet,' she replied and I thought, 'she's always such an optimist... that's what I like about her... but I ask you... who were we likely to meet on a Monday night in a country pub?'

As we made our way towards the little pub I told her about Samantha living in New York and when I had finished she said, 'well that's good isn't it?'

'I think so, but dear Mother doesn't.'

'Well I suppose that's understandable.'

'You may be right.'

'And if she goes it'll mean that you can forget all about your silly ideas of revenge,' she said firmly.

'After what she's done to me?... never in a bloody month of Sundays!' I shouted.

There was a few moments of silence before Emma said, 'do you know, Kate... I'm seriously worried about you these days.'

'And why's that?' I asked as we pulled to the pub car park.

'Because you've got this crazy bee in your bonnet about Samantha and it will end in tears,' she replied.

'It'll end in her tears... not mine!' I replied as I parked the car and switched off the engine.

'Kate... will you stop and listen to me for a moment?'

'No... let's have a drink... then I might... but not if it's anything to do with Sister Sam!'

'You're mad... do you know that?' she asked as I opened my door and got out. I ignored her and locked the car.

The pub had a few drinkers at the bar and other than them it seemed quite empty, which was not surprising for a Monday evening. The barman glanced at us, smiled and asked, 'what can I get you ladies?'

I looked at Emma and asked, 'so, what are you having?'

'Oh, a gin and tonic I think.'

'And I'll have the same.'

'Ice and lemon?' the barman asked.

'Please,' I said with a smile and Emma nodded.

'Right,' he said before he picked up the glasses, put tinkling ice cubes in them and drained two gins from the optic. He added the tonics and lemon slices then said, 'there you are, ladies.' Emma paid him while I picked up my drink and looked around for somewhere to sit. I noticed a small empty table in the corner and as Emma turned away from the bar with her glass, I said, 'over there,' and started to walk towards it. Suddenly I was aware of somebody sitting alone at the next table and when I sat down I glanced at the stranger and to my horror saw the handsome face of Eric smiling at me.

'Oh my God... it's you Eric!' I exclaimed in total surprise.
'Hello Kate.'
Emma looked at him, her eyes widened and she whispered seductively, 'ohhh, yes!'

CHAPTER 4

SO MANY GORGEOUS MEN... AND SO LITTLE TIME TO SEE TO THEM ALL!

After Sunday lunch with Mother and her new artistically funny friend, George from Am Dram, not forgetting tiresome Kate, who waltzed off later and I didn't see again... thank God, I was driving back to Tania's flat to get some rest before flying out to Boston when the bloody accident happened. I had stopped at the lights, just before the turning to the flat, when this silly prat of a man crashed into the back of me! My head jolted back and forward, pulling hard at my neck and I felt as if I had been in a wrestling match and lost. I was shocked for a moment and started to think what unmentionable things I would call him for damaging my car when a very handsome face appeared at my driver's window.

He smiled and said firmly, 'I saw what happened, so stay still... please keep quite still...'

'Why?'

'I'm a Doctor and you may have a neck injury,' he replied.

'I don't think so.'

'You may think you're alright but I'm telling you not to move!' he said in a very firm tone... I do like a man who takes control... don't you? I sighed and did as I was told while he opened my door and the gormless git who had caused the accident suddenly appeared.

'Are you alright?' he asked anxiously.

Before I could say anything the Doctor said firmly, 'No, she's not!'

'Oh dear,' said the gormless one.

'I'll send for an ambulance...' began the Doctor.

'An ambulance? I don't need a bloody ambulance!' I interrupted.

'Oh yes you do... you may have a whiplash injury which could cause you problems in future unless we're careful now,' said the handsome one.

'Oh, hell!' I said loudly as I knew that my flight to Boston on

Tuesday was now unlikely... which made me angry.

'So keep still, until we can get a neck collar on you and get you out of the car,' said the Doctor, as suddenly a Police officer arrived and peered in at me.

'Is this young lady injured?' he asked.

'I'm a Doctor and think she may be.'

'Right... have you sent for an ambulance, sir?'

'Not yet, officer,' he replied as another Police officer arrived and looked quizzically at me.

'We'll take care of that, Doctor... now are you the other driver concerned?' the first officer asked the gormless one.

'Yes, yes... I am,' he replied hesitantly.

'Come with me to my car and I'll take a statement from you and I will require you to take a breathalyser test, sir.'

'But I haven't been drinking, officer.'

'Then you've nothing to fear have you, sir?'

'No... I suppose not.'

'Come with me now, sir and we'll get things under way,' said the officer in that no nonsense tone they use. They all disappeared from my view and the Doctor said with a smile, 'it was a lucky chance the police arrived when they did... and I think they may have seen what happened.'

'Yes... I suppose so,' I mumbled, not caring whether the police were there or not... it was my trip to Boston that I was thinking about. Why is it that when everything is going along nicely something unexpected hits and knocks you off course? I thought about the next flight to New York on Friday and hoped I would be fit enough to go as I didn't want to miss the party at Wills penthouse. The Doctor interrupted my thoughts asking, 'so how do you feel now and are you in any pain?'

'No... I'm fine thanks.'

'Good... keep still... now let me take your pulse,' he said as he gently took my wrist and glanced down at his wristwatch. This gave me the opportunity to look at him carefully and I thought, 'he is so bloody good looking, tanned with dark curly hair, big brown eyes and long eyelashes... oh yes... but I bet he's married to some bossy 'nursey' type. He looked at me, smiled and said, 'there... you seem to be alright.'

'I told you so.'

'Well it's better to be safe than sorry, Miss or is it Mrs?'

'Oh it's definitely Miss... Miss Samantha Harris... I'm an air hostess.'

'I thought you might be,' he replied with a smile.

'And how could you tell?' I asked, fishing for a compliment.

'You're slim, lovely and sophisticated... and we're close to Heathrow,' he replied... oh yes, that was a spot on answer and I was just about to say something like, 'well you're my idea of a perfect Doctor...' when the sound of an ambulance siren interrupted me.

'Ah, here they are,' said the handsome one and he left me. Suddenly I was aware of the passing traffic with people staring in at me. I felt very exposed until the Doctor arrived back with the ambulance men who smiled and one said, 'we'll soon get you out of there and away to A and E, love.' He produced a neck collar and proceeded to gently fix it around my neck, asking, when he had finished, 'is that alright, love?' I hate being called 'love' all the time.

I smiled and replied, 'it's okay, thanks.'

'Right, now we can move you.'

The ambulance ride with its sirens blaring to A and E was exciting but when I was taken into the emergency reception it all suddenly stopped dead. After being poked, prodded and peered at for ages and asked a lot of silly questions by 'teenagers' in white coats, called Doctors, I was whisked away to the x-ray department. When they had finished with me I was left on a trolley for what seemed hours before one of the 'teenagers' in a white coat came along and said, 'well everything appears to be normal with no discernible signs of damage to your neck vertebrae.'

I smiled and asked, 'does that mean I can go now?' thinking of my trip to Boston.

'Yes, but you must see your GP and take some time off work and rest,' he replied.

I thought, 'bugger that... I'm off to Boston and then to New York on Friday!' but smiled and replied, 'yes of course, Doctor.'

I planned to take a taxi back to the flat and phone the Police to find out where my poor car had been taken. As I made my way out through reception a voice called out, 'Miss Harris' and I turned to see the handsome one smiling at me.

'Oh hello, Doctor, I didn't expect to see you here.'

'I had to find out how you were and I understand that you are now alright.'

'Yes, apparently so... thank God.'

'That's good to hear... now may I give you a lift home?'

'Oh yes... thank you.'

We went outside and he made his way towards a fantastic looking silver sports car. He clicked the key fob and opened the passenger door for me to slide into the opulent interior. The smell of leather was almost overpowering and I guessed the car was quite new. Suddenly he was sitting beside me and he started the engine, which had a fantastic roar and I asked, 'so what car is this?'

'It's an Aston Martin DB 7,' he replied.

'It's new isn't it?'

'Yes, I've only had it a month,' he replied then asked, 'so where to Miss Harris?'

I thought, 'to heaven with you in this car,' but replied, 'I live near the scene of the accident, just in the next turning after the traffic lights.'

'Right... that shouldn't take us long to get there,' he said as the Aston accelerated away with a growl.

'I'm in no hurry.'

'I don't suppose you are.'

As we drove away from the hospital at speed I said, 'now I'm curious, you came to my rescue, organised everything, waited for me and now you're driving me home in this fantastic car and I don't even know your name.'

He smiled, glanced at me and replied, 'I'm Martin... Martin Palmer.'

'Doctor Martin Palmer,' I repeated slowly.

'Yes... I'm a GP.'

'Really... now I thought all young Doctors were poor these days... and this is an expensive car... so how...'

'GP's starting out generally are... and Aston's are expensive... but there are some exceptions,' he interrupted.

'And you're one of the exceptions!' I said with a smile.

'Yes I am.'

'Well lucky old you.'

'You could say that,' he replied with a grin.

'So would you like to tell me about your exceptions?'

'Yes I will... over dinner whenever you're free,' he replied and I thought, 'oh yes please,' but said in a nonchalant tone, 'and why not?'

'Good... so when are you free?'

'Ah, let me think... I'm flying off to Boston on Tuesday...'

'I wouldn't advise that... you should take some rest for a few days after the accident...'

'I'm perfectly okay ... the Doctor's said so,' I interrupted.

'You may think you are but I am sure you will feel some trauma in the next few days.'

I sighed and replied, 'I may do... but I'm sure I'll be alright at work.'

He sighed and said, 'well I just hope so.'

I decided to change the subject and said, 'well I'm back on Wednesday... so how about dinner on Thursday?'

'That would be fine... I'll pick you up at eight,' he said with a smile as I suddenly realised we were close to my flat.

'We're nearly there now... so take the next turning to the right before the lights,' I said and he nodded. The car swung smoothly round as if it were on rails and I was impressed.

'Stop just up there... behind that red car... that's Tania's, she's my flat mate' I said.

'Okay.'

The Aston pulled up and I looked at Martin and said with a smile, 'well thank you so much for everything, Doctor.'

'My pleasure... and its Martin,' he replied before stepping out of the car and hurrying round to open my door.

As I slid out of the comfortable leather seat, he said with a smile, 'so, I'll see you on Thursday then.'

'Yes... you will.'

'Please take care in Boston,' he said and I nodded, whispering, 'yes,' before I made my way to the front door of the flats. I turned and gave him a little wave before I opened the door to the hallway.

As soon as I entered my flat, Tania looked up from the settee, put down her 'goss' magazine and demanded, 'where the hell have you been, Sam?'

I sighed and replied, 'you just wouldn't believe it,' before I slumped down next to her.

'Well do tell then.'

'I was on my way home from Mother's…'

'That was hours ago and she's been on the phone every twenty minutes since you left… she's going frantic!' Tania interrupted.

'Oh God,' I sighed

'You'd better call her now.'

'I will in a minute.'

'So… where have you been?'

'As I said, I was on my way home and some gormless idiot crashed into my car at the lights…

'Oh my God!' she interrupted.

'Yes… then I was taken to hospital by ambulance…'

'Oh, no!'

'Oh yes… and there I was poked and asked silly questions by kids in white coats, then x-rayed before being driven home by the handsomest Doctor you could ever imagine in his new Aston Martin.'

'Oh… my… God!'

'And he's taking me out to dinner on Thursday!'

Tania's eyes widened in disbelief for a moment then she asked, 'would you like a scotch before you tell me how the bloody hell you manage to find gorgeous men everywhere?'

I didn't reply but smiled, fluttered my eyelashes at her and she sighed before casting her eyes up to heaven.

While we sipped our scotch I went over everything in detail with Tania. I phoned Mother, who was in a state and when I told her what happened she said, 'my God! I knew it, I just knew it… I thought you must be dead in a ditch by now… are you sure you're alright?' I assured her I was and would phone to let her know how I was feeling before I went to Boston.

The first thing I did in the morning, after several cups of black coffee, was phone the Police to find out where my car had been taken and was given the name of the vehicle recovery garage. I phoned my insurance company and gave them all the details and the helpful person said that they would handle everything and asked if I was injured. I said that I wasn't and would be at work and away until Wednesday. So everything was now okay but as the day wore on I felt my neck getting a little stiff. I shrugged it off as I was determined not to miss the trip to Boston. In the evening I soaked for a long time in a hot bath whilst Tania cooked dinner, I phoned Mother and managed to placate her. I felt a little better after the meal but went to bed early to recover completely for the trip to Boston.

After a slight delay in our departure time the flight was smooth all the way and we made good progress across the Atlantic. The passengers, on the whole were quite amenable, and nobody became obnoxious or particularly drunk, which was a blessing as I was not in any mood to tolerate a gormless git after the experience with the one who had damaged my car. However, I believe there is always an upside to everything in life and I had met the handsome Doctor Martin Palmer as a result of the crash. I wondered where he would take me for dinner… somewhere intimate and expensive I hoped as I served a fat American lady with a gin and tonic, just as she burped! Some people are very vulgar.

When we approached Boston we held in a pattern before we could land, which seemed to concern some passengers when Mac announced the slight delay over the speaker system… why do passengers always think something is wrong because we have to wait for a landing slot? Don't they know it's busy down there as well as up here?

Eventually we touched down smoothly and taxied to the hub where the passengers disembarked, with smiles of relief. Once they had all left the cabin we tidied up, checked the overhead lockers and prepared to leave the aircraft. I was excited and so was Tania and we wondered what adventures Boston would have in store for us. We waited with Ricky and some of the other girls by the door for Mac and John to arrive and when they did, I smiled at Mac and asked, 'so, where are you taking us tonight, Captain?'

'Nowhere I'm afraid.'

'Oh,, why not?' I asked.

'I'm sorry to disappoint you girls but the truth is I have to get some rest… I'm getting too old for constant partying.'

'You're never too old,' said Tania, Mac smiled and replied, 'but I'm sure John or Ricky will take you somewhere interesting,' he said before stepping out of the aircraft. We looked hopefully at Ricky and John and Tania asked, 'well, guys?'

John smiled and replied, 'I know a little place…'

'Oh good!'

'We'll eat first then I'll take you to the Zanzibar Club and…' he began.

'After that we'll go somewhere really interesting,' interrupted Ricky with a smile before he strode out. John looked a little perplexed so I said, 'the Zanzibar Club sounds just fine to me,' and he smiled.

We took a cab to the Excelsior, which was our crew hotel, booked in and went to our room, which was comfortable and spacious. I slumped down on the bed and felt my neck give a slight twinge, but it soon passed and I wondered if Doctor Palmer would examine me on Thursday… after an intimate dinner and hopefully, somewhere very private. Tania interrupted my thoughts and asked, 'do you think Ricky is a bit jealous of John?'

'Probably… after all, he is very good looking and he's a pilot… and most stewards are a bit envious of them,' I replied.

'Yes I suppose so… and I wonder where Ricky's taking us after the Zanzibar Club?'

'I've no idea… we'll ask him.'

'Do you think he'll tell us?'

'No… he will say it's a surprise… I think I'll have a shower before we eat.'

'Yes, I will too.'

We went down to the bar an hour later all made up and ready for the evening ahead. John and Ricky were already there but there was no sign of Mac. After Ricky ordered scotch on the rocks for us, I asked John, 'so where's our Captain?'

'He's just a bit tired and needs to rest before our flight back to Heathrow tomorrow,' he replied.

'He's alright isn't he?' asked Tania.

'Yes, he's fine, he just needs to sleep... he says that the jet-lag takes longer to wear off when you get older.'

'I know the feeling,' said Ricky with a smile.

Tania smiled and said, 'you're not old... I bet you could dance all night.'

'I probably could with you,' he replied and Tania blushed slightly before she asked, 'so where are you taking us after the Zanzibar Club?'

'Ah, that's a secret,' he replied.

'I told you he'd say that,' I said with a grin.

The restaurant was busy so we had to take our time over the meal as the waiters were rushed off their feet. Some of the other girls joined us as we finished eating and Jasmine sat beside me and asked me where we were going later. I told her we were off to the Zanzibar Club and she gave me a funny look before saying, 'well mind how you go in there.'

'Why?'

'Usually there are too many guys and not enough girls to go round... so you'll be fighting to keep them off!'

'Oh good... now are these guys handsome and rich?'

'Some are.'

'And how will I know?'

'Well you can see for yourself who the handsome ones are... and they'll tell you they're rich... but they're all bloody liars!'

'So have you been burnt recently?' I asked with a grin... guessing she had.

'Yes... he told me he wasn't married and was just concentrating on becoming a billionaire with his real estate business before looking for a sophisticated woman to be his wife and help him spend money along with the other wealthy ones in Boston.'

'And you fell for it?'

Jasmine sighed and replied, 'yes I did… it turned out he was married with three kids and worked in the local tax office.'

'I guess that was after he'd screwed you,' I said, she nodded and whispered, 'yes.'

I smiled and said, 'well don't give up trying… you might meet a lying frog who's really a Prince!'

'Not in Boston I won't.'

We left the restaurant and made our way out to the reception where I suddenly felt a twinge in my neck and needed the pain killers that I kept in my overnight bag. I stopped and said to John,' just wait a moment would you while I go up to my room for something?'

'Yes of course,' he replied while Tania glanced at me and asked, 'are you okay, Sam?'

'Yes, I'm fine thanks… won't be a minute,' I replied before heading towards the lift.

I stepped into the lift, pushed the button for the fifth floor and hoped my neck pain would not get any worse during the evening. I wanted a good night out at the Zanzibar Club and where ever else Ricky was taking us afterwards. The lift stopped at the fifth with a 'ping' and the doors opened. I stepped out, walked towards my room and saw bloody Eric sitting comfortably on a chair in the hallway.

'Oh, no… not you again!' I exclaimed.

'Hello Samantha,' he replied with a smile. I ignored him and carried on walking with my head held high to my room. He followed me and as I unlocked the door I said firmly, 'you're not coming in Eric!'

'Please let me give you some healing for your neck…'

'How do you know about that?' I asked angrily.

'Listen… I just know, alright? So let me heal you.'

I looked at him and melted… he was so handsome and his smile was captivating. I thought, 'well this could all end with being a toss-up between wealthy Wills, who was the front runner with his money, the lovely Doctor Martin with his new Aston

Martin and Eric blue eyes, who was probably poor, which is a shame, but I think all Norwegians are poor, don't you?... nevertheless... how lucky can a girl get?'

I nodded and said with a sigh, 'okay, if you think it will do any good.' He just smiled as I unlocked the door and he followed me into the room. He pulled the stool from in front of the dressing table and said, 'please sit down there.' I did and looked at myself in the mirror while he stood behind me.

'I hope you're not going to strangle me!'

Eric laughed and said, 'no of course not... I wouldn't dream of hurting you... now please just sit still and be quiet while I concentrate.' He held his hands above my head, closed his eyes and after a few moments I felt a warm glow around my neck and a tingling sensation in my head. The twinge in my neck was beginning to fade and I wondered what magic this gorgeous man was working on my body... it made me think of other things he might do to me that would send me into ecstasy... you know what I mean?

'Are you feeling anything?' he asked.

'Yes... I am.'

'Good... now just relax.'

I did and wondered if I could persuade him to work his healing powers on me down on the bed as I was feeling just a little overtired after the flight and needed something to pick me up before I went out for the evening. Within a few minutes the twinge in my neck had completely disappeared and I was just about to tell him when he said, 'I feel that your neck is much better now.'

'Yes it is... thank you.'

'Good... now I want to talk to you about...' he began when he was interrupted by a knock at the door and Tania calling out, 'are you alright, Sam?'

'Yes!'

'Let me in then.'

'Oh God,' I whispered under my breath... there is always someone or something!

I glanced at Eric in the mirror... he smiled and drew his hands away from me. I hesitated for a moment before getting up and opening the door. Tania followed me into the room looking concerned but stopped dead when she saw Eric.

'And who is this?' she asked in wide eyed amazement.

Before I could answer, Eric said in his clear, clipped voice, 'my name is Eric... and I am pleased to meet you, Tania.'

'Oh... do I know you?' she asked in a breathless, hopeful tone.

'No, but I know all about you.'

'Do you now?'

'Yes.'

'Well I hope it's all good.'

'It is.'

'Then I'll just sit for a moment while you tell me everything,' Tania said with a smile as she sat on the bed.

'We haven't got time now,' I said hastily and added, 'John and Ricky are waiting for us.'

'Let them wait while Eric tells all,' she said.

I sighed and replied, 'It'll take too long.'

Tania ignored me and asked, 'so who are you Eric?'

Before he could answer I said, 'he says he's my guardian angel... God help him!'

'Oh really... how wonderful... and are all angels as good looking as you, Eric?' she asked with a disbelieving grin.

'I'm not good looking only...'

'Let me be the judge of that!' interrupted Tania and he laughed, saying, 'as you wish.'

'So are you my guardian angel too?'

'I'm afraid not...'

'What a pity.'

I glared at her and said firmly, 'yes it is a pity... now let's leave Eric alone and go down stairs!'

'Oh, Sam, you're always in such a bloody hurry...'

'I am... and I'm also sure that Eric will soon turn up unexpectedly once again... he always does!'

'Oh, you lucky girl!'

'So some say... now come on, Tania.'

She got up from the bed and said, 'bye for now Eric.'

'Goodbye, Tania.'

She turned when she reached the door and said with a giggle, 'and Eric, if you happen to see my guardian angel... ask him to visit me as soon as he's free.'

'Yes I will,' he replied before he followed us out into the corridor and whispered to me, 'I'll see you later,' before disappearing through the door to the stairs.

Once safely in the lift heading downwards, Tania asked, 'now Sam, who is he really?'

'I told you, he says he's my angel and keeps popping up at all sorts of funny times.'

'That's all silly nonsense and you know it... so where did you meet him and what did you tell him about me?'

'Nothing... absolutely nothing,' I replied.

'I don't believe you, Sam.'

'Well you can believe what you like!'

'I bloody well will!'

'And if you must know I met him in New York and he says he knows Kate...'

'Your sister Kate?'

'Yes... there's only one Kate I know.'

'So where was he at Wills party because I didn't see him there?'

'He wasn't at Wills party... I first saw him in the restaurant at the hotel then when I went down to the bar he was there,' I replied.

'You didn't tell me about him.'

'No, I didn't, because you were asleep when I got back to our room and I just forgot to say anything on the flight to Heathrow... we were busy... remember?'

'Yes I do... but how could you forget to tell me about meeting a guy like Eric?' she asked as the lift stopped, the bell 'pinged' and the doors opened. I ignored her question with a shake of my head and strode across the foyer to where John and Ricky were waiting for us.

The Zanzibar Club was more than a bit of a disappointment and I thought that all the rich, handsome men must still be on their luxury yachts or at elegant parties for the very wealthy. There was no sign of anybody remotely interesting and I thought they'd hardly be likely to break away from their hobnobbing to come down to a dump like the Zanzibar to pick up something in a dress that they could play with for a night. Ricky and John took it in turns to buy us drinks and danced with us to the tuneless music of a hopeless trio before some old guy, who reminded me of Mum's Am Dram friend George, asked me to dance and I did... and wish I hadn't. He was all hands and smelled of a powerful fly repellent or was it cheap aftershave? As he clung to me like a limpet, he asked in a hoarse whisper, 'so what's a nice girl like you doing in a place like this?'

'I have no bloody idea,' I replied and he gave a chuckle before suggesting we went back to his place for drinks and to enjoy something a little more refined. He seemed quite annoyed when I said firmly, 'no thanks.' Our fleeting romance stopped right there and I made my way back to the bar through the half drunk, smooching dancers, joined the others and asked, 'so Ricky... where are you taking us next?'

'Well you're in a bit of a hurry to leave aren't you?' he asked in a surprised tone.

'Yes I am because this place is a toxic dump full of ugly old smelly men!'

'Oh dear... I'm sorry you think that, Sam,' said John apologetically.

Ricky smirked and said to him, 'I told you so.'

John sighed and replied, 'yes you did... well let's drink up and go then.'

Tania was as relieved as I was to leave the Zanzibar and we remained silent in the cab that took us across town to a night club called 'The Blue Windmill.' First impressions from the outside were good but I suppose we were expecting too much after New York. We were quite disappointed when we reached the bar, which was very gaudy with blue concealed lighting that hurt my eyes. John bought the first round of drinks awhile Tania and I surveyed the scene, which did not fill me with any confidence... the place was even more of a dive than the Zanzibar! The so called 'Jazz Quartet', wearing bright blue jackets, struggled to stay in tune and tried to cover it with a fat coloured guy occasionally playing his trumpet loudly.

'Oh dear God... what a hole this is,' whispered Tania.

'You can say that again,' I replied as I caught the eye of another strange looking middle aged man sitting alone at a table.

Tania sighed and said, 'I suppose this place is alright for men who have to drink themselves silly to forget whatever they need to forget…'

'… and for old guys looking for someone new to shag!' I interrupted while I glared at the old man still giving me the eye.

'Oh yes… I couldn't put it better,' said Tania as John handed us our drinks.

'Well cheers girls… here's to a good night,' said Ricky.

We said, 'cheers', and Tania whispered to me, 'somehow I don't think so.'

I replied, 'neither do I,' before sipping my scotch on the rocks.

'So let's make some excuse and go, Sam… we'll say we've got headaches or something,' whispered Tania.

'That's a good idea.'

'And when we get back to our hotel we might find Eric and chat him up… which would be better than staying here,' said Tania.

'I doubt it,' I replied before finishing my scotch in one go.

Tania finished her drink and when John asked her to dance she replied, 'I don't think I can, John… I've got a terrible headache.'

'Oh, dear… are you alright?' he asked.

'I will be when I have had some rest… I think I did too much on the flight out and I'm feeling completely knackered now.'

'And if you don't mind, guys… I think we'd better call it a night… I'm quite tired too,' I added.

'Yes of course,' said John while Ricky looked decidedly unhappy. Perhaps he thought he would get his leg over with Tania tonight… no chance!

In the cab taking us back to our hotel I thought about lovely Doctor Martin and our dinner date on Thursday and wealthy Wills party in New York on Friday night… life could not be better for me… oh, wasn't I a lucky girl? I was sure nothing could possibly go wrong… then I thought of Eric and hoped that he would not suddenly appear and screw things up for me… if he did… then I'd have to kill him!

CHAPTER 5

TRY AND STAY CALM, SAMANTHA... THIS MIGHT UPSET YOU A LITTLE BIT!

Eric did not stay long with us in the pub before he made some lame excuse about helping to 'guide' someone else... whatever that means. He said he'd see me again quite soon and left quickly, leaving me more confused than ever and Emma wide eyed and mesmerised. She looked at me and said in a whisper, 'well he's absolutely bloody gorgeous, Kate.'

'Yes he is... but he's a bit peculiar don't you think?'

'No I don't... so let me get some more drinks and you can tell me again how you met and everything you know about him,' she said before she made for the bar.

We sipped our gins and I went over it all again in detail, but I could not satisfy her curiosity and she kept asking questions about Eric that I couldn't possibly answer. In the end I gave up trying and told Emma about Samantha's so called 'accident'.

'Oh dear God... was she hurt?'

'Of course not!'

'Why do you say it like that?'

'Because the Devil takes good care of his own and she will never come to any harm, believe me!'

Emma sighed and said, 'I just wish you wouldn't say things like that, Kate... it's not like you and I know how upset you are over how she has behaved in the past... but you must stop this 'hate' thing and move on otherwise it will destroy you... and it just isn't worth it is it?'

'Oh yes it is... she'll be made to suffer as much as I have... I'll see to that!'

We stayed silent for a few minutes before Emma said, 'let's go shall we?'

'Already?'

'Yes, I'm tired and have had enough excitement for one night.'

The next two days at work were run of the mill and Emma

seemed a bit distant when we met in the canteen... which I put down to what I called the 'Eric effect'. Mother dear worried about Satan's Handmaiden until I was quite sick of it. The whole situation was getting out of my control... and I blamed Eric and Sister Sam for that... dear God, when would I ever find a solution to it all?

As I drove home from work on Thursday, I thought, 'perhaps if she went to live in New York, it really would be the answer to everything... Mother dear would obviously still worry about her favourite child but I could ignore her and Eric would be satisfied about his 'guidance' and leave me alone. I was still deep in thought when I parked the car and went into the house. I heard Mother dear talking to someone and then she laughed as I opened the door to the drawing room and ... bugger me... I saw Eric sitting on the settee with a cup of tea!

Mother glanced up at me and said, 'oh, hello dear... you're late.'

'Hello.'

'Eric has just dropped in to see me... which is a nice surprise... but you and Samantha already know him of course,' said Mother with a silly grin on her face.

'We have met,' I replied, wondering what on earth he was doing here... surely he wasn't interested in seeing my Mother... or was he?

'Hello Kate,' he said with his captivating smile which made me go weak at the knees... why does he have that effect on me?

'Eric was just telling me that he saw Samantha in Boston,' said Mother with a big proud smile.

'Oh, how nice,' I replied before slumping down on the settee near Eric.

'She's back now... and she phoned earlier to let me know she was alright.'

'Oh, good.'

Mother dear glanced at Eric and said, 'you must have been on the same flight as Samantha.'

He smiled at her and replied, 'no I wasn't on her flight... I always have to make my own arrangements to fly.'

'Oh... have you a private plane or something?' she asked.

'Yes... something like that.'

'Well that sounds very interesting, Eric,' said Mother and I just grinned, thinking, 'if he is an angel... which I very much doubt... he'd be quite tired after flapping his wings all the way across the Atlantic!'

'It has its advantages, Mrs Harris,' he replied looking quite calm and not tired at all, which was proof that he did not fly with angel's wings!

'Now would you like some more tea, Eric?'

'No thank you... I really must be going... I've still so much to do this evening you understand,' he replied.

'Yes, yes, of course...but tell me, Eric, what line of business are you in that keeps you so busy these days?' asked Mother and I thought, 'now this answer could be very interesting.'

'I'm on a special commission from a very high authority looking into people's life objectives and how I can help them reach their goals with fulfilment and happiness,' he replied with a smile.

Mother dear gasped before saying enthusiastically, 'oh, how wonderful, Eric... is it government funded?'

'I'm afraid not, Mrs Harris.'

'Well, as you're a Norwegian it must be the United Nations or something,' she persisted. I sighed, rolled my eyes and wished she would shut up.

'I really can't comment any further I'm afraid,' he said and Mother gave him a knowing nod and said in a whisper, 'I understand perfectly, Eric... it's all hush-hush.'

'You could say that, Mrs Harris.'

'Oh how very exciting!'

'Now I must leave you,' he said as he stood up and added, 'thank you for the tea.'

'You're most welcome, Eric... and please drop in any time you're passing,' she said with a broad smile as she stood to shake his hand.

'Thank you... I will... goodbye Kate.'

'Goodbye,' I mumbled as he strode to the door with Mother dear following. I could hardly wait for Mother to come back after seeing him out of the house to question her about his visit.

'So what was he doing here?' I asked as soon as she came into the room.

Mother didn't answer my question but said, 'he's such a nice young man... and he seems very keen on Samantha you know.' Well that did it!

'Bugger Samantha... what did he want for God's sake?'

'Kate... you are becoming so offensive these days that I hardly know what to do or say anymore... you're worse than your bloody Father!'

'Well that's all your fault!'

'My fault?'

'Yes... you and Samantha... you're the cause of all my troubles and unhappiness!'

'Well...'

'In fact you both get on my bloody nerves!' I shouted before storming out and going up to my bedroom.

Work was a drag all day on Friday and Emma was not at her best when we met in the canteen at lunchtime. She was very surprised when I told her about Eric's visit and asked why he came to the house.

'I don't know... Mother dear didn't say before we had a row,' I replied.

'Oh dear, Kate... you do seem to be constantly at war these days.'

I sighed, nodded and replied, 'yes and its all my bloody sisters fault!'

'Well... take my advice and give it a rest over the weekend...'

'I can't Em... I just can't,' I interrupted.

She sighed, glanced at her watch and said, 'it's time to get back... give me a call tomorrow.'

'Okay.'

The first thing I decided on Saturday was to go for a walk in the park to clear my head and think what to do next. As I wandered along towards the park gate I wondered if Eric would suddenly appear as he was always popping up these days. I half hoped he would so I could ask him about his unexpected visit on Thursday. I made my way towards the seat under the tree where we had met and talked previously and to my surprise he suddenly appeared from behind the tree. I gasped as he said, 'hello Kate.'

'Hi,' I replied as I sat down, hoping he would sit close to me... and he did.

'And how are you today?' he asked with a smile.

'I really don't know.'

'Why is that?'

'I'm confused...'

'Oh dear, I'm sorry to hear that... so what is confusing you?'

'You are.'

'Me?'

'Yes... why did you come to see my Mother?'

He looked away for a moment as if thinking what to say before he turned, looked into my eyes, smiled and replied, 'I came to see you... but unfortunately I was not able to be alone with you.'

I sighed and said, 'my Mother always gets in the way!'

'No she doesn't,' he replied and we sat for a moment in silence before I asked, 'so what did you want to see me about?'

'You are now at a crossroad in your life, Kate... and I am concerned that you do might make a mistake and take the wrong path.'

'And what path is that?'

'One which you will regret in future,' he replied in a serious tone.

'Well if you're an angel won't you guide me?'

'I will always be here for you, Kate... but I cannot interfere with your free will.'

'Perhaps you should,' I said with a grin and he shook his head, looked away then whispered, 'I only wish I could.'

'So what's stopping you?'

'The instructions from my higher authorities... which I have to obey.'

'Well just ignore them... I mean to say, if you really are an angel, which I don't believe for a moment... you must have super powers to do anything you want...which includes saving little me from some fate worse than death,' I said as calmly as I could.

'You don't understand, Kate...'

'No I don't Eric!'

He did not reply and we sat looking at the children playing on the swings for what seemed an age before he turned to me and said, 'Kate…'

'Yes, Eric?' I interrupted with a silly grin.

He sighed and continued, 'you must stop this business of seeking revenge on Samantha…'

'Not in a million years!' I said firmly.

'Then you will come to regret it and I am sad about that because it means that I have failed in my duty to guide you.'

'Well you could try and persuade me to stop.'

'And how may I do that?'

'By taking me out and spoiling me of course,' I replied and he looked at me with his blue eyes twinkling and said, 'then let me try!'

'Oh, yes, Eric… please do try,' I replied and thought, 'now it's time for me to make sure I have more allure than the Devil's handmaiden!'

'Right… now we will go back to your house and while I have a cup of tea with your Mother, you pack a bag for two or three nights, because we are going away,' he said and my heart leapt.

'Where are we going?' I asked breathlessly.

'To France.'

'Paris?'

'You'll have to wait and see,' he replied with a smile before he stood up and strode away towards the park gates with me trying to catch up. My heart was beating like mad as I thought, 'where is this gorgeous man taking me for days… and nights?' I kept repeating to myself, 'days and nights… alone with him… dear God, this was what I needed!'

Mother was surprised to see me back so soon but she was all smiles when she saw Eric who wished her, 'good morning, Mrs Harris…' then asked for a cup of her tea which he said he enjoyed so much last time he came to visit. Mother melted and was all of a 'tizz' when he said that and I rushed upstairs to pack leaving Eric to explain that he was taking me away to France for a couple of days… bless him. I quickly phoned Emma and told her the good news... she was struck dumb with excitement, which was a good thing in the circumstances as I hadn't time for a long conversation with her. I hurriedly packed and rushed downstairs with my bag full of everything I thought I needed... black lacy negligee, my push up bra, stockings, several pairs of high heels for dancing, two low cut dresses for dinner, my little black one and my red one with matching knickers... and I crammed all my makeup into my handbag. I was now ready to be whisked away to Paris, dined and romanced... and then afterwards... you know what... well a girl has got to have hope!

Eric was sitting on the settee calmly drinking tea with Mother dear gazing at him with far away misty eyes when I arrived in the room.

He glanced up at me and I asked, 'are you ready to go yet, Eric?'

'In a minute, Kate.'

'Well I'm all packed and ready.'

'Good.'

'Have you told Mother where we are going?'

'Yes I have,' he replied as Mother looked at me and said, 'you're a very lucky girl.'

'Yes... and for once I think I am... so where is it?'

Eric replied, 'it's a surprise,' before he finished his tea, put his cup on the coffee table, stood and said, 'goodbye Mrs Harris... we will see you in a few days time.'

'Just phone me when you're nearly home and I'll cook something for you,' she said with a smile... it's amazing what effect Eric has on everybody.

'We will... thank you.'

I followed him out of the house and he stopped by my car, saying, 'we'll go in this, Kate.' I was puzzled, thinking, 'surely were not going all the way to Paris in my little car?' so I asked, 'where to?'

'Southampton,' he replied.

'Southampton?'

'Yes, that's where the boat is,' he replied and my mind went into overdrive but I said nothing. I put my case on the back seat before starting the car and waving to Mother as I reversed out of the drive. We drove out of Bracknell towards the motorway that led down to Southampton and I started asking questions... but Eric was not in any mood to say much so I just stopped asking... I really didn't want to spoil this hopefully romantic trip to France.

As we reached the outskirts of Southampton he guided me off the motorway towards Lymington and told me that was where our boat was moored. Well, I didn't like the sound of this... I wondered, 'what sort of boat was it?' but decided not to ask. Eventually we reached Lymington and drove into a small car park near a jetty where several yachts of various sizes were moored. After stopping the car in a vacant bay I looked about and asked, 'so is this it, Eric?'

'Yes... our boat is at the end,' he replied, pointing casually towards the yachts bobbing at their moorings. I grabbed my bag from the car and locked it, wondering if it would be safe for a few days, then followed him along the jetty to the last yacht, which was much bigger than the others. He took my bag and helped me to climb on board this shiny new yacht which I guessed was about forty feet long. Once aboard I asked, 'is this boat yours, Eric?'

He shook his head and replied, 'no... and I'm only allowed to use it on special occasions.'

'So am I a special occasion?'

'Indeed you are, Kate,' he replied with a smile.

'Oh how nice,' I said in a whisper before following him to the steps down to the cabin.

My first impression of the spacious interior was superb as it was beautifully finished in gleaming varnished wood with fitted cream coloured cushions. He led the way forward and through a door before turning to me, saying, 'this is your cabin.'

'And where's yours?' I asked thinking, 'this is not my idea of romantic days away with a gorgeous man.'

'I'll be out there,' he replied as he dumped my bag on the double bunk and I thought, 'not if I have anything to do with it!' but replied, 'okay.'

'Get changed into something warm and comfortable, Kate... as we set sail in half an hour and I will need your help.'

I thought, 'bugger me... I've never been on a yacht before and he expects me to help sail this bloody thing... that certainly is not my idea of romance!'

As you already know I had only packed things for romantic nights in Paris and had nothing warm to wear on a yacht for goodness sake! I opened my bag, sighed and took out my dresses and hung them in the fitted wardrobe and left my cabin dressed as I was in a sleeveless pink blouse and jeans. Eric was up on deck fiddling with some ropes and a winch thing. He looked at me and asked, 'haven't you got something warm to wear?'

'No, Eric... I was expecting a trip to Paris... I didn't think you'd be asking me to help sail a boat... so I only brought dresses!'

'I'm sorry... I should have told you... and we're not going to Paris,' he replied whilst still fiddling with the winch.

I put my hands on my hips and thought, 'well that's another bloody disappointment!' then asked, 'so what do you want me to do?'

'Nothing for the moment, Kate,' he replied and I thought, 'oh that's good... now I'm a useless thing once again... this is not going at all well!' I glared at him and he must have felt something was wrong because he looked up at me, smiled and said, 'why don't you make yourself comfortable on the helm seat?'

'And where might that be?'

'Just behind the wheel,' he replied and pointed at the bench seat behind the large steering wheel. I nodded and made my way to the back of the boat, sat down as told and fumed slightly. Although it was now late afternoon the sun was still warm, so I settled back for some relaxation while he buggered about with the boat.

I watched Eric as he went from one side to the other making adjustments and doing things with various ropes and winches. To me it remained a complete mystery how the two of us were going to sail this boat to wherever in France, as I knew absolutely nothing about sailing and usually felt sick on the Isle of Wight Ferry when Dad used to take us on holiday when we were young. As the time passed I decided that I was not looking forward to this sea adventure with handsome Eric and hoped things would improve… but I somehow doubted it!

Suddenly I was aware of him standing front of me and he said, 'we're all ready to go now, Kate.'

'Good… so where are you taking me in this boat?'

'We're going across the Channel and then south along the French coast to Le Touquet.'

'Le Touquet?'

'Yes.'

'And what's so special about Le Touquet?'

'Ah, that's a secret.'

'Well I hope I'm not going to be disappointed again,' I said firmly and he just smiled then hurried away to the front of the boat where he undid a rope. We drifted out a little way and I began to feel anxious knowing I could not get off and go home. I watched Eric pull some strings around a sail at the front of the mast which billowed out and caught the light summer breeze. He hurried back to where I was sitting, took hold of the wheel and quickly moved it hard over and the boat swung gently round to face the harbour entrance and the open sea beyond. I heard the slap of the water against the hull as the boat moved forward and felt a little more relaxed… he seemed to know what he was doing… and if he was my guardian angel then nothing awful could happen to me… could it?

Once passed the harbour entrance and out into the sea the boat began to move up and down more than I expected and I worried about being sick all the way to France… oh, God help me. Eric turned round from the wheel, looked down at me huddled on the bench seat and said with a smile, 'we're on our way now,' and seeing I was going a pale shade of green, asked, 'are you alright, Kate?'

'I'm not really sure.'

'Well come and take the wheel while I get you a drink…'

'I don't want a drink so just leave me alone for a moment!' I interrupted sharply.

'Kate... the drink will settle you down and you will feel much better, please trust me,' he said with that wonderful smile of his. I shrugged then nodded and he said, 'now come and hold the wheel for me.' I did as I was told and clung onto the bloody thing with my white knuckles showing and he said, 'just keep her straight.' I nodded as he disappeared down into the cabin leaving me feeling very anxious and alone. Within minutes I saw another yacht under full sail coming towards us and I wanted to shout to Eric but it seemed as if I was in a dream where whatever you shouted could not be heard by anyone else. For a few moments I felt paralysed before myself preservation instinct made me swing the wheel to the right, the boat heeled over and I heard Eric shout in alarm from the cabin. I thought I'd overdone it and the boat was going to topple over into the sea but it moved to the right and away from the oncoming yacht so I turned the wheel back and it carried on as if nothing had happened. We passed the other yacht as Eric emerged from the cabin clutching a glass and looking anxious, 'whatever are you doing, Kate?' he asked.

'We nearly hit another boat... so I turned away and it missed us... there it goes,' I replied pointing at the fast disappearing yacht. He looked at it and said, 'oh well done, Kate.'

I smiled and replied, 'so it seems I'm not just a pretty face.'

'I know you are much more than that,' he said as he handed me the glass and took the wheel. I sat back on the seat and sniffed at the red liquid in the glass... it was brandy mixed with something so I asked, 'what's in this Eric?'

He turned round and replied, 'it's port and brandy... it'll make you feel better, Kate.'

I nodded, took a sip and it was really quite nice so I quickly finished it hoping I would soon feel well.

We sailed on and I felt better but began to feel cold and hungry as the sun set.

'Have you brought anything for us to eat on this boat, Eric?'
'Yes, we'll have something soon,' he replied.
'Good... so what is it?'
'You'll see... and I'm sure you will like it.'
'So I suppose it's another one of your surprises.'

'Yes,' he replied and laughed.

'And I'm getting cold now.'

He looked round and said, 'I will see you are warm in a moment,' and I thought, 'oh good… some cuddles will be just fine before we eat.'

Nothing happened for what seemed an eternity before Eric turned and said, 'we're passing the Needles at the end of the island now and when we have passed them I will prepare our meal.'

'Good,' I replied as I looked out at the white chalk cliffs standing in a row at the end of the Isle of Wight, Dad brought us to look at them every time we came on holiday… oh, what happy memories.

The boat sailed on and I was beginning to enjoy the slow, easy up and down movement as it gently rode the waves… but I was impatient for something to eat and getting colder by the minute. Eric seemed to know and he turned and said, 'now take the wheel again, Kate, while I get our food.' I did and felt quite pleased to be doing something and after he had disappeared down into the cabin I swung the wheel gently round and then back again… it was fun as the boat did as I wanted and I do enjoy being in control. Within moments Eric appeared again carrying a long white fur coat which he draped over my shoulders saying 'now this will keep you warm until the food arrives.'

I couldn't believe it as I stroked the fine white fur and said, 'wow, Eric… this is something a bit special!' He smiled, nodded and said, 'yes it is… and I will tell you about it later,' before he returned to the cabin. I soon felt very warm and pleased to be in charge of the boat and now only needed some hot food and a cuddle from this gorgeous man to make this sea trip to France more enjoyable. As it became darker I suddenly noticed the large silvery moon shining down and it seemed as if its moonbeams were dancing on the sparkling waves. I began to feel very dreamily romantic as Eric appeared, now dressed in a leather waistcoat lined with fur over his white shirt and carrying a large wooden bowl.

'Hold this for a moment while I lash the wheel,' he said, handing the bowl to me. I sat down on the seat and smelled the liquid in the bowl. I was not sure what it was but obviously some kind of soup with little bits floating in it and he had only brought one large wooden spoon to eat it with. After Eric had tied the wheel, he sat next to me, put his arm around me and I asked, 'what is this?'

'It is a Norwegian dish... a fish soup that is delicious,' he replied.

'And you've only brought one spoon?'

'Yes, we will share it and I will feed you,' he replied and I thought, 'oh... my... God,' and said, 'well let's try it then.' While I held the warm bowl he took a spoonful of the soup and I opened my mouth... the soup was savoury, smooth and delicious.

'Oh this is very good, Eric.'

'I knew you'd like it.'

'Some more please.'

'Of course.'

He fed me several spoonful's before he had some himself... it was so romantic sharing a spoon with him. When we had finished eating the soup he returned to the cabin and brought back a tray loaded with bread, cheese and fruit. He cuddled me as we helped ourselves and occasionally I fed him with a morsel or two of cheese and grapes.

The boat sailed gently along and as the night grew darker the moon lit up the shimmering sea. I turned to Eric and said, 'this is really lovely.'

He nodded and replied, 'as a Viking it is in my blood and I am very happy to be at sea... it's where I belong.'

'So tell me truthfully, Eric... are you really what you say you are... a Viking and all that other nonsense about being an angel?'

He looked at me with his twinkling blue eyes and said in a whisper, 'yes, I am, Kate.'

'I find it hard to believe.'

'Most people do... but it is the truth.'

'So do you always tell them?'

'Yes I do... I find it helps in the long run.'

'And when you guide people do they usually do what you tell them?'

He smiled and replied, 'not always... sometimes I have to persuade difficult women like you...'

'I'm not difficult!' I interrupted and added 'now don't spoil my romantic mood, Eric.'

'I did not intend to, Kate... I only wanted to tell you the truth.'

'Well that's okay then... so give me a kiss to show I am forgiven.'

'You're forgiven,' he said before giving me a long breathless kiss. As our lips parted I sighed and thought, 'now this is very good and just what I need at the moment.'

After a few minutes I asked, 'when will we reach France?' thinking if it was a few hours then perhaps I could persuade him to come to my cabin and satisfy my needs... you know what I mean.

'I have only set the jib sail which means we will have a longer crossing but smoother than if we were under full sail... so I think it will be some hours yet, and we will have to stand off the coast until it is light before entering the harbour.'

I thought, 'good answer, Eric, so that means I've got you to myself all night,' and I made plans to lure him to my cabin.

'Now let me tell you all about this fur coat,' he said with a smile but I didn't want to listen to any of his fairy tales I just wanted him... right now.

'I'm feeling a little bit cold... so can we go to my cabin where you can tell me?'

'Yes of course, Kate,' he replied and I thought, 'Yes!'

'I'll go down then,' I said and stood up.

'I'll be down in a minute when I have checked our heading,' he said.

'Don't be long,' I replied before making my way down into the main cabin and along to mine where I slipped out of the fur coat and lay on my bunk waiting for my new lover to arrive. I felt all tingly inside when he stepped into the cabin and sat down on my bunk.

'Now long ago we had a ceremony to...'

'Don't you think it would be better if you lay down here with me to tell me a romantic story?' I interrupted, patting the bunk.

'Yes... if you like,' he replied and I thought, 'oh yes, Eric... I definitely would like!'

He lay beside me and started telling me a story about some Snow Princess with a fur coat or something, but I wasn't paying any attention, then, after he had finished his short story and I was just about to make myself fully available to him, he said, 'I have to go up and check our heading.'

I thought, 'bugger me! I bet this never happens to Samantha!'

When he returned I was still anxious to carry on but he stopped my intentions to have him by saying, 'I'll have to remain on deck from now on to look out for other ships... it is very busy in this part of the Channel.'

'Yes, of course... will it still be busy when we reach France?'

'No,' he replied before he left the cabin and I thought, 'that's where I'll have him!'

Shortly afterwards I put on the fur coat and followed him up to the deck and sat on the bench seat behind the wheel. He was pleased to see me and smiled saying, 'we'll be arriving off the coast within a few hours.'

'Oh good,' I replied as I gazed out across the moonlit water. It was very beautiful and I did feel a sort of inner peace... perhaps it was the sea or more likely Eric... I looked at him as he stood at the wheel... his broad shoulders and slim waist, were so attractive... I sighed and thought, 'would I manage to catch him tonight?'

It seemed as if I was in a lovely dream with the man of my choice but it came to an end when he said, 'we're now near the coast, Kate... so I'll have to stay at the helm until its daylight.' I sighed, said nothing and thought, 'shame... but perhaps I'll have a chance to have him on the journey back to Lymington.'

The dawn was beautiful and as the sun came up I felt calm but excited at the prospect of a couple of days in France with Eric. We eventually sailed into the small harbour at Le Touquet and after tying up at a berth I made tea for us in the cabin before Eric went off to see the harbour master, while I waited on the seat for him and enjoyed the morning sunshine. He returned quite soon and said we could go ashore... I don't know what he told the harbour master but apparently everything was in order. We walked through the picturesque town and although it was a Sunday there were many interesting shops open getting ready for the day ahead. He led me out of the town towards the pine forest which he said held a secret place where I would feel relaxed and content... I wondered what he meant. As we strolled along the road into the forest I was impressed by the luxurious houses that had been built standing in their own grounds, surrounded by pine trees. Eventually we turned off the road onto a small track that led steeply up between two large houses and through the thickest part of the wood to a small clearing from where we could look down at the town and the sea beyond.

Eric held my hand looked into my eyes and said, 'this place is very special and I hope that by being here with me you will change from the path that you have been travelling along.'

'I suppose you mean my sister and everything?'

'Yes... I must guide you away from your desire to avenge yourself for her treatment of you.'

'Well you must admit she has behaved bloody badly!'

'Indeed she has... but revenge is not the answer to your long term happiness.'

'Is that so?'

'Yes.'

'Well, let me be the judge of that, Eric!' I replied angrily, he just sighed and looked out at the blue sea. We stood silently for some time both deep in thought before he said, 'let's sit awhile on this stone and talk,' as he pointed to a large slab of smooth slate which was set in the grass. The stone was surprisingly warm when I sat down on it and Eric joined me and gave me one of his disarming smiles. He spoke for some while telling me stories about people he knew and loved in the past. I was only half listening as I knew he would use his experiences to try to change my attitude towards Samantha but I had no intentions of changing my mind about her... I would have my revenge and nothing would stop me!

I think he realised that it was a waste of time and finally told me that he had brought the love of his life to this place many years ago. She was called Rowena and was a Saxon whom he wanted to marry but he was killed before he could do so... as if I believed this fairy tale nonsense, but hoped he might see me as the love of his life... and that would upset Samantha and put her back in her box!

Sometime later we drifted back into the town and looked for somewhere to have lunch. After looking at the menu outside a little café called 'Le Moulin', Eric decided that we would eat there. My prawn salad with avocado was delicious and Eric's moules and salad looked really good. We had a bottle of white wine with the meal and tea afterwards. Luckily I had bought my handbag with me, thinking I could buy something with my plastic in the town...well you never know what you might find... some shoes or sexy French underwear, but I had to pay the bill for lunch as Eric calmly said he didn't carry money!

We wandered about for a while looking at the shops before Eric said that we should return to Lymington. I was disappointed as I thought we would be away in France for a few days but I realised that as I had to pay for everything it would not be a good idea because I was almost at my credit limit. It was late afternoon when we boarded the yacht and set sail back across the Channel. Once outside the harbour Eric unfurled the main sail so we would make the crossing at a faster speed... not that I was in any hurry to get back. I decided to have one more try at Eric, using my allure to capture and keep him. The sails caught the wind sending the yacht simply whizzing through the sea with Eric standing proudly at the wheel. I gazed at him and thought, 'you really are at home here and I wonder if you will ever settle anywhere.'

As the evening wore on and it grew dark I went down to my cabin, put on my 'push up' bra and my red dress then returned to sit on the seat behind Eric. He looked at me as I appeared from the cabin and smiled, saying, 'you look very lovely, Kate.'

I fluttered my eyelashes and replied, 'thank you my angel.'

He laughed out loud and said, 'what am I going to do with you?'

I didn't hesitate, replying, 'make a fuss of me, Eric ... I need you in my cabin,' and kissed his cheek. He put his arm around my waist and drew me close to him, kissed me passionately and when our lips parted he said in a whisper, 'I can't make love to you.'

'Why not?'

'It is my duty to guide you and not get romantically involved.'

'So don't you love me?'

'I do indeed... but unfortunately I can't take you as I would wish to,' he replied and I went weak at the knees when he said the words, 'take you'... oh dear God, if only he would!

'So you're more like a brother then?'

'Yes I'm afraid so, Kate... but I wish it were otherwise.'

'So do I,' I said with a sigh and pulled away from him and sat on the seat.

We made the crossing in quick time and arrived at Lymington where Eric brought the yacht into the small harbour and tied up to the jetty. I sat motionless in the seat for awhile feeling desperately disappointed. It had all gone wrong... I thought he was taking me to Paris but we ended up in Le Touquet for a day! To cap it all, I had not managed to get him to make love to me as he should have... I was very sad and frustrated.

Thankfully my car was still parked where I left it and I slipped behind the wheel. We did not speak much on our way back to Bracknell and I knew Eric realised that I was very disappointed. Occasionally he tried to cheer me up but as we got closer to home I was determined to make sure that I had my revenge on Samantha... my life, unlike hers, seemed to be just one bloody disappointment after another! The Devil's handmaiden would pay for her sins and knowing she would suffer as I had done, I suddenly felt a lot better!

CHAPTER 6

WOULD KATE BE JEALOUS WHEN SHE FIRST MEETS MY MAN? I HOPE SO!

The flight back from Boston was routine and quite easy for us as there were only a few passengers on board and none of them were difficult... thank heavens. After landing at Heathrow we said goodbye to the passengers, tidied up, checked the overhead lockers and, other than finding some silly person's bag, everything was clear. Tania and I said goodbye to Mac, John, Ricky and the girls, left the aircraft and took a taxi home.

After we had each taken a shower to freshen up, Tania cooked us a quick meal of lasagne, which was straight out of the freezer and into the microwave... what wonderful time saving gadgets we have today to help working girls like us. We enjoyed a bottle of rich red Burgundy with our lasagne and I felt quite squiffy afterwards... which I put down to tiredness after the flight. I phoned Mother to let her know I was safely back and had to listen to all her problems before we said 'goodbye'. Tania talked for a little while about Boston before I decided to get some sleep so I would be at my best for my dinner date with Martin the next evening.

After a well deserved lay-in and a brunch of well done toast and black coffee that Tania prepared, I started getting ready for my date with the handsome Doctor.

I believe you can never spend too much time on getting ready for your next lover when you want to really impress him... can you? And I wanted to impress this handsome man, with his Aston Martin and 'special exceptions'... whatever they might be. As I lay soaking in the bath I thought of the trip to New York on Friday and wondered if I really had any chance with Wills. He was surrounded by glamorous women of all types and sizes so it was obvious that he had the pick of them all. He was very rich, good looking and single... the three most attractive things that a girl looks for in any man. Wills was just perfect for any woman so why shouldn't that woman be me?

I spent a long time on my hair, which didn't go the way I wanted at first but eventually it was just right and I was satisfied. Next I concentrated on my make up but dithered about the colour of my lipstick before deciding on Bermuda Blush to match my red dress. Suddenly I realised that the time had quickly disappeared so I slipped into my black lace undies, wriggled into my dress before giving a dab of Givenchy 'L'intense' in all the right places. I stopped in front of my full length mirror for a final check and decided that I looked presentable and very alluring to any red blooded man... so Doctor Martin I am all yours for the night!

I heard the sound of the Aston Martin pulling up outside just before eight and said to Tania, 'he's here now... so don't wait up!'

'I won't... but remember we're off to New York tomorrow.'

'Don't worry... I'll be back well before we're due to go,' I replied, slipping on my coat as I made my way to the door. I hurried down to the entrance and found him waiting for me with a lovely smile.

'Hello Samantha.'

'Hello.'

'You look absolutely gorgeous tonight,' he said with an even bigger smile.

'Why thank you, Doctor, and I'm already feeling better after hearing that.'

'Well I'm glad I have that effect on you... so shall we?'

I nodded and he led me to the silver sports car that looked so sleek and fast. He opened the door for me and as I slipped into the comfortable seat the smell of soft leather wafted around me. I thought, 'now this is my idea of a car... I wonder if Wills has one.'

As the Aston roared away down the street Martin said, 'I'm taking you to my favourite Italian restaurant in Ascot... I hope you'll like it.'

'I'm sure I will.'

'Good, now how is your neck... have you fully recovered

from the accident?'

'Yes... I feel okay,' I replied, but thought, 'perhaps he would like to examine me later,' so I added, 'but I do have a slight twinge now and then.'

'Oh dear... well to be on the safe side perhaps I had better have a look later.'

'Oh that's very kind of you... are you sure you don't mind?' I asked naively.

'No not at all,' he replied as the Aston accelerated to an even faster speed... I was really enjoying this and the evening had only just begun!

We arrived outside the 'Figaro' restaurant in Ascot in very quick time and Martin helped me out of the super car. He led me into the beautiful little, dimly lit restaurant where we were greeted by a smiling elegant man dressed in a white tuxedo, who said in a thick Italian accent, 'ah, gooda evening, Doctor, youra table isa ready fora you, sir.'

'Thank you, Tony.'

'This way if you pleasa,' he said as he gestured us to follow him. We were taken to a candle lit alcove with a table for two at the back of the busy restaurant which was very private. I sat in the alcove surrounded by red plush buttoned velvet while Martin was helped to his seat opposite by the ever smiling Tony. After placing the menus in front of us he asked, 'nowa, whata can I get you to drinka whilea a you choosa, sir?'

'What would you like, Samantha?'

'I'll have a scotch on the rocks please.'

'And I'll have my usual tonic and orange, Tony.'

'Very gooda, sir,' he said before hurrying away and I thought, 'oops... perhaps I should have ordered something a little less alcoholic... I didn't want him to think I was a lush.'

Martin smiled and said, 'I have to be sensible about what I drink when driving the Aston.'

'Of course... but is there a time when you're not sensible?' I asked coyly.

'Oh yes... I have no inhibitions at all when the time is right,' he replied with a smile.

'And when is that?'

'You may find out when I examine your neck,' he said with a

grin before he glanced at the menu and I thought, 'well here's hoping!'

So I asked in a whisper before I looked down at my menu, 'so is it your place or mine later?'

'Oh most definitely mine,' he replied with a chuckle.

I thought, 'I'm glad we've got that sorted as I do like certainty,' and replied, 'good… now I think I'd like the avocado and prawns to start with… then the lobster salad.'

'An excellent choice, Samantha… I'll join you with the avocado and prawns followed by steak Il Napolitano, it's delicious,' he said as Tony arrived with our drinks.

'Hava youa decided yeta, sir?' he asked as he placed the drinks on the table.

Martin nodded and ordered while I sipped my scotch. Tony was all smiles before he handed the wine list to Martin and hurried away.

'I don't think we should have anything more to drink unless you would like something from the list,' said Martin.

'No, I'm quite happy with just this,' I replied.

'Good.'

'So now tell me about your 'special exceptions'.'

'Ah, it's a long story…'

'I've got all the time in the world tonight,' I interrupted, giving him a quick flutter of my eyelashes. He smiled and replied, 'well I'm a very lucky man…'

'Oh, I like lucky men,' I interrupted again and he chuckled before saying, 'good.'

'So do go on.'

'I will if you'll let me.'

'I will.'

'Well my parents are wonderful and quite wealthy,' he began which pleased me… especially the wealthy bit… and I smiled.

'Dad is a commodities dealer in the City and has done very well over the years.'

'How interesting,' I murmured.

'Yes and he always said that he would see that my brother Robert and I had a good education then we could do whatever we wanted…'

'How nice.'

'So he sent us to Stowe School and up to Oxford where I studied medicine and Robert studied marine biology.'

'That's wonderful,' I whispered as Tony arrived with our starters and asked if we wanted any wine. Martin declined and went on with his story as I started on my prawns and avocado.

'Robert is two years older than me and is happily married to Rebecca, who is also a biologist and they now travel around the world together making underwater films for television.'

'How fabulous,' I said.

'It is... they both have deep tans and look very well when we occasionally see them.'

'Your parents must be very proud of you both,' I said with a smile.

'They are, but now they hint at having grandchildren and as Robert and Rebecca are so busy and I'm not married they have almost given up hope,' Martin replied.

'And are you looking for wife at the moment?' I asked with a coy smile... happy to know that he was single, rich and good looking.

'Possibly... but it all depends if the right girl comes along,' he replied.

'Oh I'm sure she will.'

'You seem very confident about that.'

'I am,' I replied with a smile.

'So can you predict the future?'

'No... but I know a man who says he can,' I replied thinking of Rafael in New York.

'Is he local?'

'No, he's in New York and is writing a book about his predictions.'

'That's a shame... I could have asked him about my future wife,' he said with a large grin.

'Well I'll be seeing him at a party tomorrow so would you like me to ask him for you?'

'Would you?'

'Of course... but I know what his answer will be.'

'So tell me then.'

'He'll say that you already know her.'

'Really?' Well I just wonder who that could be,' he said with a chuckle.

'I've no idea,' I replied, Martin laughed out loud then said, 'Samantha... you are very amusing.'

I smiled and asked, 'may I have another scotch?' as I finished the starter.

'Of course.'

'So it seems that your parents are responsible for your 'special exceptions'.'

'Yes, it was Dad... he gave us both a considerable sum last year so I bought my flat and the Aston and Robert bought a boat.'

'Really?' I asked in surprise then asked, 'would he like to adopt me?'

'Possibly.'

'Well, put in a good word for me next time you see him.'

'Oh I will... before you meet him.'

'Meet him?'

'Yes, I think that you should both meet.'

'Why?'

'Ah that's my little secret.'

'I'm not sure I like secrets.'

Martin smiled and said, 'let me order you another scotch.'

'Would you make it a double?... I feel all my inhibitions slipping away!'

'That what I like to hear,' he said with a chuckle.

Within moments Tony arrived with our main meals and Martin ordered my scotch and another tonic and orange. The food was delicious and we hardly spoke as we both knew that we would end up as lovers before the night was over and we wanted to get to that happy blissful moment without any unnecessary time wasting. After a sumptuous helping of Italian soft ice cream covered with chocolate sauce we stopped for a quick coffee before Martin paid the bill. We said 'goodnight' to Tony, promising him to come again soon, and left the little restaurant.

'My flat is quite close by,' he said as he led me to the Aston.

'Oh, good.'

The silver sports car literally flew across Ascot to Martin's flat.

He guided me through the carpeted entrance hall and upstairs to his spacious luxury flat with picture windows that overlooked the racecourse. I was enchanted by its comfortable homeliness and sank down into the cream coloured, soft leather settee with a contented sigh.

'Would you like another scotch?' he asked.

'No thanks, it's not necessary... but I would like a kiss,' I replied in a slightly slurred tone and he smiled, sat beside me took me in his arms then kissed me until I was breathless... I do like to be kissed like that. When our lips parted I said in a whisper, 'oh, Martin... I need you.'

'And I need you, Samantha.'

'I can't wait any longer... I'm so very hungry.'

'So am I, my wonderful darling,' he replied before he stood up, took my hand and led me through to the bedroom. We kissed as we undressed and in a moment I was stroking his lovely warm naked body and he mine. We caressed for a few minutes before he kissed my nipples and gently fingered me... I was wet and his touch was so gentle which made me even more aroused. He laid me down on the bed then climbed on top and I felt him slowly enter me with care. He was quite big and I became more excited the further he went up into my yielding body... oh God, this was lovely! His rhythm was slow, long and deep, which was fantastic. I wrapped my legs around his waist while he gently held my head and kissed me passionately for a long while. I felt my climax coming on and whispered to him that I was close so he went faster heaving himself up before we reached that wonderful moment and exploded into violent, convulsive passion. When it had passed, I lay gasping and so did he before rolling off my sweating body.

'Oh dear God, Samantha... that was fantastic,' he whispered.

All I could say in a whisper was, 'oh, yes it was.'

We lay silent for some time recovering before I said, 'I would like to stay here all night with you but I must be ready for work in the morning so please take me home.'

'Of course, my darling.' That was the second time he called me 'darling' and I liked it.

As we drove leisurely back to my flat he talked about our next meeting which would be on Sunday after I returned from New York. We kissed for some time after he stopped the Aston outside my flat and we finally said 'goodbye' as if we had been lovers for ages. Martin waved to me as I turned at the entrance to the hallway and I blew him a kiss before he roared off in the sleek silver car down the road and disappeared.

Tania glanced up from the settee and asked, 'well?'

'Oh, yes, very well!'

'And did he examine your neck?'

'No... but he did examine the rest of me!' I exclaimed as I slumped down beside her.

'Then I'd better get us a scotch so you can tell me all... and I want to know all the sordid details!'

So as we sipped our scotch I told her everything. When I finished, Tania said slowly, 'you lucky, lucky thing, Samantha,' and I just smiled.

After a wonderful night's sleep, I showered and dressed in my neat uniform feeling very happy and pleased with myself. We left the flat and arrived at Heathrow well before our flight time for departure to New York. From the moment we boarded the aircraft everything somehow seemed to go wrong... as if it was a warning not to go and felt a bit uneasy. The 'in-flight' food was late arriving which put us in a bit of a panic then the sink in the galley got bunged up. Ricky sorted that out after fiddling under the unit and we breathed a sigh of relief. We had only moments to get ourselves organised at the entrance to welcome the passengers on board. As they filed in I noticed one or two who looked as if they'd been drinking too much in the departure lounge and hoped that they would not become a nuisance on the flight... there's nothing worse than having to deal with a drunk passenger. When everybody was settled in their seats ready for departure, Ricky spoke to them over the address system while we carried out the life jacket drill and pointed at the emergency exits. After we had finished we strapped ourselves into our seats at the back of the cabin and waited for the take off. The aircraft taxied out and stopped in the queue behind the others waiting to depart... and we waited and waited. There was a growing atmosphere of unease and impatience amongst the passengers before Mac came on over the address and said that there had been a call from an aircraft ahead of us in the queue with a technical problem, which meant we had to hold until it had cleared the taxi way. Tania and I looked at each other and raised our eyebrows as we both knew this could be a difficult flight with disgruntled passengers.

It was almost half an hour before we began to move again and I was relieved when at last the engines roared and we rolled along the runway, picking up speed before we lifted off and climbed away, gently turning on to our heading for New York. From the very start we were busy serving drinks and meals to the passengers who kept asking when we would arrive at Kennedy as it seemed they all had appointments they couldn't possibly miss... except the drunks! Two hours into the flight I felt knackered but the thought of seeing Wills again in his luxury apartment kept me going until we landed at Kennedy.

After all the relieved passengers had left the aircraft Ricky told us to stay back because Mac wanted to speak to us all... I was anxious about this because I thought somebody may have complained about me... in particular one over-weight drunk who told me I was too bloody slow bringing him drinks! Tania whispered that she thought we were all in trouble and when Mac arrived with John in the main cabin looking serious we held our breath.

Mac cleared his throat and said, 'this flight has not been the best and to cap it all our ILS, that's our instrument landing system, has gone unserviceable as we approached Kennedy... which means we'll have to stay in New York until our engineers have sorted out the problem because we can't fly back to Heathrow with the system down.'

'How long will it take to fix, Captain?' I asked thinking about my hot date with Martin on Sunday.

'I've no idea, Samantha... but I'm sure our boys will get it sorted as soon as possible because it's costing the company serious money to stay here on an emergency stop over,' replied Mac. I felt relieved that nobody had complained about me or the other girls and we all left the aircraft before making our way to our hotel.

An hour later Tania and I went down to the bar hoping that Mac would be there and able to tell us when we would return to Heathrow. He was sitting up at the bar with John and Ricky and smiled when we got close.

'So, I see you're all dressed up for the night,' said Mac and I replied, 'we are, Captain.'

'Well, wherever you're going it will be without us because we have to stay here to talk to our engineers and we may go back to our maintenance hangar tonight,' said Mac.

'I thought we were all going to Wills,' I said.

'Yes... you can go with Ricky but unfortunately we have to stay here,' said Mac.

'It's a shame but it can't be helped,' added John with a sigh.

'So tell Wills what's happened and I'm sure he'll understand... now what do you girls want to drink?' asked Mac.

After a scotch on the rocks we went into the busy restaurant for our evening meal. I sat next to John and during dinner he said that the last time the ILS went down it took three days to fix, so he thought we may have to stay quite a few days in New York, which I was not best pleased about because it meant I would miss my date with Martin. I was in a so-so mood when I climbed into the taxi with Ricky and Tania which hurried us across busy New York to Wills apartment block.

The door to Wills luxury apartment was opened by a tall blonde, dressed in a low cut revealing black number and it looked as she had been poured into it by someone who didn't care about her appearance... her tits were positively bulging out the sides!

We looked her up and down as she asked, 'yeah?'

'We're friends of Wills,' replied Ricky and the blonde remained silent for a moment as her brain cell clicked in and she was thinking, 'should I believe him and let them in?'

Suddenly we heard Wills voice asking, 'who is it, Yo, babe?' Did I hear, 'Yo, babe?'

The blonde did not answer him but opened the door wide as Will came in to view and smiled at us.

'Hi, great to see you guys... come on in!' We smiled, said, 'thanks,' and entered his sumptuous palace overlooking Central Park.

'Where's Mac and John?' asked Will and Ricky explained what had happened.

Wills shook his head and said, 'well, I am sorry to hear that... but I guess you'll all be staying in New York for a few days 'til the plane's fixed.'

'It looks like it,' replied Ricky with a sigh and my heart sank again at the thought of missing my date with Martin.

Wills smiled and asked, 'so while you're waiting how about you all come with me and spend the time on my boat?'

'Your boat?' I asked as my heart lifted a little.

'Yes... I keep it down at Delaware Bay... its big and sleeps twelve,' he said with a smile.

'All in the same bed?' I asked, he grinned and replied, 'that could be arranged!'

'How very interesting,' I said and Wills laughed.

'Okay... so you'll come then?' he asked.
Ricky looked at Tania and me, shrugged his shoulders, nodded and said, 'I guess so... but we'll have to let Mac know where we are in case our engineers fix the ILS in double quick time.'

'Sure... just give Mac my mobile number and when he calls I'll have you all back here within a few hours,' said Wills.

'Sounds good to me,' I said and Tania nodded before asking, 'so are we the only guests on your boat?'

'No, there's a few more but you know most of them.'

'So who is this lady?' asked Ricky looking at the overweight, top heavy blonde.

'Ah, sorry, folks, this is Yolanda Vecchio, I call her Yo... she's another new author of mine... and she's fantastic!' replied Wills and I thought, 'I bet she is... I could see the attraction straight away because if she couldn't write she could suffocate any man with her tits alone!'

Wills added, 'Yo's writing a book about the position of women in the board room,' and I thought, 'well , looking at her it's probably on her back on the board room table.' He introduced us to Yo, who looked quite annoyed, so I guess she was not best pleased at having us along on the boat... she knew competition when she saw it!

Suddenly Kristal Day appeared with another scraggy looking woman clutching a glass and said, 'hi, Sam, glad you could make it.' I wanted to reply, 'well we lesbians must stick together,' but said, 'hi, Kristal... I've been looking forward to coming back to New York.'

'It's the greatest place on earth to be... now this is Lottie Franks, Wills editor... she's tough as old boots and doesn't let me get away with a single thing... her blue pencil is all over everything.'

I thought, 'I bet it is... the old boot is right enough and I bet she's always the one on top,' but said with a smile, 'hi, Lottie.'

Lottie smiled curiously at me, glanced at Wills and said, 'come on Wills, get us some drinks while we get to know these pretty little things.' I cringed slightly but smiled and glanced at Tania, who I could tell was also cringing inside at the very thought of Lottie getting too close and 'knowing' us... you know what I mean.

'Okay... what'll you have?'

'Scotch on the rocks,' I replied.

'Me too,' added Tania, Ricky settled for a beer.

'Coming right up,' said Wills before he hurried away to the bar where I glimpsed Fiona raising a glass and talking to a tall guy with a beard. I wondered where Yo fitted in with Wills... I mean, was she just another supposedly talented author or something else? Perhaps she fancied herself as the next Mrs Wills Hurst but Fiona was in her way... this boat trip could be very interesting. As I looked around at the other guests I noticed Rafael, he spotted us and came over.

'Hi, guys... so glad you could make it again,' he said with a broad smile.

'So are we, but we're stuck here for awhile because our plane's broken down, so whilst they fix it we are coming with you on Wills boat,' I said.

'That's fantastic!'

I spent a tolerable evening with Tania dodging all the inane conversations and comments by the lesbians, the over-weight blonde and Fiona, who constantly referred to Wills as 'her man.'

Yo was not too happy about that and I guessed she saw herself as a permanent resident of the apartment and Wills bed... if she could get rid of Fiona.

Wills made arrangements with Ricky for us to meet him in the morning at Newark airport, where he kept his private jet... I liked the sound of that! We would fly down to Baltimore and take taxis out to the small harbour in Delaware Bay where his boat was moored... I wondered just how big this boat was... a rich handsome man with an apartment to die for, a private jet and a big boat... what more could any girl ask for? Back at our hotel, and after talking about the party morons with Tania, I hardly slept that night just thinking about Wills and my possible future with him... but there was Fiona and now Yo in my way... I had to get rid of them if I was to stand any chance with Wills. What could I do?

Next morning at breakfast Mac told us that the engineers thought it would take at least three days to fix our plane's instruments as they had to wait for parts, so we were safe to go off with Wills, which pleased me no end.

We said 'goodbye' to Mac and John, climbed into a taxi with our overnight bags and headed out to Newark airport where we found Wills and the others waiting in the VIP departure lounge. We smiled and said 'hi' to the bleary eyed lot who obviously drank more and partied long into the night after we had left. Fiona and Yo looked particularly the worse for wear and I was pleased about that and hoped they were not good sailors so they would be stuck in their cabins while I made progress with Wills. The thought came to me as we excitedly boarded the sweet little jet parked on the executive ramp at Newark that Martin was now my man of second choice... poor boy, but he'd get over it... because whatever you don't get over... you die of!

The flight down to Baltimore was smooth and quick. During the journey I occasionally glanced at Fiona and Yo's anxious faces and noticed that they became even more pale faced when the plane suddenly turned sharply and rapidly descended to land... they obviously did not like flying and I hoped that they did not like boating!

There were nine of us altogether in the party and we made the trip out to the picturesque harbour in three taxis. I noticed that Will shared the first taxi with Fiona and Yo whilst Kristal, Lottie and Rafael climbed into the next one and we had the last cab. On arrival I was impressed by the sheer number of boats of all sizes and shapes bobbing at their jetty moorings in the warm sunshine. There were several very large motor cruisers moored at the far end of the nearest jetty and I hoped that one of these fabulous boats was Wills.

'Come on everybody… let's get aboard and crack open some Champagne before lunch!' said Wills with a big smile as he turned and led the way along the jetty. We were the last to follow him and as I walked along with Tania, I glanced at the yachts moored up, some with their busy owners getting ready for a day's sailing. Tania walked ahead trying to catch up with Ricky and I didn't notice the man with his back towards me bending down tying a rope. As I walked passed him he whispered my name. I turned back quickly as he stood up and stared open mouthed at Eric.

'Oh… my… God!'

'Hello, Samantha.'

'What on earth are you bloody well doing here?'

'Looking after you.'

'Well I don't need looking after thank you very much!'

'Oh yes you do, Samantha… you've already met the man you should marry and who would make you happy…'

'I know,' I interrupted impatiently.

'But you must be careful that you don't let him down on the boat,' said Eric with a knowing smile… that's the trouble with so called angels… they think they know everything!

'Don't you worry, Eric, I won't!'

'I wish I could be sure of that, Samantha… so please listen to my guidance.'

'No… you listen to me… I know what I'm doing and I'm going to have a good time on Wills yacht!'

'Well I hope you do and have no regrets afterwards,' he replied with a smile before he turned away and strode back along the jetty and what he said made me think for a moment. Suddenly I heard Tania calling my name and looked at her beckoning me from the end of the walkway. I hurried towards her as she called out, 'come on, Sam... Wills is waiting!'

I glanced up at the biggest cruiser moored alongside the jetty, Wills was standing on the upper deck of this fabulous boat waving at me. Tania clambered up the short gangplank to the deck at the back of the boat and I followed while glancing up at Wills and giving him a little wave.

As I stepped on to the deck, Tania asked, 'who were you talking to on the jetty?'

'Oh just some guy...'

'Was it Eric?' she interrupted.

'Well if you must know...'

'I must.'

'Yes.'

'I thought so... what is he doing here?'

'That's what I asked him but he didn't answer... just told me to be careful and then walked off.'

'How peculiar.'

I nodded and replied, 'I think so.'

Kristal and Lottie were looking out towards the open water of the Bay while the rest of the party were already inside the spacious lounge. I said to Tania, 'this is absolutely fabulous,' as I led the way through the huge open glass doors into the lounge.

'It is... and I didn't think it would be this big.'

'I did,' I replied as Wills appeared from a doorway at the other end of the lounge.

'Come on everyone... let's roll with the Champagne before we lunch and float this boat,' said Wills with a broad smile as a young man, dressed all in white, appeared behind him carrying a silver tray supporting nine Champagne flutes, with the golden liquid bubbling away. Yo and Fiona were served first followed by the rest of us while Kristal and Lottie made a late entrance.

For the next hour or so we drank Champagne, talked loudly and laughed at Wills jokes before the young man in white announced that lunch was served. We were all a little bit unsteady as we followed Wills into the dining room where a buffet lunch was laid out on a large polished wooden table. There was everything imaginable to eat, from crisp salads with oodles of dressings, piles of king prawns, cold beef steaks and rich trifles with cream; so we tucked in to this feast of fattening goodies. I noticed that Yo and Fiona picked and poked at the food as I guessed they did not want to get any fatter than they already were. That is the trouble when you're overweight... the fat doesn't come off very easily and it seems you only have to look at food to put it all back on... or so I've been told!

After lunch Wills gave us a tour of the boat and we met the Captain and his first officer on the bridge. They were suntanned, handsome guys and they gave Tania and me quite a look when we were introduced. Captain Peter hoped we all would have a good cruise and enjoy the Bay scenery before we headed out into the Atlantic. When I heard that I wondered where Wills was taking us... I thought of Mac calling us back to New York for the flight home and wondered how we could make it in time. Tania glanced at me and whispered, 'so where are we going?' I shrugged my shoulders and shook my head before we followed Wills and trooped down to the sundeck at the front of the boat. I noticed two guys busy untying ropes and felt the throb of the engines as they started up. Within a few minutes we were pulling away from the jetty and turning out towards the open waters of the picturesque Delaware Bay.

The young man in white appeared as if by magic and showed all of us to our cabins, where our bags had already been taken, and I was impressed with ours. It was spacious, beautifully furnished with two single beds and an en-suite.

Tania lay down on a bed, sighed and said, 'I could quite happily live here forever.'

'So could I... and I wonder what Wills cabin is like?' I asked.

'You'll soon find out, Sam... he's got his eye on you and you'll be hitting the sack with him so get yourself ready for action.'

'Not with Yo and Fiona hovering around I won't,' I replied as I lay down on the other bed.

'Wanna bet?'

I smiled and replied, 'no... but it would be good to push them out of my way.'

Tania laughed and said, 'they're no problem, Sam... Wills is after you and he'll get you for sure.' I thought, 'how romantic... a cruise with my future husband aboard his luxury yacht... and having all my needs met... fantastic food, Champagne and sex!'

We rested for quite a while as all the food and Champagne were having an effect and making us sleepy, we eventually pulled ourselves together and went up on deck. Lottie, Kristal, Rafael, Ricky and Wills were there gazing out across the Bay to the green rolling scenery but there was no sign of Fiona and Yo. As the boat moved gently up and down in the water I hoped that the two creatures were not feeling well.

Wills smiled at us when we joined them and asked, 'so what do you think of that?' as he waved his hand towards the scenery.

'It's fabulous... but where are you taking us?' I asked.

'To Bermuda,' he replied.

'Bermuda?'

'Yup.'

'But that's miles away in the middle of the Atlantic.'

'It's nearer to the East coast than you think.'

'So what happens if Mac calls us back to New York?' I asked, now worried that if we failed to show up then our jobs would be on the line.

'Oh, that's easy, Sam... I'll just call my pilot in Baltimore and get him to fly out to Bermuda and take you straight back to Kennedy so you won't miss your flight,' Wills replied.

I smiled and said, 'well you seem to have thought of everything.'

'I hope so... now how about a drink before we get ready for dinner?'

We sat on the sun deck watching the scenery pass slowly by whilst sipping more Champagne. I casually asked Wills about Fiona and Yo and he replied, 'they're not good sailors but I guess they'll try and make an appearance at dinner.' I smirked said, 'oh I'm sorry to hear that,' but thought, 'oh bloody good...my way was now clear to try and catch this handsome millionaire.'

Dinner was a candlelit affair in the dining room served by the young man in white assisted by an attractive dark haired girl, also dressed all in white. Tania and I were wearing our little evening numbers and I had splashed on more perfume than necessary. Wills looked gorgeous in full evening dress while Lottie and Kristal looked quite presentable and Rafael was wearing a white tuxedo and black tie. We had just been served our starter of prawn salad when the two harpies suddenly appeared looking like death warmed up.

Fiona bent down and kissed Wills on his cheek and said, 'so sorry we're late, honey, but we just slept for a little too long... I guess it was all the Champagne.' Yo nodded and whispered, 'sorry, folks,' before she sat down next to me. My heart sank and I glanced at Tania sitting opposite. She gave me a funny little knowing smile as if to say, 'don't worry, these two will not last the evening... so he's all yours.'

We enjoyed tender fillet steaks cooked in red wine and followed those with pecan pie, oodles of ice cream and all accompanied by various wines. Our conversations became more and more loud and boisterous with Wills saying the most outrageously funny things about his business competitors. I watched in fascination as Fiona and Yo slowly disintegrated into drunk, mumbling, giggling, incoherent witches oblivious to us. Wills gave Fiona a final disapproving look and said, 'babe... I think it's time that you got some rest.' She looked at him, nodded and replied, 'guess you're right, honey... will you come and tuck me in?'

'Of course.'

'And me as well?' asked Yo.

'I'll see to you both,' said Wills with a smile and I thought, 'oh bloody hell... I've lost him to the witches tonight.'

The two overweight drunks staggered from the dining room after mumbling 'goodnight', and were helped away by Wills. Tania and I went out onto the rear deck to get some air while the others sat around in the lounge. The breeze was warm and gentle as we stood at the rail watching the twinkling lights on the coast.

'Well, I'm sure Wills will be busy with those two for the rest of the night,' I said.

'He'll be back, Sam… you only have to wait,' she replied with a smile and lo and behold about ten minutes later he appeared. He put his arm around me as we stood at the rail and said, 'they're out for the night… thank God.' I smiled and replied, 'glad to hear it.' We stayed silent for a few moments then he asked, 'are you enjoying all this?'

'I am.'

'Good, now come with me … I've something for you.'

'What is it?'

'You'll see soon enough.'

I like a mystery, so when he held my hand and led me along the walkway towards the front of the boat I was more than happy. He opened the door to his master cabin and said, 'this is where I like to entertain my very special guests.'

'Am I a very special guest then?' I asked as I stepped into the fabulous cabin.

'Very… but I think you know you're more than that to me… so make yourself comfortable,' he replied as he closed the door. The walls were panelled wood hung with pictures of sailing ships lit by soft concealed lighting, which was very romantic. The cream coloured leather curved settee was fitted all along one side of the cabin and half way around the back wall with a huge black glass coffee table in front of it. I sank down into the soft leather as Wills asked, 'would you like a drink?'

'Please.'

'What'll it be?'

'Scotch on the rocks,' I replied, he nodded and made his way across to a bar in the corner with a black glass top. As he poured our drinks I asked, 'so what is it that you have for me?'

'Patience, Sam… patience.'

'Waiting for something is not what I'm best at.'

'I'm sure you'll be pleased when you see what I have for you,' he said as he brought the drinks over, placed them on the coffee table and sat very close to me.

'Aren't we going to say cheers?'

'Not until after I've kissed you,' he replied as he came close, paused for a moment, and kissed me very gently.

As our lips parted I sighed and whispered, 'mmm... that was good.'

'Yes it was,' he said as he handed me my Scotch.

'Cheers... here's to our future,' he said and I liked the sound of that. We drank in silence with my mind absolutely whirring with thoughts about this lovely man. Was I really his chosen one? Oh dear God I do hope so!

As I put my empty glass down he kissed me again and said, 'now it's time for you to see what I have for you.' He stood up, disappeared through a door and returned moments later with a dark blue velvet, box and sat next to me. He opened the box slowly to reveal a large diamond and emerald necklace saying, 'Samantha, this is my 'hello' to you and welcome to my world.'

I gazed at the glittering necklace and was struck dumb... which is not something I often experience.

'Oh... my... God,' I eventually whispered.

'Here... let me put it on for you,' he said as he took the exquisite piece from the box and placed it around my neck.

'Oh, let me look at it,' I whispered.

'There's a mirror through there,' he said pointing at the door. I stood up, rushed into the bedroom, sat down at the dressing table and looked in the mirror at the glittering diamonds around my neck. I was totally amazed at this wonderful gift. Wills appeared behind me and smiled, saying, 'you are truly beautiful, Samantha.'

'Thank you... and so is this necklace.'

'I hope you like it.'

'Like it? It's fabulous!'

He put his hands gently on my shoulders and said, 'I thought you'd be pleased... now let me tell you how I feel about you.' I smiled at him in the mirror and thought, 'this is interesting and possibly bedtime is now only minutes away.'

'From the moment I first saw you I had the feeling that you were somebody who would be very special to me and as I got to know you better I was totally convinced... so now you are now a part of my world and you must never leave it.'

I whispered, 'that's so wonderful to hear, Wills, because you are so very special to me.'

'My darling,' he whispered before he kissed my neck. I stood up and flung my arms around him and kissed him passionately. When our lips parted he said, 'let's make love now my darling, Samantha.'

'Oh yes... let's.'

'Please keep your necklace on... I want to see you naked and wearing only diamonds,' he said as he lay back on the bed while I slipped out of my dress and paraded for him in my black lace undies.

'Truly beautiful,' he whispered and I smiled as I undid my bra and let it fall to the floor.

'My God.'

I turned slowly away from him, slipped my knickers down and showed him my bare bum before stepping out of them then turning back to let him see me naked except for the diamonds.

'Just come here and let me have you!'

I did as I was told and he struggled out of his trousers while I undid his shirt. As soon as he was naked I lay on top of him, kissed him then sat up and guided him into my moist body. I rode him while he fondled my breasts and kissed my hard nipples as the diamonds slapped against my skin... that was a wonderful sensation!

It was only a matter of time before he shouted out, 'oh God... oh God... oh God!' and I felt his release... lovely... he was now my prisoner!

I rolled of his sweating body as the phone on the bedside table rang. He picked it up and still gasping, said, 'yes?'

'Hi, Wills... its Mac... the ILS is fixed so can you bring my crew back to New York now?'

CHAPTER 7

THIS IS NOT REVENGE, SAMANTHA… IT'S NATURAL JUSTICE!

After my lovely, but frustrating trip to France with Eric, the days at work ground on relentlessly with me still in a quandary to know what to do about Samantha. Emma was no help when discussing my annoyance and frustrations over lunches in the canteen and I almost gave up and took Eric's advice about revenge, when the opportunity I had been waiting for suddenly appeared.

The Devil's Handmaiden had arrived back from New York. Apparently, as a result of some trouble with the plane she had been stranded there for a few days. She was full of it when she came over to see Mother, who was concerned to hear that the plane had broken down in America and now worried about her favourite daughter's safety. I had to listen to find out what she had been up to so I put down my magazine and looked interested.

'Flying is quite safe, Mum,' cooed Samantha while looking smug.

'Well I hope it is, dear.'

'You've nothing to worry about… now, while we were waiting for the plane to be fixed, Wills invited us to spend a few days on his boat.'

'How lovely… did you enjoy yourself, dear?'

'It was simply fabulous and I had two super days with Wills,' she replied with a broad grin which meant he'd probably screwed her.

'Oh wonderful… so tell us all about it,' said dear Mother and once Satan's sister started she didn't stop for breath. We heard all about Wills again, his peculiar friends, the Champagne, the food and then the final crowning glory… the diamond and emerald necklace… which meant he'd definitely screwed her! I was still thinking about that when she dropped the next bombshell and announced, 'Wills says he wants me to be part of his life from now on… so he will probably marry me when I live with him in New York.'

Mother's jaw dropped open and there was a stunned silence for a few moments before she said in a whisper, 'you're going to live in New York with this man you hardly know?'

'I am,' she replied and I thought, 'anything in trousers, so no change there then!'

'But dear, have you thought carefully about this sudden decision of yours to live with some rich man, who's a stranger, just because he asks you to?' persisted Mother but it was no good, the Devil's Handmaiden had made up her devious mind and whatever the future held for her she was going to have Wills... and his money.

'I know he loves me... and I love him!' she replied and I thought, 'and his money!'

Mother sighed, shook her head slightly in disbelief and said, 'but if you go, when will we ever see you again?'

'New York is not the end of the world you know, you can come and stay with us in Wills apartment anytime you like,' replied Samantha and I wondered if Wills knew about this convenient arrangement.

'I know, but if you do go then I will hardly see you... and travelling abroad is not my favourite thing... besides, the airports are so crowded with foreigners these days and I really don't like any of it,' said Mother in one of her sad, lonely tones.

I smiled as I asked, 'so are you going to still carry on working for United?'

'I don't have to... Wills is a multi-millionaire and will take good care of me,' she replied firmly and I thought, 'I bet... 'till he finds out what you're really like then he'll dump you faster than the speed of light!'

Mother put one of her distraught faces on and asked, 'so when do you plan to go to New York, dear?'

'I'm due to fly out next Friday so I will stay with him and make arrangements then return on Monday, hand in my notice to United and leave as soon as possible after that,' she replied.

'Oh Samantha... this is all so sudden,' whispered Mother before she started to weep a little.

'Oh please don't cry... just be happy for me... it's all for the best and I know I'll have a wonderful life with Wills.'

Mother just nodded as she dabbed her eyes with a handkerchief and it was at that moment I thought of a cunning way to upstage my sister with her 'Wills' in a way she'd never, ever, forget! The plan for revenge is so sweet when it suddenly appears in front of you on a plate!

Over dinner the Devil's Handmaiden went on and on about Wills, his luxury apartment in Madison Towers overlooking Central Park, his private jet, his boat, his wealthy friends and while Mother dear looked totally bemused I listened carefully and made plans. After Samantha left us to return to Tania's flat, Mother asked me, 'so what do you think of her hasty move to live with this man?'

I shrugged my shoulders and replied, 'well it's up to her… she's old enough to make her own decisions about what she wants to do with her life.'

'I know… but it's all so sudden, Kate.'

'It is… she says she's in love with this Wills and he with her… so I guess that's okay.'

'I don't know how you can be so uncaring about your sister.'

'It's easy, I just have to put myself in her place and think what she would say if I was the one going off to New York to live with some rich guy… she wouldn't give a shit!'

'Kate!'

'I'm going to bed… goodnight.'

I lay awake making plans and decided that I would keep the plan to myself and not tell Emma… that would be best because if she didn't know then she couldn't talk me out of it. I was going alone to New York after the Devil's Handmaiden arrived back on her last flight and looked forward to meeting Wills in his apartment… which would be a surprise for him!

At work the next morning I put in for three days holiday for the following week and booked a flight for Tuesday with American Airlines to Kennedy Airport. I didn't bother to book a hotel as I would stay with Wills, although he wouldn't know that until I arrived… how exciting is that? Once all my arrangements were made I told Mother dear that I was going away to Scotland for a few days with friends from work. She didn't seem a bit interested and only said that I would probably miss Samantha when she returned from New York... as if I cared. The days dragged by at work but I became more and more excited as the trip got closer. The weekend with Mother nearly drove me up the wall so to survive I concentrated on my trip. Monday dawned at last and I went off to work feeling very happy. At the end of a boring day checking colour patterns I said 'goodbye' to Emma and everyone in the lab and hurried home to pack.

After telling Mother that I would be back on Thursday I drove to Heathrow, parked in the short stay car park and made my way to Terminal 5 and checked in. I was bubbling with excitement and anticipation when I went through into the departure lounge. With a little time to spare I wandered over to the book stall and browsed through the paperbacks trying to find something interesting to read on the flight and chose 'Amorous Angels'. According to the notes on the back of the book the story was all about handsome Angels who came to Earth in medieval times and had affairs with noble women... well they would wouldn't they? As usual the peasants would have to take care of themselves! I paid for the book, made my way over to the coffee bar and ordered a latte. I perched up on a bar stool and waited for my coffee and as the latte was placed on the counter a voice behind me said, 'hello, Kate.' I turned and looked into the handsome face and twinkling blue eyes of Eric.

'Oh... my... God! What are you doing here?'
'I need to talk to you before you go to New York,' he replied.
'About what?'
He sighed and replied, 'your intentions.'
'And what about them?'
'I have to try and guide you away from taking these foolish actions that will hurt you and Samantha...'
'Never mind about her!' I interrupted angrily.
'Is this man bothering you, Miss?' asked the barman who was waiting for me to pay him.
'No, no,' I spluttered and added, 'everything is okay, thanks,' as I handed him a five pound note. He nodded and looked warily at Eric, rang up the till and gave me a few coins change.
'Let's sit over there and talk... its more private,' said Eric

pointing towards an empty table in the corner. I nodded and clutching my expensive latte followed him, thinking, 'whatever he says I am going to New York to teach her a lesson she'll never forget!'

We sat down before Eric gave me one of his drop dead gorgeous looks and said, 'Kate, your future happiness is all I care about and it is my duty to do everything I can to persuade you to leave this path of hate and revenge…'

'It's not revenge, Eric… its natural justice!' I interrupted.

'You may think that, but you're wrong,' he said calmly.

'No I'm not… you don't know what that bloody cow has done to me over the years!'

'Yes I do… but revenge is not the way forward for you.'

'So what is then?' I asked before sipping my latte.

'You need to take time and reflect on what the future holds for you… the past is a country we can never return to… so you must concentrate on your future happiness which I know will come to you.'

I thought for a moment and asked, 'so you don't want me to go to New York?'

'No I don't… so stay here with me.'

Now, this sounded tempting, so I asked, 'stay with you? Where exactly?'

'At home,' he replied with a smile.

'You mean you're going to live with me somewhere?' I asked as my heart lifted.

'Oh, no, no, Kate… I mean you stay at your home with your Mother and I will see you occasionally,' he replied.

I sighed and said, 'just forget it Eric.'

He was about to speak when the tannoy went 'Bing-bong' and a woman with a high pitched, plummy voice announced that passengers on flight AA1272 for New York should report to gate 12 for boarding. I smiled, took a long sip of my latte, stood up and said, 'goodbye, Eric… I expect I'll see you when I get back… then you can tell me how foolish I've been!'

He sat open mouthed and I gave him a final glance before I flounced off towards gate 12.

The flight was smooth after we hit a few little bumps on our way up and I was served coffee by the smart hostess as we cruised along, then a reasonable airline lunch an hour later. I stopped reading 'Amorous Angels' and gazed out at the clouds way below as they slipped by, and thought, 'was Eric right about my trip?' I decided that it was necessary to have some revenge on the Devil's Handmaiden for all the harm she had done to me... a sort of justice which would then settle my mind for good. I finished reading my erotic book by the time tea was served and soon afterwards the captain announced that we would be landing at Kennedy in an hour. The plane touched down with a slight, gentle bump and we slowed before taxiing to the terminal. My stomach was starting to turn somersaults now I was here and about to face Wills... if he was at home. New York is about five hours behind us so as we left Heathrow at eleven o'clock and the flight took six hours it would be about midday local time... I hoped Wills had not gone to his office yet and was having an early lunch at his apartment!

I eventually cleared immigration and took a yellow cab from the airport into New York. The driver was a chatty guy who told me all about his family living in New Orleans, which helped take my mind off the meeting with Wills. The cab stopped outside Madison Towers and I paid the driver, who smiled and wished me a good vacation... if only he knew!

I plucked up courage and after entering the plush building, took the elevator to the top floor and when it pinged and the doors opened I hardly dared to step out. I took a deep breath, marched out of the lift and along to the large wooden door at the end of the corridor and rang the bell. My heart was racing like mad as I heard some movement inside the apartment before the door was flung open and there stood Wills.

'Sam!'

I smiled and said, 'da-dah!' and made a funny open gesture with my hands.

'Oh...my... God, Sam... you're still here!'

'I am.'

'So you obviously didn't fly home to London last night.'

'No I didn't, because I just wanted to be with you a little longer so I told Mac I was not feeling well and another girl took my place,' I lied convincingly.

'Well come on in, honey... I'm glad and so surprised to see you,' he said with a smile as I swept into his swish apartment.

It was much better than the She Devil had said... which, was a surprise to me because she normally exaggerates everything.

'Like a drink, Sam?'

'After I've had a kiss,' I replied, he smiled and he took me in his arms and gave me one hell of a plonker! I thought, 'wow! The She Devil must have really given the performance of her life last time he screwed her... but then she's had plenty of practice!'

As our lips parted he whispered, 'now, what about that drink?'

'My usual, darling... but after that kiss you'd better make it a double,' I replied before sinking down into the large, soft cushioned sofa. He laughed and made his way over to the bar and I thought, 'I'm really beginning to enjoy all this.' I looked around at the spacious room with its picture windows overlooking the Park and wondered what it cost Wills to live here... no wonder Satan's sister wanted to move in with him. As he handed me my scotch with tinkling ice cubes he asked, 'so, have you had lunch yet, honey?'

'No.'

'Great... I'll take you to my favourite Italian restaurant in Manhattan... then I have to drop into the office and see Lottie about the cover design for Rafael's book, afterwards we can come back here and spend the rest of the afternoon together before I take you out for dinner later... how's that?'

'Sounds fabulous,' I replied and lifted my glass up to him, he said, 'cheers,' before we clinked. The Scotch hit the spot and I felt very good.

'So how long are you staying, Sam?'

'I think I must go back on Thursday otherwise my boss will be suspicious,' I replied.

'Well I'm sure you'll be back here soon,' he said with a smile and I wondered why he didn't say anything about moving in with him... perhaps the She Devil had exaggerated this time!

'Yes I'm sure I will.'

'Good... then we can have more fun together here and on the

boat,' he said and I thought, 'so it seems that Sam is just his bit of English 'totty' to screw whenever she's available.' For a moment I felt angry for her at this... but it soon passed!

Half an hour later we left the apartment and took a cab to 'Mario's Restaurant' in Lower Manhattan. The place was very Italian and quite romantic with red candles in goblets at the centre of the white clothed, round tables. We were shown to a table for two by a smiling, talkative Italian with a Brooklyn accent wearing a white tuxedo and given large menus by the attentive waiter.

'So what do you think of my favourite restaurant, Sam?'

'It's very nice and I presume the food is good.'

'It's the best in New York, honey, so what'll you have?'

I chose a starter of a mixed salad dressed with olives followed by lasagne. Wills had the same starter followed by Tournedos Rossini and he chose a bottle of Chianti. As we sipped the wine Wills chatted about his publishing business and all the new authors he had discovered.

'How interesting,' I murmured occasionally when he paused for breath before taking another mouthful of Chianti.

'Yup... and I've got great plans for the future,' he said in a confident tone as our starters arrived.

'And what is at the top of your list?' I asked with a smile thinking it might be his future with Sam.

'I'm gonna open an office in Los Angeles... so I can be nearer to the movie business for book adaptations,' he replied with a smile.

'How exciting... are we going to live there?' I asked... well I had nothing to lose.

He looked puzzled and stopped chewing his salad for a moment then shook his head and replied, 'no, honey... I'll stay here in New York.' I noticed the 'I'll stay here' rather than 'we'll stay here,' so I guess I was right and Samantha is his English 'totty' for bonking pleasure and nothing else... the bastard! But she deserves him!

'Oh good... I'd hate to have to fly down to Los Angeles to see you,' I said with a smile.

'You'll never have to do that, honey... and if I go when

you're over I'll take you with me in my private plane.'

That would be fantastic,' I said enthusiastically and he nodded.

We finished our salads and he carried on about the prospects of getting his books adapted for screenplays, which would bring in a fortune for the authors, and his business, if the agents did what they were paid to do. Our main course arrived and he stopped talking to eat... I was relieved to have a moment's peace.

After a few minutes he asked, 'so how's your lasagne?'

'It's good, thanks,' I replied and he gave a small nod and carried on eating his steak.

We had almost finished the main course when he said, 'so tell me all about your family and friends in London honey.'

'Well I've a sister...'

'A sister... so what's her name?' he interrupted.

'Kate.'

'Is she older than you?'

'No, she's younger.'

'That's nice... I've got an older sister and she's always bothering with some dumb assed thing that's not important.'

'Oh, shame,' I replied and thought, 'I know the feeling.'

'So is Kate as lovely as you?' he asked with a smile.

'She's prettier.'

'Oh really... then I must meet her sometime.'

'I'm sure you will,' I replied with a grin.

'Well, I plan to come over to London soon, so I guess we can all meet up then,' he said and my heart fluttered and I thought, 'this could get very complicated!'

'And how about your parents?'

'They're divorced.'

'Shame, but that's the norm now... everyone gets married in a hurry then regrets it soon after... the damn lawyers are making a fortune out of other peoples misery,' he said, I sighed and nodded.

'So, what about your friends?'

'I've Tania of course and then there's Emma,' I replied and thought, 'if she could only see me now!'

'I guess you don't see much of Emma now you're flying all

the time.'

'No... but we meet up occasionally and go for a drink,' I replied.

'In one of your quaint old English pubs I guess?'

'Yes.'

'Have you told them all about your present?'

'What present?' I asked with my mind desperately trying to think.

'Your diamond necklace!' he exclaimed.

'Oh, yes, yes, of course...'

'And what did they say?'

'It was absolutely fantastic,' I replied.

'Good... and you can wear it for me when we get back... and nothing else,' he said with a grin.

My confused mind went into free fall wondering what I was going to do... I mean, had Satan's Sister take it back to London with her? Or did she leave it here with him to take care of? How would I explain this to Wills? Oh God... what a mess this could be. I needed time to think so I smiled and replied, 'I like wearing it with nothing else.'

'That's what I like to hear, honey.'

I giggled knowing that after lunch and the quick visit to his office, it was bonking time back at the apartment... well, there's worse ways of spending an afternoon than a session of sweaty horizontal line dancing with a handsome millionaire in his luxury penthouse.

We finished the meal with soft ice cream smothered in chocolate sauce followed by black coffee.

The yellow cab pulled up outside the skyscraper office block on 42nd Street and I asked, 'do you want me to come in?'

'Sure, honey, Lottie will be pleased to see you,' he replied and my heart sank... would she somehow realise that I wasn't Samantha? All women have a sixth sense about things that are curious and matter to them.

We took the lift to the fifth floor and stepped out into the carpeted corridor. Right in front of us were enormous glass doors with 'William T. Hurst Publications', boldly written on them in gold lettering. Wills led the way in through the swing doors to a huge reception area with the walls full of large framed book covers and where two attractive girls sat behind a desk. They smiled and wished him 'good afternoon, sir,' and he nodded before leading me through into a plush corridor, pausing outside a door.

'Lottie's in here, so just say 'hi' to her,' he said before opening the door for me. A middle aged woman wearing horn rimmed glasses looked up from her cluttered desk and managed a half smile at Wills then gave me a disapproving glance. I guessed she thought I was the Devil's Handmaiden, so I felt relieved.

'Hiya Lottie, it's good to see you so busy,' said Wills.

'Is it?' she asked.

'Oh come on now... don't tell me you're in one of your 'nothing's gone right today' moods,' said Wills with a grin.

'You could say that.'

'Hi Lottie,' I said with a smile.

'I thought you'd gone back to London,' she said firmly as she dropped her head slightly to look at me over her thick spectacles.

'Sam was a little sick so Mac told her to stay and rest until Thursday,' volunteered Wills with a smile.

'Well she looks fine to me,' replied Lottie before she glanced down at the paperwork in front of her.

'I always recover quickly so I think it's probably jet lag I'm suffering with,' I said with a smile.

Lottie gave a nod and said, 'yup... possibly... now, Wills, I guess you've come in to see the first God awful attempt at the cover design for Rafael's book?'

'Is it that bad?' asked Wills.

'I can't look at it for too long... it makes me feel sick,' Lottie replied as she handed him a white folder which he opened.

'Oh... my... God... it is awful!'

'Told you so... and only God Almighty knows why you pay those damned kids in Design thousands of dollars to produce such crap!' she said angrily.

'Well, Lottie, everyone deserves a chance...'

'A chance! We're trying to run an upmarket publishing business, Wills... not a charity kindergarten for dumb, talentless 'no hopers'!' she interrupted. He sighed, gave a nod, closed the folder and placed it back on her desk.

'Well?' she demanded.

'Tell Jo it's not acceptable and to try again.'

She fixed him with a stare that could kill at any distance and said in a menacing tone, 'just leave it all to me!'

'Yup... you're in charge, Lottie.'

'And you may regret that after I've finished with Jo and her department of silly kids!' she said firmly, he laughed and turning to me, added, 'I think we'd better go and leave Lottie to her work.'

'Yes of course...'bye, Lottie,' I said with a smile and she just grunted as she looked down at her desk.

Going down in the lift, Wills tried to excuse Lottie's abrupt tone but I wasn't interested in her, I was preoccupied with the whereabouts of the diamond necklace which I was supposed to wear when I was naked! In the cab he carried on talking about his plans for the business while I was getting more and more concerned the closer we got to Madison Towers, where I knew I'd have to have a good answer regarding the diamonds.

I was shaking inside when the cab pulled up outside the building and I felt sick as Wills helped me out. My heart was beating fast when Wills opened the door to his apartment and I followed him in then sank down on the sofa while he wandered over to the bar.

'Let's have a drink before we get started, honey,' he said.

'Sure... and make mine a double,' I replied in a nonchalant tone.

'Coming up... then you can just slip everything off... except your necklace and parade up and down for awhile... that'll make me so horny,' he said and I shuddered, thinking, 'God, whatever shall I say?' He left the bar with our drinks, handed me my Scotch and sat next to me. He smiled and said, 'just give me a little kiss to get me going,' so I did and when our lips parted we both said, 'cheers.' I took a large mouthful of Scotch hoping that somehow it would give me courage to tell him that I hadn't got the bloody necklace. We sat in silence and finished our drinks with my heart beating so fast now that I was sure I could hear it!

I thought, 'I must tell him now,' but before I could speak, Wills said, 'you go and get undressed, honey, and I'll get your necklace from the safe.' I sighed with relief when he said that and thought, 'Oh dear God, thank you, thank you... you've just saved me!'

'Don't be long now, babe,' I said with a relieved smile before getting up and heading for a door which I presumed led to a bedroom.

'No, I won't, honey,' he called after me.

I found the bedroom off the corridor and quickly slipped out of all my clothes. I just kept my high heels on and then strode out to pose and parade naked for the Devil's Handmaiden's lover... and I would be wearing her bloody diamond necklace!

I took a deep breath, entered the lounge and heard Latin American music playing gently in the background. Wills smiled at me and said, 'honey, you look fucking gorgeous, now let me put the necklace on you.' I nodded and turned around for him. He placed the glittering piece round my neck, fastened the clasp then stroked my breasts upwards and gently tweaked my nipples, which made me go all weak... mainly from relief! He turned me round to face him, kissed me until I was almost breathless then let me go and said, 'now, honey, just parade up and down while I sit and watch you.' I nodded and began to walk suggestively up and down in time with the music with my hands on my hips while occasionally giving him a coy glance. He kept whispering, 'Sam you're gorgeous, absolutely gorgeous.' Which is so nice for any girl to hear... although I'm Kate and he doesn't know it... revenge is so sweet! Don't you think? I kept walking, turning around and really enjoyed showing off my body in front of this handsome man for what seemed an age before he said, 'now let's go and do things!' I thought, 'oh yes!' and replied, 'why not?' He stood up and kissed me gently before leading me through to the bedroom where he pushed me slowly down on the bed. He slipped out of his clothes and stood for a moment holding his large rigid prick before he lay beside me and felt my moistness with his fingers while I sighed with pleasure.

'This is so good, honey,' he whispered before he rolled on top and eased himself into me gently.

'Oh yes,' I whispered as he began to ride me slowly at first then faster and faster until I felt myself edging towards a fabulous climax! He pinned my wrists down above my head on the soft pillow while I put my legs around his waist so I could feel him deeper inside me. Within a few hectic minutes he started shouting out, 'oh God... oh, God... oh, God!' before he rammed up into my body and exploded and I felt myself gripping him hard before I joined him in ecstasy!

As we finished moving, we gasped like swimmers who had just come up for air before he rolled off me and said, 'that was wonderful, Sam.'

'Yes it was.'

'You are a dream.'

'Glad you think so.'

'I do. Let's rest before we go out for dinner... then we can come back here and do this all over again!'

'That'll be so good, Wills, darling,' I said before I kissed him.

I was almost six o'clock when we were disturbed by the telephone on the bedside table. Wills answered it in a dreamy voice and I could hear it was Lottie on the line.

He murmured, 'oh, heck,' several times then, 'oh God,' and finished by thanking Lottie before he hung up.

'Is anything wrong?' I asked.

'It's nothing I can't handle, honey,' he replied with a sigh.

'Well what is it?'

He didn't answer my question and said, 'I think we'd better shower and have an early dinner this evening.'

'Why?'

'Do you always ask so many dumb questions?' he asked and it was obvious he was rattled by something Lottie had told him.

'Oh, I'm sorry I'm sure... just wanted to know if...'

'What?' he interrupted as he climbed off the bed.

I sighed and replied, 'never mind.'

He glared at me... as if I'd done anything wrong! ... men! He made his way into the en-suite and I heard the shower start. I didn't know whether to join him or not... I mean to say... he seemed to be in a foul mood just now... I suppose that's what you have to expect when a man has had his fill of your body and has other things on his mind. I decided to stay in bed and wait for Mr Grumpy to arrive after his shower… he certainly would be cleaner if not in a better frame of mind. He came back wearing a white towel around his waist and said with a smile, 'sorry, honey, I didn't mean to get so uptight with you just now.'

'Don't worry, babe, I do understand you must have lots of pressures with the business,' I replied with a smile before I slipped out of bed, gave him a kiss, handed him the necklace and waltzed off into the en-suite. After a refreshing shower I got dressed and made myself look reasonably presentable before I went into the lounge to find him. Wills was standing out on the balcony looking over the Park and clutching a drink. He gazed at me and I said, 'a penny for your thoughts.'

'What?'

I sighed and replied, 'it's a funny old English thing we say when we want to know what someone's thinking,' I replied with a smile before giving him a quick kiss on his cheek.

He grinned and said, 'let me get you a drink, honey.'

'Good idea… and make it a double!'

'Coming right up!'

As he went inside to the bar I gazed out at the view across the Park to the skyscrapers, now in the early evening beginning to show lights in thousands of windows. I thought New York was a magical place and could understand why everybody was so captivated by the city. I decided to take some photo's on my mobile to remind me of Wills and to show the Devil's handmaiden that I had been here with him… which was the purpose of my revenge…I felt so good about that! Moments later he appeared with my Scotch and we touched glasses and said, 'cheers.'

After taking a good sip of my drink I asked, 'so where are you taking me for dinner tonight?'

'That's a little surprise… but I know you'll like it.'

'Good… and can I wear the necklace to where ever you're taking me?'

'Fraid not, honey, you'd be overdressed,' he replied with a smile so I guessed it was back in the safe.

I said, 'shame…now let me take a photo of you looking out

across the Park so I can show you off to Kate and my Mother.' Wills grinned and replied, 'okay, honey, but make sure you get my best side.'

'And what side is that?' He laughed and I added, 'both sides look good to me,' as I kissed him on his cheek.

'Sam, you really are something special.' He posed and I snapped away and thought he was very handsome.

'There, I think that's enough,' I said.

'Okay, honey... now let's go to dinner.'

I slipped on my coat, grabbed my bag and he opened the door for me and standing in front of us was a tall dark haired, well dressed woman. Wills whispered, 'oh my God!'

'Hi, Wills... and who's this little fat hooker?' she asked in a strident tone as she looked me up and down.

'Her name is Samantha and she's not a hooker!'

'You could have fooled me, honey, but then you always did!'

'Samantha is from London, she's an air hostess...'

'Wow, that's a helluva long way to come for a lay with you!' she interrupted.

He sighed and said, 'you do appear at the darndest times, Maria!'

'Don't I just,' she replied before she pushed passed me into the apartment and slumped down on the sofa. Wills looked at me and said, 'Maria is my first wife...'

'Ex!' she shouted out, Wills nodded as she added, 'and one of many!'

I didn't know what to say or do in this dreadful situation and suddenly I just wanted to go home. I was about to ask Wills if I should wait outside when he said, 'Lottie warned me that Maria was in town and on her way over so I thought we'd go out before she arrived.'

I nodded and replied in a whisper, 'good thinking... so shall we go?'

He sighed and said, 'I'll see what she wants first... it could be anything... she's Argentinean and unpredictable... and very emotional.'

'And bloody rude,' I added and he nodded.

Maria glared at him and asked impatiently, 'so what have I got to do to get a drink round here?'

Wills closed the door and told me to sit while he poured some drinks. I sat down at the far end of the sofa and looked at this horrible aggressive woman while she glared back at me. We stared at each other until he arrived with the much needed Scotch. Wills sat in the easy chair opposite Maria said, 'cheers,' took a large swig of his drink and asked, 'so, what the hell do you want now?'

'Nothing that money can't fix,' she replied before downing her Scotch in one go. He sighed and said, 'I guessed as much.'

'Well think about it while I have a pee!' she said aggressively before she stormed out of the room. I looked at Wills and said, 'quick, let's leave her!'

'I can't honey… it's better that you leave, so take a cab and go to the office, Lottie will still be there and wait with her until I get rid of Maria… then we'll go to dinner,' he replied taking out his wallet and giving me a 50 dollar bill. I nodded, took the note and made for the door as I did not want to witness the oncoming row with his bad tempered ex-wife. I breathed a sigh of relief going down in the lift and smiled at the doorman outside the building after he hailed a cab to take me to 42nd Street.

There was no one at the reception desk at William T. Hurst Publications so I walked into the corridor that led to Lottie's office and knocked gently before going in. She looked up at me and said, 'well I guess madam arrived before you could both escape.'

'Yes, I'm afraid so.'

'She was here panting and snorting like an Argentine mare looking for Wills before she galloped out so I guessed she was on her way to his apartment,' said Lottie with a grin.

'Thanks for calling.'

'No problem, sweetie… shame you didn't manage to get clear of her in time.'

'It was… she's bloody awful.'

'You don't know the half of it… could you use some coffee while you wait for Wills?'

'Please,' I nodded.

'Make yourself comfortable because somehow I think you're in for a long wait,' she said as she stood up and went over to a table with a large coffee percolator. I sat down and wondered what I should do. I had got what I wanted and so really there wasn't any point in staying in New York any longer. While I was still thinking, Lottie placed a cup of coffee in front of me, resumed her seat at her desk and said, 'Wills life is a little complicated and it's all to do with money... that's other people's money.'

'Is that so?'

She nodded and carried on, 'add that to his string of disastrous marriages and you get some idea why he latches onto any sweet young thing like you to get his rocks off.'

'Really?'

'Oh, yes indeedy... so my advice to you is to high tail it out of here and back to London.'

'And why should I want to do that?'

'No reason, sweetie, other than it might stop you from being involved with his two timing confused life and going mad,' she replied before she sipped her coffee.

'I don't think so.'

'Well have it your way... has he given you the diamond necklace yet?' she asked with a smile and I was taken aback.

'Yes... yes, he has.'

'And I guess he's locked away in the safe for the very next time you're over in New York.'

'I suppose so.'

'Well I know so... he gives that little piece of real estate glitter to every new kid on the block!'

'Dear God,' I whispered.

'So, take my advice and leave.'

'I might just do that.'

'Good... now I guess he'll call soon and tell you he can't make it as something's come up... so I'll take you to MacClusky's for a bite to eat and book you into the Metropole for the night so you can catch the first flight out to London in the morning.'

'Well, that sounds good to me,' I said feeling quite relieved.

We talked for awhile about publishing as I did not want to know any more about Wills and his life dramas and she obviously didn't want to say any more. After about half an hour her phone rang and it was Wills. Lottie handed the phone to me and he said that things, 'were a little complicated at the moment and he was sorry, but Lottie would take me out for dinner at MacClusky's, book me into the Metropole then I could go back to London and he'd catch me the next time I was over.' We said, 'goodbye,' and I handed Lottie her phone and felt relieved.

Dinner at MacClusky's with Lottie was very enjoyable and she seemed to be more relaxed and less prickly. After the meal we took a cab to the Metropole and I was booked in on the William T. Hurst Publications account. I slept like a baby that night and felt okay when I went down to breakfast in the morning. I managed to get aboard the early flight back to Heathrow and felt as if I had accomplished my mission… to have my sweet revenge on Samantha!

CHAPTER 8

KATE... YOU ARE LOOKING AT THE NEXT MRS WILLIAM T HURST!

I could hardly wait for the next flight over to New York where I would see Wills and make our final plans to get married. Mother and dear Kate looked stunned when I told them, but I didn't care... I was going to marry a handsome millionaire and live in New York. I asked Tania to be my bridesmaid and she seemed even more excited than I was.

However, have you noticed that when things start to go wrong it seems they never stop and it's just one damned thing after another?

It started on the flight from Heathrow at midday on Friday. We were an hour into the flight when I had to deal with a drunken woman passenger who was obviously terrified of flying, and had got herself well plastered in the departure lounge, she then made it worse by ordering more Scotch from the trolley. A typical loud mouthed New Yorker, she complained bitterly when I said I thought she'd had enough. It ended up with her throwing her empty glass at me and demanding to see Ricky. I smiled and said I would get him so she could complain to him all she liked, but I wasn't bothered because I knew that this would be my last trip before I resigned from United. Ricky was diplomatic as usual and managed to listen carefully to the drunk before he suggested that she might like to have some coffee while he explained that alcohol had a serious effect on everyone flying because of the pressurised cabin. The woman was pacified while I poured the coffee and Ricky told her that her well being was all he cared about. She melted, calmed down and thanked him for his concern. Ricky smiled at her before turning to me and giving me a quick wink before he hurried away to the rear of the cabin. After that little episode we suddenly hit jet stream turbulence and Mac asked everyone to fasten their safety belts. The drunken New Yorker was immediately sick, either from too much alcohol or nerves, which caused two other passengers sitting beside her to reach for the bags... oh, God, I was so glad this would be my last trip! As I made my way back to the galley to get some coffee the plane lurched and fell like a stone which caused me to lose my balance and fall down in the aisle. I was not sure what I had done to myself but Ricky suddenly appeared above me and started to help me up.

'Are you okay, Sam?'

'I think so,' I replied but as I stood up my left ankle went and I slumped into his arms and yelled with pain.

'Oh Christ,' he murmured before he picked me up and hurried back to our station at the rear of the cabin, put me gently down on a seat and looked at my fast swelling ankle.

'I don't think it's broken... probably you've just sprained it,' he said calmly.

'Oh that's bloody good!' I replied thinking if that was true then all my plans would be straight out the window.

'Just rest and I'll get a cold compress for it,' he said as the plane took another lurch downwards. Tania appeared and asked, 'how on earth did you do that, Sam?' I glared up at her and replied impatiently, 'I damn well fell over!' Well, she does ask daft questions every so often.

'I do hope it gets better before you get married,' she said innocently as Ricky arrived back with the cold compress.

He looked quizzical and asked, 'who's getting married?' I sighed, shook my head and was about to say something when big mouth Tania blurted out, 'Sam... she's marrying Wills!' I could have killed her! Ricky looked stunned and after a moment's pause asked, 'are you really, Sam?' I smiled weakly, gave a slight nod and whispered, 'yes.'

'Good God! When did this all happen?' he asked.

'Oh... it's really hurting me now,' I said with a whimper so he bent down and placed the compress on my swollen ankle.

'Now, does that feel better?' he asked.

'Yes... thanks, Ricky.'

'Well, you should stay quiet and rest it until we land.'

'I will,' I replied with a smile as the plane lurched once more and this time some of the passengers let out little anxious cries.

'Tania, we'd better go and calm the passengers and clean up

any sick,' said Ricky with a smile.

'Okay,' she replied, as they left me in peace. My mind was in a whirl and other than Jasmine and Jane asking me what had happened I was left alone. Tania came and went but I didn't feel like talking to her much other than telling her I thought the swelling was going down. As time passed the turbulence slowly died away and we resumed a smooth flight, to the relief of everyone on board

After landing at Kennedy my first thought was to get to our hotel and see if I could manage to shower and pull myself together. My ankle felt a lot better and when Mac knew I had fallen and hurt myself he was very concerned. The passengers had all left the aircraft when Mac and John came back to see me.

'I think you'd better see our Doctor and take a few days off to recover,' he said as he looked down at me still sitting at our crew station.

'Yes... thank you Captain,' I replied with a demure smile thinking, 'oh goody...I can spend more time with Wills before I have to go back.' Ricky and Tania helped me up and I hobbled off the aircraft.

The Doctor saw me immediately and after an examination stated that I had suffered a sprain but nothing serious. So I was allowed to leave the airport with strict instructions to rest my ankle and report back in three days time so the Doctor could examine me and allow me to fly once again. Three whole days with Wills! This could not have been better. Once back at the hotel I had a shower and lay on the bed while Tania got ready for the evening's round of drinks and dinner with the others.

'Oh poor old you... stuck in for the night,' she said and I replied with a sigh, 'it can't be helped.'

'Well take care, Sam, and get some rest... I'll try not to disturb you later,' she said before she left our room. Once she was gone I hurriedly dressed and made my way out of the hotel where the doorman hailed me a cab to take me to Madison Towers. I was shaking with excitement when the lift pinged and the doors opened on the penthouse floor. I limped up the corridor, rang the bell of Wills apartment and Fiona opened the door.

'Oh dear God, it's you again,' she said in a slightly slurred voice so I guess she had been well oiled already.

'Yes,' I replied and limped passed her into the apartment.

'Sam!' Wills called out from behind the bar and I saw Lottie and Kristal sitting on the sofa clutching drinks.

As he came over to greet me he noticed my limp and asked, 'what ever has happened to you, honey?'

'We hit turbulence on the flight over and I fell and twisted my ankle,' I replied.

'Oh my God! Well take a seat and I'll get you a drink,' he said, I nodded said, 'thanks,' with a smile and sat down on the easy chair opposite the two on the sofa.

Lottie glared at me and said, 'so you didn't take my advice.'

'What advice?'

'To stay away,' she replied.

'I don't know what you're talking about,' I said as Wills appeared with a large Scotch tinkling with ice.

'There you are, honey... now tell me about your accident,' he said with a concerned look. I went over it all in detail and was conscious of the two women looking at me as if I was exaggerating my accident. Wills tut-ted in all the right places and asked how long I'd be staying in New York.

'For at least three days,' I replied.

'Well that's fine, honey... and as things have been a bit hectic around here recently...'

'You can say that again,' interrupted Lottie.

'So I think a few days away will help us all recover... don't you agree?' Wills asked, I nodded and Lottie said, 'you can't be serious!'

Wills looked at her and replied, 'Lottie, you stay and mind the fort with Kristal while I slip away for a break with Sam and Fiona.' When I heard that, I asked myself, 'Fiona? Why does Wills want her along with us?'

'My God, you're more of a fool than I thought,' said Lottie.

'I may be, but always remember who pays your Goddamn salary every month!' replied Wills before he downed his Scotch in one gulp.

There was moment of stunned silence before Fiona asked in a slurred tone, 'so where are we going, babe?' and I groaned inwardly.

'I'll think of somewhere nice and sunny,' he replied.

'Oh good... meantime... get me another drink, babe.'

The atmosphere was getting a little prickly so I decided to go back to my hotel and rest. Wills came with me downstairs and while the doorman hailed a cab, he said, 'have a goodnight honey... and I'll call by and collect you from your hotel about ten in the morning.'

'That'll be lovely... but why are you bringing Fiona on our trip?' I asked with a smile as the cab pulled up. Wills gave me a nice gentle kiss and replied, 'don't worry about her she won't be in our way... I promise... see you tomorrow honey... sleep tight.'

'I will,' I whispered before climbing into the cab feeling distinctly uneasy.

I was in bed and thinking about the trip to somewhere sunny with Wills... and Fiona... when Tania arrived back. She flopped down on her bed with sigh and asked, 'how are you feeling now, Sam?'

'Better, thanks... have you had a good night out with the others?'

'Oh, yes, shame you missed it... Ricky was on top form and danced with me, Jane and most of the girls at a night club somewhere in Brooklyn,' she replied.

'What about Mac and John?'

'Oh, we left them in some bar,' she replied.

'So they'll need a rest before you fly back.'

'No chance, we've been routed to Boston in the morning before we have a rest day,' she replied.

'Oh dear... it's all work these days for you.'

'You can say that again... are you really going to marry Wills?'

'I am.'

'And are you really sure about it?'

'Yes I am sure.'

Tania sighed and said, 'well rather you than me, Sam.'

'Why do you say that?'

'I just think you don't know what you're letting yourself in for… I mean, I know he's very rich and all that, but he is not right for you,' she replied.

'So tell me what I'm missing, before I marry this handsome guy with too much money, and spend my life worrying about things that don't bloody matter?' I asked angrily thinking, 'she's only jealous.'

'Well if you really want the honest truth…'

'Oh I do, believe me I do!' I interrupted.

'He's just so… so worldly, so difficult to understand…'

'Aren't all men?'

'I suppose so, but Wills life is complicated…'

'I know that, Tania.'

'And I don't think he'll make you happy… at least not for long before he starts to stray with other women,' she said, which touched a raw nerve as I thought of Fiona.

'Well I'm prepared to take the chance,' I said firmly.

'Good luck then.'

'Thanks.'

'I suppose you'll be leaving United?' she asked.

'Of course I will… I'm marrying a millionaire… remember?' I replied.

'I shall miss you, Sam.'

'And I'll miss you,' I replied and that was the end of our conversation.

Tania was up and in the shower the next morning getting ready for her flight to Boston while I was still sleepy in bed. I became fully awake when she said, 'goodbye, Sam… I'll see you back at the flat sometime.'

'Yes… hope you have a good trip.'

'Thanks,' she replied with a nod and with that she was gone. I looked at the clock by my bedside and realised I had only an hour to get ready for Wills. I hurriedly showered, dressed and plastered on enough makeup to look okay and packed my bag. I was waiting outside the hotel for just a few minutes when a large black limousine pulled up, the rear window wound down and Wills smiling face appeared.

'Get in, honey… we're running a little late.'

I smiled and said, 'okay, babe,' as the door opened and I stepped into the enormous car and snuggled up next to him on the leather seat. The limousine accelerated away at speed as I asked, 'so where are you taking me?'

'To Bermuda.'

'Bermuda?'

'Yup, I've got a little holiday villa over there,' he replied and I thought, 'oh this just gets better and better!'

'How fabulous, babe... and where's Fiona this morning?' I asked, hoping she was too drunk to travel.

'She's waiting at Newark,' he replied and I thought, 'oh, damn!'

On the journey out to Newark airport I tried to get Wills to talk about us and our future together but he just kept making excuses, saying, 'I've got important business to cope with at the moment, honey, so don't push me until things settle... then we'll have time to get sorted.'

I sighed and looked out the window at the busy traffic wondering what was in his mind... was he really going to marry me or was I just his English 'totty'? My mood was made worse when we arrived at the Executive Terminal and were met by an overdressed, heavily made up Fiona.

'Hi guys,' she burbled with a cheesy grin and I thought, 'this is going to be a ghastly few days!' but managed to say, 'hi' with a smile.

Wills attended to some flight documents before he said, 'okay, ladies, let's go.' We trooped out to his private jet and were met by the pilot before climbing aboard the luxurious plane. At the entrance the hostess said 'hello,' and gestured to the seats. We sank into the deep, soft leather and waited for the jet to taxi out. The take off was smooth and we climbed to cruising altitude before the hostess brought us drinks. As we all touched glasses Wills said, 'so here's to a few days of perfect peace in the sun,' and I just wondered how peaceful they would be with a blousy, overweight drunk in tow.

The jet touched down gently on the Island, shimmering in the sun. The passenger door was opened to a rush of warm air and I stepped down to the tarmac with Fiona following. Wills stayed to speak to his pilot while our bags were brought from the luggage compartment by the co-pilot, who smiled and wished us a happy few days in Bermuda.

After we cleared the quaint little terminal a taxi took us out to Wills beach villa. I was impressed by the place, with is glittering white walls and green tiled roof, swaying palm trees encircling the villa and velvety green lawns surrounding the split level house.

'This is lovely, Wills,' I said.

'Glad you like it, honey... and we have our own private beach too,' he said and Fiona added with a grin, 'it's great to swim here late at night when nobody can see you.' So I wondered how many times had she been staying with Wills and swimming late at night? No doubt it had always ended up with rampant sex on the sand!

'I'm darn hot, so let's get inside for a drink,' said Wills.

'So am I, babe,' said Fiona with a nauseating grin before we climbed out of the taxi.

Wills led the way into the villa and introduced us to his housekeeper and cook, Blossom, who promised to prepare such delicious food that would make our stay in Bermuda one we'd never forget. I thought, 'you may be right about that, Blossom cookie... but not for your food... more likely what Wills and Fiona would get up to on the beach!

Wills showed me to my room while Fiona already knew the way to hers, which did not please me. There was a large double bed, which bode well, and a spacious en-suite with all the soaps, shampoos and potions any girl could wish for. Huge glass windows opened onto a patio with a wrought iron surround containing a table and chairs and a covered swinging sofa... bliss... provided I could share it with Wills... alone! He gave me a quick kiss and said, 'come on down when you're ready, honey,' then left the room.

I opened the sliding windows and stepped out onto the balcony, breathed in the air, gazed at the blue glistening ocean and thought, 'this is better than living near Heathrow with Tania!'

We sat on the cool veranda drinking more Scotch while Blossom started lunch. I occasionally glanced at Fiona and when our eyes met I could see her dislike for me and I guess she wondered why Wills had brought me along to his island paradise villa. Presumably, she thought I was a straight laced diversion, who just lay back silently and let him finish, in contrast to whatever outlandish tricks she could perform on the sand or the bed.

Wills gazed out to sea and said, 'I think I'll go for a swim after lunch… so how about it, ladies?'

'Why not?' I replied.

'Oh no babe, it's too darn hot for me… so I'll just rest in my room 'til supper,' said the blousy tart.

'Okay,' Wills said slowly while nodding and turning to me gave a knowing look followed by a quick wink. I wondered, 'what on earth is he up too?'

In a little while Blossom arrived and announced that lunch was ready so we followed her into the dining room. We sat at the large glass topped table and Blossom served up a concoction of melon and fruit with a sweet sauce followed by a 'fish of all sort's' salad, which was quite tasty. We finished off with soft ice cream smothered with coffee liqueur.

I was feeling quite full and a little tipsy by the end of the meal and when Wills said, 'so let's go swim, honey,' I was tempted to say, 'no,' but just nodded and replied, 'okay.' Fiona gave me a peculiar look and said, 'well, while you go and get tired in the sun, I'll take a rest… so I can swim later.' I didn't know what to say to that so just nodded and left the room to get changed into my bikini.

Wills was waiting on the veranda for me dressed in his striped beach robe and asked, 'you okay about this swim, honey?'

'Oh, yes.'

'Good… and we can talk later,' he said with a smile.

'Fine.'

He led the way across the soft lawn and down the steps to the white sandy beach.

'This is all ours,' he said as he gestured in both directions and threw off his robe.

'How wonderful to be so private.'

'Yup, I like to think so,' he replied before he made towards the glittering sea gently breaking on the shore. I followed him into the cold but clear blue water and began to swim after him. He turned after we had gone out a little way and asked, 'isn't this just dandy?'

I nodded and replied, 'yup... it sure is.' I thought, 'I'm beginning to sound like an American these days.'

Wills smiled, turned and swam off out to sea but I decided not to follow. I swam up and down for awhile before I felt a little queasy... it must have been Blossoms rich food... so I got out of the water, collapsed down on my towel and started to improve my tan. The afternoon sun was now really hot and I thought I'd ask Wills to get some cream and rub it all over me... how nice!

It was quite awhile before he came out of the sea and slumped down next to me saying, 'boy, that was so good.'

'You must be fit.'

'Well, honey... I do work out when I can,' he replied.

'And it shows,' I said with a grin, adding, 'now I'm really burning up here, so would you get some sun cream from my room and rub it all over me?'

'Of course, honey... I'll be right back,' he replied.

'Thanks, babe.'

I lay there on the hot sand getting more and more burned until I could stand it no longer so I went in search of my millionaire fiancé and the sun cream. I hurried back to my room to find my cream and fiancé and was met by a ghastly, horrid sight I'll never, ever forget.

Fiona was stark naked and kneeling on my bed... yes, my bed... she was cross eyed, open mouthed and her huge tits were swinging gently as Wills pounded into her from the back, his hands clutching great folds of white flesh scooped up from her fat arse!

I screamed, 'Wills how could you... how bloody could you?' before storming out of my room. I heard him call out, 'oh God... oh God... oh yes! It's not what you think, honey!'

I thought, 'I've heard that before!' as I burst into tears. I made for the veranda and wondered how I could get rid of the fat blousy tart forever... or if I failed I knew I would give Wills up, our bedroom would be bloody overcrowded with her body rolling about on the bed... and I couldn't stand that! I sat and gazed out at the ocean as I tried to think clearly before he eventually arrived, gently touched my shoulder and whispered, 'I'm so sorry, honey.'

'Is that sorry you got caught or sorry for what you've done to me?' I asked angrily. 'I'm really sorry... so sorry,' he sighed as he sat down next to me.

'I just don't understand, Wills... what has she got to give that I haven't already given you?' I asked as the tears streamed down my face in utter disappointment. It's always men who mess up women!

'Honey, I know it's difficult...'

'You can say that again!' I interrupted.

He sighed, shook his head and said gently, 'I have special needs...'

'Like what?' I demanded.

'I need to...'

'You can tell me... I don't suffer from shyness you know,' I interrupted firmly.

He hesitated before he replied, 'I have to have a woman who'll do things that any respectable woman like you just wouldn't do.'

'So tell me then,' I said, now full of curiousness... I mean, what could the blousy fat old tart do that I couldn't do for him... or to him?

'I think the world of you, Sam, believe me...'

'Huh... oh really? So is that why you had to shag her on my bed while you're supposed to be engaged to me?'

He shook his head and replied, 'I need to use her to do things... like getting caught by somebody in the middle of it... and when I'm about to unload into her gives me the biggest kick of all that I can't resist... and I have to finish while they watch.'

I looked at him, thinking, 'oh you kinky, handsome bugger, you,' and said slowly, 'so you wanted me to catch you at it?'

He nodded and replied, 'well sort of... but I didn't mean to hurt you, Sam.'

'Well you did.'

'I'm sorry about that... and you must believe that she means nothing, absolutely nothing to me.'

There were a few moments of silence while I quickly thought of all the money, the apartment, the villa, the boat and the private jet and decided to go with the flow saying, 'so what makes you think I wouldn't do kinky things for you?'

'Would you?' he asked in an incredulous tone.

'Yes... I'll do whatever you want, babe... provided you get rid of her forever... and I mean forever!' I replied.

'Oh honey... I will, I sure will if you'll perform like she does,' he said enthusiastically and I thought, 'job done...now he can tell me everything... well, a girl's got to know what she's letting herself in for... hasn't she?

'So, babe... just tell me everything you want me to do and I'll just do it... because I love you,' I said with a triumphant smile... oh there's nothing like winning!

Wills kissed me passionately and when our lips parted he whispered, 'honey, you are the best thing that's ever happened to me... do you know that?'

I nodded and replied, 'you'd better believe it, babe!' and thought, 'goodbye, fat Fiona... you're history now!'

We sat talking for a while and he told me some of things he got up to with the blousy tart, which didn't surprise me. Quickies in lifts, back's of cabs in traffic jams, toilets in trains and planes... you name it they did it... which made me think I was about to enjoy sex with this kinky millionaire, anywhere he fancied that we might get caught. Men are funny creatures and quite hard to understand... don't you agree?

Half an hour later Blossom arrived carrying a silver tray with tea and sandwiches. She looked at me as she put the tray down and said, 'my word, missy, you've caught the sun today.'

'Yes, I have.'

'Well, mind how you go... too much of it can be really bad for you.'

'I will,' I replied as the fat blousy one came out onto the veranda dressed in a white almost transparent beach robe. She grinned like a contented cat, sat opposite Wills and asked, 'so how was it for you this time, babe?'

'It was absolutely great, Fiona,' he replied and she grinned even more as she looked at me... as if to say, 'see... I can give him what he wants any time I like and you are so out of it now... and no competition!'

'I'm so glad you enjoyed it, babe,' said Fiona with a smirk and I could have slapped her silly face!

Blossom began pouring the tea as Wills said, 'but that's the very last time, Fiona... Sam and I are engaged...'

'What!' shrieked the fat one loudly which made Blossom jump and spill tea all over the sandwiches.

'Oh dear, sorry, Boss,' said Blossom.

'Don't worry,' said Wills as Fiona glared at him and said, 'well... I'm waiting for an answer!'

'There's nothing to answer... Sam and I will be getting married so you are now no longer part of my life,' he said coldly which made me feel warm inside and I thought, 'that's the way to do it!'

The fat one burst into tears, stood up and threw the plate of soggy sandwiches at Wills before rushing away sobbing. Wills sighed and said calmly, 'she'll get over it soon and move on,' before he picked the remnants of a tea stained cucumber sandwich from his face and I giggled.

'Shall I make some more sandwiches, Boss?'

'Please.'

Blossom smiled and said, 'okay... well many congratulations, Boss... and you too missy,' before she wandered off to make the sandwiches and I thought I heard her giggling.

The fat blousy one locked herself in her room from then on and would only open the door to Blossom when she arrived with a tray of food. This suited me down to the ground and I enjoyed being with Wills and having him all to myself before it was time to leave the villa and return to New York. On the morning of our departure Wills eventually managed to coax the red eyed, blousy tart from her room and without looking at me, we climbed into the waiting taxi. The flight back to Newark airport was smooth and I thought I could now enjoy this wonderful life style with handsome Wills. After we landed, left the jet and were walking towards the terminal, Fiona turned to me and said, through clenched teeth, 'you'll regret this... and, my, oh my... that's for certain!' I did not answer her but just looked straight ahead and thought, 'we'll see... you blousy old tart!'

Fiona caught a taxi outside the terminal without saying 'goodbye. Wills and I were whisked us off to the apartment in the waiting limousine where we had unbridled sex until we were totally exhausted... which is what I do enjoy.

The next morning I presented myself to the Company Doctor at Kennedy airport for examination and he pronounced me fit to resume flying. I arranged to catch the midday United flight back to Heathrow which gave me enough time to say 'goodbye' to my fiancé and confirm our arrangements for my to return to New York as soon as possible, so we could make the final plans for our marriage. I went to the office but Wills wasn't there so I found Lottie at her desk and asked her where he was. She looked up at me over her thick glasses, paused for a moment and said, 'he's at the apartment with Yolanda and Kristal... they're having a meeting about their new books... *if* you can believe it.' She smirked before looking down at the paperwork on her desk and I felt quite uneasy. I said innocently, 'right... I'll catch him there then before I leave.' She glanced up at me again and said in a firm tone, 'if you know what's good for you you'll stay away from Wills... I've told you before, it's all too complicated and you'll just crash and burn, believe me.'

I didn't know what she was talking about and thought, 'another jealous old bag,' but said with a smile, 'goodbye, Lottie.'

As the cab drew closer to Madison Towers I became more and more anxious, wondering what my fiancé was up to with Yolanda and Kristal. I had bad vibes about the situation but hoped I was wrong. I paid the cabbie, hurried into the building and caught the lift to the penthouse suite. My knees were shaking as the lift pinged, the doors opened and I walked towards the large wooden door with my stomach turning cartwheels. Kristal opened the door, looked surprised and asked, 'Sam, what are you doing here?'

'I've just come to say goodbye to Wills before I fly back to London,' I replied as I brushed passed her into the lounge. I looked about for Wills but couldn't see him or Yolanda and my heart began to pound even more as rushed to the bedroom. I flung open the door to see Yolanda on the bed on her back with her stocking clad legs wrapped around Wills naked body as he thumped into her. I was just about shout at them but Kristal appeared as Wills said, 'give me some more whipping, Kristal for Chrissake and make me finish!'

Kristal replied, 'you've got a visitor…'

'What?' he interrupted and stopped thumping Yolanda before he turned his face away from the busty blonde underneath him and glanced at me.

'Sam!'

'Yes I'm here, babe.'

'Oh, Sam…'

I didn't hesitate because I knew in a second that I could not tolerate this man's behaviour and said, 'goodbye Wills… I'll catch you next time I'm over in New York… and you can tell me all about your kinky sex dates with fat old women!' I stormed from the room as he called out my name and begged me to stop but I just kept on going… into the lift… down to the ground floor, out into the avenue and taking a cab to Kennedy, wait there and composed myself.

On the flight back to Heathrow I sat and pondered on what might have been with the handsome millionaire but I guess there's never a happy ending to a love affair.

CHAPTER 9

I CAN HARDLY BELIEVE WHAT YOU'RE TELLING ME, SAMANTHA!

The first thing dear Mother asked when I arrived home from my trip to New York was, 'and how was Scotland?' I looked at her in surprise and thought, 'she's never taken any interest in me before... so could it be that now Satan's Sister was about to disappear off to New York and marry Wills that Mother dear realised she only had me to care about?'

'It was fine... a bit cold though, especially at Inverness,' I lied convincingly.

'It always is... but I'm glad you're home, Kate... I'll make some tea,' she said and wandered off to the kitchen while I carried my bag upstairs to my room. I plonked down on the bed and thought for a few moments, wondering if it had all been worth it. Still, never mind, my revenge was now all over and done with... and I decided that I felt much better for it. I enjoyed being in New York for the first time and having steamy sex with handsome Wills in his apartment. Lucky Samantha... but she'd be as mad as hell when I tell her that I had worn her diamond necklace and paraded naked for her fiancé before he screwed me... oh, decadent revenge is such bliss!

Over tea, Mother dear asked so many questions about Scotland that I struggled to keep up with the answers. She had been there a few times with Dad before they were married and so knew a lot of places that I didn't, which made it difficult to answer her. I kept telling her we didn't have time to go everywhere. I was relieved when she eventually stopped asking and said she'd start dinner.

I decided to go to the Park and stretch my legs, breath some fresh air and clear my mind for work tomorrow. As I strolled along in the evening sunshine I wondered when Satan's Handmaiden would come over so I could torment her in front of Mother dear. That would be so wonderfully sweet for me and my revenge would be complete... don't you think?

As I walked into the Park, I immediately noticed Eric sitting on the bench under the tree and sighed. I went across to him and as I approached he smiled a gorgeous smile and I melted a little. I sat down next to him and expected another round of moral righteousness from my supposed Angel.

'Hello, Kate.'

'Hello there.'

'Did you enjoy your trip to New York?' he asked with his blue eyes twinkling.

'Yes I did and it was something I'll always remember,' I replied, thinking about my fabulous naked romp with Wills.

'That's good to hear but please make sure that you don't use your meeting with Wills to hurt Samantha,' he said calmly and I went mad.

'I'll do whatever I want and say whatever I want to Satan's Sister!'

He sighed and replied, 'Kate, what you do is more likely to hurt you than Samantha...'

'Well we'll wait and see about that won't we?' I interrupted angrily.

'Yes we will, but you are choosing a path that will lead to regret,' he said firmly.

'It'll be Samantha who will be the one to regret for what she has done to me in the past!'

'You may think so, but you are quite wrong, Kate.'

'Well I may be... but I will feel a lot better when my horrid sister realises how deeply she has hurt me!'

He sighed once more, looked into the distance then turned and kissed me gently on my cheek, saying, 'I feel sorry for you, Kate.'

'Well please don't bother yourself about me!'

'I will meet you again when you realise that you have chosen a path of revenge and bitterness that will eventually hurt you.' With that he stood up and walked quickly away towards the trees at the far end of the Park and disappeared. I sat dumbfounded and tried to think what I should do about Satan's sister. In the end my righteous revenge won and I decided to tell her everything that I had done with Wills the very next time I saw her... that would make her realise that she wasn't the only one who could play around with her sister's fiancé!

At work the next day, whilst having lunch in the canteen, Emma was full of questions about my short holiday in Scotland. I decided to tell her the truth now that my deed had been done.

She looked totally surprised when I told her and asked, 'you went to New York?'

'Yes.'

'Why?'

'To see Samantha's fiancé…'

'But why would you do that?' she interrupted.

'For my revenge!'

'Kate I do wonder about you sometimes,' she said firmly as she stirred her tea.

'Well 'wonder' away, Em.'

She gave me a knowing look and asked, 'so what did you do with her fiancé to have your revenge?'

'I paraded naked up and down in his apartment wearing a diamond necklace he'd given to Satan's sister before he screwed me,' I replied and Emma's jaw dropped in surprise.

'Oh… my… God,' she whispered and stopped stirring her tea.

'And it was so good!'

'Was that the trip or the screwing?' she asked.

'Both!'

'Well do tell all, Kate,' she said enthusiastically… so I did… and showed her my phone photo's of Wills and his apartment just finishing by the time our lunch break was over.

I returned to the lab to carry on checking paint colour patterns for the rest of the boring afternoon. While thinking about my trip to New York I began to wonder if I should go again when Satan's sister was back here. I thought of handsome Wills in his luxury apartment… and his smooth sex techniques… so I decided that I should have some more revenge! I was smiling to myself with the thought of it all when Roger came over to my desk and said, 'there's a new bloke in original finishes who wants some colour samples checked for Land Rover… can you do them now?' I sighed and replied, 'I suppose so.'

'I'll let him know then,' said Roger before he disappeared to the other side of the lab. About twenty minutes later Roger brought a good looking guy to my desk and said, 'this is Tony Simpson... he's the new bloke in original finishes... and he wants some samples checked.'

'Hi there,' said Tony with a captivating smile as Roger wandered off.

'Hi... I'll check them for you now,' I replied, thinking, 'he's not bad looking for a guy in original finishes... they're all dowdy old farts up there who think they are above earthly mortals.

'I do hope I'm not putting you to too much trouble,' Tony said as he handed me three sample panels.

'No, no, not at all... it won't take me long to check them,' I replied as I took the painted panels from him.

'Thanks, er, er... I'm afraid I didn't catch your name,' he said with a smile.

'I'm Kate... Kate Harris.'

'May I call you Kate?'

'Yes... why not.'

'Thanks... I guess we'll be working together quite a lot from now on,' he said.

'Possibly,' I replied before taking the panels over to the master panel exposure rack and selecting the control panel for each colour. I wondered what had happened to old Jack Wood, who usually came down from the original finishes lab looking for colour checks.

'So are you replacing Jack Wood?' I asked as I selected the panels from the rack.

'Yes... yes, I am.'

'What's happened to him then?'

'He's been moved over to electro-coat primers,' he replied.

'Oh... how nice,' I replied... as if I cared.

'It is for me.'

'And why is that?'

'Because it means I can come down here and see you,' Tony replied with a smile. I sighed inwardly and thought, 'here's another fast sex worker hoping to get his leg over!'

'Well I'm always very busy so I may not be able to do these

checks right away,' I said firmly, hoping it would put him off. I mean, he was hardly any competition to Wills.

'That's okay... I understand,' he said and I thought, 'an understanding guy... that makes a change.'

I checked the panels in our variable light cabinet, told him that they matched the master panels, signed the test certificate and handed them back to him. He smiled and said, 'thanks, Kate... see you soon.' I just nodded and went back to my desk as he wandered off upstairs to his lab full of old farts.

I waited impatiently for the weekend and hoped that Satan's Sister would come over to see Mother dear so I could confront her and make her squirm. It was after dinner on Saturday evening that she phoned and had a long chat with Mother dear, arranging to come over for Sunday lunch. I was delighted at the news and didn't pay much attention to Mother dear as she warbled on about Samantha.

On Sunday morning I went for a walk in the park hoping to see Eric but, although I sat on the usual bench under the tree, he didn't appear. I felt let down somehow and remembered he did say he would not see me again until I had gone down my path of revenge... which would be soon!

Samantha arrived just before lunch and looked her usual self. It seemed as if she hardly knew I was there, which would make my devastating revelation all the more deadly to her. As we munched through the roast beef and Yorkshire pudding we heard all about New York and the interesting people she had met once again and when she paused for breath I decided to strike!

'I went to New York this week,' I said proudly. Mother looked at me aghast and said, 'I thought you went up to Scotland with friends from work...'

'Well I didn't!' I interrupted.

Samantha's jaw dropped before she asked, 'so what did you go over there for?' and I guessed she knew.

'I went to see your fiancé, Wills, in his apartment,' I replied and they both looked totally shocked. I was so enjoying this... and knew I would.

'Why?' asked Mother dear.

'To see what he was like... and to screw him!'

'Oh... my... God,' whispered Satan's Sister and I beamed with absolute pleasure.

'You're disgusting!' shouted Mother.

'I am... and I have the photos to prove it!'

There were a few moments of stunned silence before Samantha said firmly, 'well, you're bloody welcome to Wills and all his ghastly mates!'

'What?' I asked, wondering what was coming next.

'He's nothing but a rich sex perve who likes to fuck anything in a skirt while strangers and his kinky mates watch him!' I was taken aback while Mother dear went very pale, dropped her knife and fork, and almost fainting at the revelation. I didn't know what to say... I was devastated... but before I could think of anything, Samantha continued, 'it's all over and I never want to see him again... never!'

'Oh, bollocks!' I whispered, realising my revenge on Satan's sister was now totally hopeless as she couldn't have cared less about what I had done... what a bloody mess!

'So, Kate, you're welcome to screw him any time you like while his cronies watch!'

'Dear God, what is the world coming to?' asked Mother.

'Does he know you've broken it off?' I asked, thinking that I might have another chance with Wills in New York ... well, I mean to say, if what Satan's sister said was true, then I wouldn't mind his mates watching... it would be a bit of a laugh and something to tell the grandchildren!

'No... I only made up my mind to dump him on the flight back,' she replied and asked, 'why do you want to know?'

Before I could answer, Mother dear said, 'well, it's a good job too, Samantha... I never liked the sound of the man, and he's American and you know what they're like!'

'No... what are they like?' I asked, enjoying winding her up.

'They're all womanising lechers!'

'As if we haven't got enough over here,' I said with a sigh.

'So true,' said Mother.

Samantha nodded and said, 'well, it's now finished and I think I'll start seeing Martin again.' I thought, 'bugger me... there's no stopping her is there?'

'Who's Martin?' asked Mother taking the words out of my mouth.

'Oh, he's the lovely Doctor who stopped to help me when that idiot crashed into the back of my car,' Sam replied in an off-hand tone as if Doctor's were just waiting in line to rescue the Devil's handmaiden… oh… my… God! The injustice of it all!

'So have you been out with him since the crash?' asked Mother.

'Yes… and I did tell you.'

'No you didn't, dear, you told me about your accident and I'd have remembered if you'd been out with the Doctor who saved you,' said Mother with a proud smirk.

'Well I did, Mum… he waited for me at the hospital and took me home then we went out on a date,' she said and I thought, 'bugger me… they just drop from the trees for her!'

'Well he sounds much nicer than that dreadful American,' said Mother dear.

'He is… and he's single, well flushed, has a lovely flat and drives a new Aston Martin,' said my horrid sister and I was now completely overwhelmed by her good luck… will it never end? Before I could say anything, she rounded on me, 'so Kate, don't think for a moment you can hurt me or Martin with your silly tricks!' but I thought, 'it's worth a try!'

I riled up and said, 'don't tell me what I can do to you… remember it was you that ruined everything and broke up my engagement to David by screwing him in the garage!'

'He wasn't right for you and what you can't stand is that he fancied me more than you!' she replied angrily.

'And after you'd finished with David you bloody well pinched Robert from me!'

'You deserved it…'

'Now you two that's enough!' shouted Mother dear as I flung down my knife and fork in disgust, left the table, went up to my room where I sat on the bed and cried. In a little while I recovered and started planning how I could do something that would stop this man eating, man pinching horrid she creature dead in her tracks for good.

I was not looking forward to going to work on the Monday and after I arrived in the lab the day went downhill faster than usual. First, Roger complained that according to the old farts in original finishes, the Land Rover panels were not correctly matched with the masters.

'Oh yes they were,' I said firmly.

'Well that new bloke Tony is coming down later with his boss, Nigel Towns, to check them again,' said Roger.

'Oh bloody hell,' I said in a half whisper as Charlie Butler, our lab chief, arrived at my desk and peered down at me. I knew I was in deep trouble.

'Kate, Nigel Towns has told me that you checked some Land Rover panels that were brought to you for verification last Friday.'

'Yes.'

'And he has complained that you wrongly passed them off, so he is coming down with his new man to see me,' said Charlie. I sighed and replied, 'the panels were to our standard commercial match... I'm sure of it.'

'So you say, but when Towns arrives I want you to come to my office where we can sort this muddle out.' Charlie walked away leaving Roger looking at me with a silly grin on his face... he's such a plonker! I tried to concentrate on my work but just couldn't and was relieved when I saw Towns and Tony come into the lab and go into Charlie's office... I knew I was in for another bollocking but it would soon be over!

Tony smiled at me as I walked into Charlie's office, I just glared at him as I believed this was all his bloody silly fault. Charlie waved me to a seat next to Tony as he glanced down at the panels on his desk. I sat down and glared at Towns as he began warbling on about 'personal responsibilities' and how things that go wrong through inattention cannot readily be put right, especially with such an important customer as Land Rover... blah, blah, blah.... I thought, 'anything can be put right... so get a life, you silly old man!' I glanced at him occasionally and noticed he looked more uncomfortable as he droned on, so I guess he knew what I was thinking. Suddenly Charlie turned the panels over, looked at the batch numbers and dates on the back then interrupted Towns, asking, 'are these the panels you sent down for verification?'

'Yes... yes, I believe so,' stammered Towns, then glancing at Tony asked anxiously, 'these are the ones aren't they, Simpson?'

'Yes I think they are,' replied Tony.

Charlie smiled and said, 'well these are dated the first of March last year so they are well out of date and not representative of the current master panels.' I could have kissed him!

Tony cleared his throat and said in a confident tone, 'then it must be all my fault and Kate is not to blame... I am so sorry.' Well, my knight in shining armour arrived just in time... I could have kissed him too!

Towns went pale and flustered before making excuses and hastily leaving the office with Tony following him. Charlie looked at me, smiled and said, 'well you're off the hook, Kate... thank heaven that Simpson owned up to his mistake, otherwise we could have been arguing with Towns for hours.' I smiled and nodded, thinking, 'I'll have to watch Tony Simpson from now on.'

I met Emma in the canteen at lunch time and she was full of woe and a few tears. Her current 'boyfriend'... if that's what you could call him... had behaved like an animal with her and then had the bloody cheek to dump her! I was now fast going off men... well, they just can't be trusted, can they?... they're all such bloody liars! Except Eric of course and I wondered where he was and if he'd appear soon. I needed someone to comfort me and made a note to go to the Park that evening and see if he was about. I listened to poor Emma wailing about her latest 'dumper', giving occasional 'there, there's' until it was time to go back to work. I felt drained with today's events and hoped nothing else would happen... but as usual I was wrong!

Over dinner Mother dear drove me absolutely crackers with her non-stop, one way conversation about Samantha and her new boyfriend, Doctor Martin. My Mother just talks *at* me, not *to* me, so I automatically switch off and try to think of other things while she goes rabbiting on. I only have to nod occasionally and grunt when she pauses to draw breath and that seems to work okay. Mother was so concerned that Samantha would not bring Martin to the house because of me admitting I had been to New York for revenge, which turned out to be absolutely useless.

'That's nonsense,' I said angrily.

'You may say that but your sister seems to want to keep Martin well away!'

'I don't blame her.'

'Why?'

'It's more likely that she wants to avoid you!'

'How could you say that?'

'Well you do go on a bit these days,' I replied and there followed a few quiet moments before she said, 'you get more like your Father every day.'

'Good!' I replied and not another word was said. I finished eating and told her that I was going out for a walk, Mother dear replied that it would do me good and put me in a better mood. I didn't bother to answer her.

I sat on the seat under the tree and waited for about half an hour hoping Eric would appear, but he didn't... so another disappointment. I wandered home and went up to my room, leaving Mother dear watching the television. I was just about to sort my clothes out for work in the morning when my phone rang, it was Emma.

'Hi, Kate, what are you doing?' she asked.

'Nothing much, just deciding what to wear tomorrow,' I replied.

'Oh, let's go for a drink, Kate... it's been a lousy day and I need cheering up.' I sighed and replied, 'why not?'

'Come and get me then... I'll be ready.'

We decided to go to a pub near to Emma's, the Carpenter's Arms, that would save me driving too far and we could have a quiet drink while talking about our disasters with men... and my sister! The pub was busy and full of locals who gave us a casual glance as we went up to the bar. Emma bought the first round of gin and tonic with tinkling ice, before we headed for an empty table near the door. She wanted to know more about my trip to New York and was completely stunned when I told her that

Satan's handmaiden had decided to dump Wills, and he didn't even know he was dumped!

'I'm sure he'll get over it,' she said with a grin. I nodded and said, 'and now she's taken up with the seriously flush Doctor Martin!'

'Doctor Martin?'

'Yes, he's the guy who rescued her when some idiot crashed into her car,' I replied.

'My God... she does have the allure!'

'More like good luck, but the Devil always takes care of his own!'

'So, Kate, what are you going to do now?' she asked in wide eyed amazement.

'Well, I think I'll go to New York for a final fling with Wills and when I get back I'll have my revenge on her by thinking up something with Doctor Martin,' I replied.

'Oh... my... God,' she whispered as she shook her head.

'Next time I'm determined to finish it for good then I'll feel free of her and can get on with my life,' I said firmly before taking a good swig of gin and fizzy tonic.

'Well when you go to New York, can I come?' she asked. I was about to say, 'yes, why not?' when Eric walked in, looked around, smiled when he saw us and came over as our jaws dropped in surprise.

'Hello, Kate... Emma,' he said as he sat down facing us.

'Hi, Eric, what are you doing here?' I asked while Emma's eyes just looked lovingly at his handsome face.

'I've come to see you and hopefully persuade you not to go to New York again,' he replied.

'How do you know that I'm going to New York?'

'Ah, that would be telling and...'

'You're not allowed to do that,' I interrupted and he gave a slight nod as he smiled.

'So, Kate, are you sure that you want to go and see Wills again?' he asked, looking at me with his penetrating blue eyes. I felt very unsure so needed some time to think, Emma came to my rescue with daft questions and asked him, 'are you really an angel?'

He smiled and replied, 'yes I am, but you're not supposed to know.'

'Well I promise I won't tell a soul,' she whispered.

'Good... '

'Are you my angel as well as Kate's?' Emma interrupted in a hopeful tone.

'No I'm afraid not,' he replied.

'Oh, that's a shame... but do you happen to know my angel?' she asked and Eric gave a gentle nod.

'Oh, what's he like and when will he come and take care of me?' she asked. Eric smiled and replied, 'he's around you every day and I'm sure he'll appear when the time is right.'

'Well I do hope so... I could do with some help at the moment,' she said and Eric replied, 'yes, he knows.'

'So when will he appear?' she persisted.

'I really don't know Emma, but if needed I'm sure he will.'

'Well here's hoping it's soon,' she said with a smile.

Eric gave a little nod to her and asked, 'so, Kate, tell me what you plan to do?'

'I'm not sure,' I replied.

He gazed into my very soul and whispered, 'please don't go... it will cause you nothing but pain and I really don't want that.' I couldn't resist him and replied, 'then I won't go.' He smiled and said, 'that's very good to hear, Kate.'

'But I mean to make my sister suffer for everything she's done to me!' I said firmly.

Eric smiled and said, 'coming events will change your mind about Samantha.'

'Never,' I replied but he just nodded, stood up and said, 'goodbye for now, Kate... I will see you soon... goodbye, Emma,' he strode to the door and left the pub.

'Isn't he just bloody gorgeous?' whispered Emma.

'Yes, he is...'

'Shame he's not available... but do you really believe he's an angel?'

'I really don't know... he confuses me,' I replied before taking a very large sip of my gin and tonic.

'Me too... but then men usually confuse me.'

I sighed, nodded and said, 'how right you are.'

'But I hope he is an angel and he tells mine to see me soon!'

she said with her eyes bright with anticipation and I just giggled. We had two more drinks while we talked about what I planned to do next... much to Emma's disquiet, before we called it a day and went home to prepare for work the next morning.

I arrived a little late for work and Charlie had a quiet word with me about it, while Roger stood close by with a silly grin on his face, I was not best pleased. It was just after ten when Tony Simpson appeared in the lab. He came to my desk so I asked, 'and what do you want this morning?' I was not in the mood to be messed about by him once again, or the old farts upstairs.

'Hi, Kate... I was wondering if you'd like to come out for a drink,' he said with a smile.

'With you?' I asked in total surprise.

'Yes... who else?'

'But I don't know you!' I replied impatiently.

'And I don't know you, but I'm willing to take a chance,' he replied and I laughed. It is nice when a man makes you laugh. I thought for a moment and was still undecided when he said, 'and I promise not to talk about work.'

'I don't think it's a good idea... but thanks all the same,' I said.

'To talk about work or go for a drink?' he asked with a broad smile. I sighed and replied, 'what part of 'no' don't you understand?'

'You didn't actually say 'no' only that it wasn't a good idea... but I'll have you know that my ideas are usually good.'

'Not this one,' I replied firmly.

There followed a few moments of silence before he said, 'well, I tried and failed hopelessly... but if you ever change your mind just let me know... I'm free every night of the week and know a super little pub.'

He walked away and out of the lab as Roger appeared and asked, 'what did he want?'

'He wanted to take me out for a drink.'

'He's got a bloody cheek!' he exclaimed and I nodded.

The rest of the morning dragged by and I was pleased when it came to lunch time. I hurried over to the busy canteen and saw

Emma sitting alone at a table. After choosing tomato soup and a ham sandwich from the server I made my way over to Emma. She looked up and said, 'hi, Kate,' as I sat down opposite.

'Hi Em.'

I was just about to take a mouthful of soup when she said, 'now, Kate... I've been thinking about last night in the pub and everything.'

'And?' I asked, wondering what was coming next.

'Well I think you should go to New York to see Wills... and you should take me with you,' she replied with a smile. I put down my spoon and said, 'you must be joking!'

'No I'm not... honestly I'm not... it would do us both good to...' she began as Tony appeared with a tray and interrupted her by asking, 'is this seat free?' I glared at him as he pointed to the empty chair while Emma nodded and replied, 'yes, it is.'

'May I join you then?'

'Okay.'

'Thanks... it's getting very busy in here.'

'Yes,' said Emma.

Tony glanced at me and said, 'hello again, Kate,' as he placed his tray on the table.

'Do you know each other?' asked Emma.

'Yes, we sometimes work together,' replied Tony.

'I've never seen you in here before... are you new?'

'Yes, I'm Tony Simpson. I've only recently started working in the original finishes lab,' he replied with a smile.

'Oh, how nice, Tony... and how are you finding it?' asked Emma.

'Well, generally it's been okay... but some of the natives are hostile,' he replied with a chuckle while Emma looked confused.

I glared at him and said firmly, 'he bloody well means me, Emma!' Her jaw dropped in surprise and she asked, 'why?'

'Because I won't go out with him for a drink,' I replied. There was a stunned silence as Emma looked at us in turn and asked me, 'why not?'

Tony smiled and said, 'now that would be telling... so Emma... what do you do here?'

'Oh, I work in marketing,' she replied brightly.

'Ah, that's where all the important work is done in any business,' he said before he bit into his sandwich.

'Oh, I wouldn't say that,' she smiled coyly as she fluttered her eye lashes before glancing down and I thought, 'she's making a play for him... dear God... I'm surrounded by women stealing men from me!'

'Well I would,' he replied and I thought, 'dear God it gets worse... he's after her now!'

'So, Tony, what did you do before you came here to work?' she asked with a big smile.

'I was in the Army... ever since leaving school.'

'Oh, that's interesting,' she warbled and I might as well been invisible to them.

'Yes, it was... I saw lots of action.'

'You must be very brave,' she said in a whisper.

'I had my moments.'

'Oh I'm sure... so what made you leave the Army and come to Delacor Paints?'

'Well, I'd spent ten years in the Army and thought it was now time for a change and my father wanted me to join in him in his business,' he replied.

'So why are you here?'

'Because I need to have some experience with car paint before I work for him,' he replied.

'And why's that?' she asked.

'He owns a garage... with my uncle... and I will run the paint shop repairing cars.'

'Oh really... is it a big garage?'

'Yes, it's quite large,' he replied.

'Do I know it?'

'Possibly... it's Bracknell Motors,' he replied and my mind raced back to David, my fiancé before Samantha ruined everything for me, so I said, 'that's where I bought my first car... a little Ford Fiesta.' They both looked at me as if I shouldn't have interrupted them.

'Yes I remember that... it was just after you passed your test,' said Emma.

'It was.'

'And where you met David,' she continued with a smug

smile... she can be such an irritating cow sometimes!

'Don't remind me,' I said while Tony just smiled.

'Do you know David Butler?' Emma asked... digging the knife in deeply.

'No, I don't know any of the people who work there yet... other than Charlie the cleaner,' Tony replied.

'Charlie the cleaner?' Emma asked.

'Yes, I've just moved into the flat over the showroom and Charlie cleans the hallway outside,' he replied.

'Doesn't your wife clean that?' she asked with a smile and I knew she was now fishing desperately.

'I'm not married.'

'Oh, shame.'

'It is,' he replied and there was a pause in the conversation before I said with a sigh, 'well it's time I got back to work... and leave you two to chat.' Tony looked surprised while Emma looked positively glad I was going.

It was just before our afternoon tea break when Tony came into the lab.

'What now?' I asked impatiently when he reached my desk.

He took a deep breath and said, 'as you won't come out for a drink... will you marry me instead?' I burst out laughing, thinking, 'he's such a clown!' and replied, 'marry you... not likely!'

'Then you'll come for a drink?'

'Well it might be less dangerous than marrying you!'

'It certainly would be... so are you free tonight?'

I giggled and thought, 'he's very persistent... and it would be laugh... so why not?'

Tony collected me from home at eight and while he chatted away about his life we drove to a quaint little country pub called 'The Pilgrim', which was all oak beams, horse brasses and a large stone fireplaces. We sat in the corner with our drinks and from the very start he made me laugh so much by telling me silly stories that I had to ask him to stop talking for a moment whilst I drank my gin and tonic. Tony was simply enchanting as well as funny so by the time we left the pub to go home I knew I wanted to see him again. I mean, I was still in two minds about him but he made me laugh, which made me feel much better. After we stopped outside my home, he kissed me very gently and said, 'well if you still won't marry me, perhaps you'll come out for dinner on Saturday?'

'Yes, that would be good, Tony... provided you don't make me laugh so much that I can't eat my meal,' I replied.

'I promise,' he whispered before he kissed me again. We said, 'goodnight', I stepped out of the car and waved as he drove away.

I couldn't wait to tell Emma about Tony at lunchtime the next day and she looked very po faced.

'I thought you didn't like him,' she said firmly.

'Well, I didn't at first but I've changed my mind.'

'Lucky you then,' she said before taking a mouthful of sandwich.

'It makes a change.'

'Now is this going to go to the next level?' she asked.

'Possibly.'

'So it's knickers off on Saturday,' she said and I giggled as she added, 'I'll take that as a 'yes' then.'

'Probably.'

'Oh, you're so bloody lucky, Kate, you really are!'

'Now don't get all fuzzy about Tony... I'm sure the right guy will turn up for you,' I said.

'Well I just hope he's like Eric the angel rather than anybody else.'

'I'm not sure he's an angel.'

'He is to me,' she said with feeling and we finished lunch without saying too much more as I knew that deep down she was upset.

On Saturday Tony took me to a little French restaurant where we had the most fabulous meal before we went back to his flat for coffee. I was impressed with the comfortable, spacious well furnished flat above the car showrooms and everything in it showed his good taste. I sank down onto the soft cream coloured settee while he made the coffee. He chatted from the kitchen and

I found him very amusing as well as very thoughtful, especially when he later told me about losing his best friend in Afghanistan. He was only sad for a moment and said, 'you must make the most of every day… as it could be your last.' I smiled and he kissed me before we sipped our coffee.

'So, what have you planned next?' I asked with a mischievous grin.

'Well, I hope you're going to let me make love to you,' he replied.

'Whatever makes you think I'd let you do that?'

'It's just a feeling I've got… especially as you won't agree to marry me,' he replied and I laughed.

'We'll have to see about that,' I said with a giggle.

'Yes, let's… so in the meantime let's finish our coffee and snuggle up in bed!' And we did! Tony was a gentle caring lover who brought me to a relaxed and wonderful climax and I kissed him so hard he nearly passed out.

From then on everything with Tony was like a dream… until Samantha made an announcement that changed everything!

CHAPTER 10

I TELL YOU HONESTLY, KATE, IT DOESN'T GET ANY WORSE THAN THIS!

The flight back to London gave me time to really think about Wills and by the time lunch was served I had made up my mind to forget him. Although all the money was something to consider, along with his 'big boy' toys, I could not face the world he lived in with its peculiar people and way-out life styles... not to mention Maria and his other ex-wives! God only knows what other surprises Wills kept hidden away from me and I did not intend to wait until after we were married to find out... I can be shocked you know.

By the time tea was served I had definitely and finally made up my mind to forget all about Wills and concentrate on Martin... dear, handsome Doctor Martin... with his flash car, flat in Ascot and who knows what else! I thought he would be a wonderful substitute for Wills as he is so down to earth, and of course he is a Doctor, which means that I could get any medical examination and opinion without leaving his flat... how good is that? By the time the plane landed at Heathrow I had made my plans to phone Martin the moment I was clear of the airport and get him to ask me out for dinner. As I hadn't seen him since my life had taken another direction I felt I owed him an apology for our missed date, I was sure I could make up some believable story to tell him.

I phoned from the back of the taxi as it hurried towards Tania's flat and Martin answered with a soft, 'hello.'
 'Hi, Martin... I'm just back from New York... how are you?'
 'Sam darling... I'd given you up... but it's good to hear from you,' he replied enthusiastically.
 'Well, you know how it is for an air hostess ... all work and no private life.'
 'Oh, don't I know... so where are you now?'
 'In a taxi and almost back at my flat.'

'Good, so if you are free for dinner tomorrow night you can tell me all about New York and apologise for standing me up!'

'Oh, yes, I'm sorry about that…but it would be great to explain everything over dinner.'

'So that's a date… I'll pick you up at about eight… is that okay?'

'It's perfect, Martin.'

'Good… I'll see you then… and you can tell me everything… bye, Sam.'

'Bye Martin.' I clicked off my phone and said, 'yes!'

Tania looked surprised when I walked in and found her draped across the settee watching some God awful talent show on TV.

'Well, I didn't expect to see you back so soon… what happened?' Tania asked as she clicked off the TV.

'It's a long story,' I replied as I slumped down on the chair opposite.

'So do tell all after I've got us something to drink.'

'Make mine a double… I need it after the events in New York,' I said with feeling.

'My God was it that bad?'

'Worse than you could possibly imagine,' I replied with a sigh.

'Well this sounds very interesting!'

After we had said, 'cheers' and I had drunk most of my Scotch, I began the long story about Wills, his ex-wives and his peculiar sex adventures. Tania looked amazed and every so often kept whispering, 'oh my God,' and, 'I don't believe it,' as the tale unfolded. She giggled when I told her about catching Wills screwing the fat tart on my bed in his villa in Bermuda and laughed out loud at the sandwich throwing incident. I told Tania that I could not marry Wills under any circumstances and made up my mind to go after Martin, as he was more my type.

'So tell me Sam, what exactly is your type?'

'He has to be handsome, rich and sexy… that's all I need in a man and I've got that in my Doctor Martin,' I replied.

'He's not your Doctor yet.'

'He will be after dinner tomorrow night,' I replied.

She laughed and asked, 'so its dinner... then back to his flat for some fantastic all night tricks?'

'You've got it in one!' I replied and she giggled while I finished my Scotch.

'So when are you coming back to work?'

'I'll think about it and let someone know when I feel ready,' I replied. Tania grinned and said, 'well if you have a good night with Doctor Martin you might not come back at all!'

'That's very true... now let's have another drink before I phone my Mum.'

I made a hurried call to Mum, told her I was okay and I'd come over for lunch tomorrow, which kept her happy. I was not looking forward to telling her that Wills and I were now history as it meant I'd failed and I was certain that Kate would make the most of it when she heard the news... she's such a miserable, spiteful little cow!

While we were having lunch, Kate dropped her shocking bombshell and claimed that instead of going on holiday to Scotland, she actually went to New York to see Wills... and pretended to be me and screw him just to spite me! She's such a bloody awful toe rag! But I got my own back when I told her I'd broken it off with Wills and she was welcome to the perve! You should have seen her face... she was dumbstruck... which made a nice change! Then I rubbed her nose in it when I told her about Martin and warned her not to try any more silly tricks! She went off in a huff to her room and I left without seeing her again... thank God. Mum was delighted I was not going to marry Wills and thought Martin sounded a much nicer person. I promised to bring him home soon to meet her, which really pleased her.

It was late afternoon when I left Mum and returned to the flat where I immediately started getting ready for my dinner date with Martin... well, you can never spend too much time preparing yourself for a special, sexy man... can you? I showered, washed my hair in the latest 'wonder shampoo', guaranteed to make you look ravishing, spent ages on my makeup and finally gave my kissable lips the final coat of lip gloss. I looked at myself in the mirror once more and thought, 'he'll never resist me tonight!' I got dressed slowly, putting on my matching black lace 'push up' bra and my very flimsy panties with the little red roses, followed by a suspender belt and fish net stockings. I slipped into my low cut, little black dress, stepped into my very high heeled comfy black shoes and looked at myself in the long mirror. There, I thought, 'you look gorgeous... and he'll never get enough of you tonight!' For the final touches I put on my matching pearl earrings and necklace followed by a good splash of Givenchy 'L'amour' down my cleavage and all the other sexy places. I was now ready for the night ahead with Doctor Martin!

He arrived in his fabulous car spot on eight o'clock and I hurried down to meet him after he rang the sonnette to announce himself. When he saw me in the hallway his eyes widened and as soon as I emerged through the glass doors he kissed me passionately.

'My God, you look absolutely gorgeous, Sam,' he whispered... which is always good to hear at the start of the evening. I smiled, gave a little nod and held his warm hand as we walked to his silver Aston Martin. We drove at speed to Windsor and talked all the way until we arrived at the Oakley Court Hotel. Martin slowed the Aston before he turned into the driveway, 'this is one of my favourite places, Sam, the grounds are lovely, overlooking the Thames... and the food is excellent.'

I nodded as I glanced at the imposing hotel coming into view, nestling amongst the trees and thought, 'this could be a night to remember... and here's hoping!'

Martin had booked a table in a corner of the opulent restaurant and we were quickly shown to it by the attentive Maître d'. We ordered aperitifs, I had a gin and tonic while Martin ordered an orange juice, being mindful of driving us back to his flat in Ascot. I was pleased because I wanted him to be on top form when we arrived home for the night... I mean to say, it's no good having a lover who is hopeless because of drink when you want some good, rigid, long lasting performance that will make the night a memorable one... do you?

I chose pâté de campagne as my starter followed by boeuf

bourguignon, Martin also had the pâté but chose Tournedos Rossini as his main course. After he had ordered, Martin listened carefully as I told him about my adventures in America but of course, leaving out all the parts which would make him jealous and perhaps unhappy. He laughed in all the right places and kept giving me 'come to bed' glances with his soft brown eyes. I hurriedly finished the pâté and hoped the main course would not be too long in coming as I was anxious to get back to his flat as soon as possible... well I do have needs you know and was now like a coiled spring just ready to go 'boing!'

The main meal was delicious and we followed it with apple strudel and creamy custard. I said, 'no,' to coffee and was surprised when Martin suggested that we walk along the path by the River. I hesitated for a moment but agreed, as I knew it was part of the evening's romance for him, although I just wanted to get to the steamy, sweaty, body entwined sex bit, followed by a good sleep in his arms.

The night air was surprisingly warm as we made our way through the picturesque, well kept gardens to the River's edge. We stopped and looked at the fast flowing water before he kissed me passionately. When our lips parted he whispered, 'I do love you, Sam.' I looked deep into his eyes and replied, 'and I love you, Martin,' and thought, 'maybe I really do.' He kissed me once again before we turned and walked along the River with our arms around one another. I only had eyes for him but suddenly I noticed a tall man approaching us in the opposite direction. I was first struck by his height and my blood ran cold when I recognised him... it was bloody Eric! What the hell was he doing here? I didn't know what to do, so decided on doing nothing, which is always the best thing when you're undecided. As Eric got closer, my heart was beating so fast I thought Martin would hear it! As Eric passed us I held myself rigid but when he smiled and said, 'good evening,' in his clipped tone with a broad smile, I was relieved, Martin replied, 'good evening.' After Eric had gone some way down the path, he said to me, 'what a nice chap... and so tall.'

I nodded and replied, 'he's probably a foreigner staying at the hotel.'

'Yes, and he certainly gave you a good looking over.'
'Oh, did he? I didn't notice.'
'Good, because I don't want any tall foreign strangers stealing you away from me,' Martin said with a chuckle.
'No chance of that… I'm feeling a bit chilly now… so can we go?'
'Of course, Sam darling… so is it back to my place for coffee?'
'Sounds good to me,' I replied and thought, 'here we go!'

We hardly spoke during the drive back to Martin's flat but once we were in and he had closed the door I just went 'boing!' I began tearing at his clothes and he mine as we kissed while struggling through the lounge and into the bedroom leaving a trail of discarded underwear and shoes. He flung me on the bed and ravished me in the nicest way possible, and I can tell you it is so nice to be ravished by a handsome Doctor, they know everything about the female body, but not the mind… that still remains a complete mystery so Martin says! We writhed in complete ecstasy and I almost squeezed the life out of him with my legs locked around his body while he urged himself up into me time after time… but slowly… until we climaxed violently, kissing with unbelievable passion. We lay panting like sweaty joggers for a while then we did it all again! After that we fell into a deep sleep that lasted until the morning and when I awoke he was fondling and kissing my breast.

I grinned and said, 'morning Doctor… are you interfering with me again?… I hope!'
He giggled and replied, 'oh yes I certainly am.'
'That's good because I thought for a moment you'd lost interest after screwing me senseless.'
'No… I only lose interest in patients…'
'After you've screwed them once!' I interrupted with a giggle.
'Oh you know me so well,' he replied with a little chuckle.
'That I do… now are you going to make me some coffee?'

While Martin made the coffee I had a quick shower, found a shirt and slipped it on but left it unbuttoned. We sat and drank our coffee at the table whilst looking through the picture window at the race course beyond.

'So tell me, Doctor, when the Queen arrives for the races in her open coach can you see her from here?'

'I certainly can.'

'And can she see you?'

'Possibly.'

'Then we'd better behave when she arrives,' I said with a giggle.

'Well, luckily it is only once a year.'

'So we can be very naughty the rest of the time.'

'And why not?' he chuckled.

'I like the sound of that,' I replied with a grin before he got up, came round stood behind me and fondled my breasts.

'So are you a breast man?' I asked.

'I'm an 'anything man' with you, Sam.'

'That's good.'

Suddenly he stopped and asked, 'how long have you had this little lump?'

'What little lump?'

'This one here,' he replied and he touched me quite hard.

'I never noticed,' I replied.

'Mmm... tell me, have you any family history of breast cancer?'

'Breast cancer?

'Yes.'

'No, Martin... not that I know of.'

'Well you'd better get your GP to have a look...'

'Martin, you're frightening me!' I interrupted.

'So sorry, darling, but I'm just concerned about you...'

'Do you think I've got cancer?' I interrupted in alarm.

'No, Sam, but it is better to get any little lumps checked... just in case.'

'Oh God,' I whispered.

The day went rapidly downhill from then on. I dressed and phoned my Doctor within the hour and was told that the earliest appointment would be in two days time. I was not pleased about that but accepted the booking with a reluctant sigh. Martin drove me to my flat and said 'goodbye' to me with a passionate kiss.

'Let me know how you get on with your GP,' he said as I climbed out of the car. I nodded and replied, 'yes, I'll phone you straight away.'

'Good... take care, darling... I'm sure you'll be okay,' he said with a smile.

'Hope so,' I replied before turning away and making my way into the flat. Tania was not there... her note said she'd been called on to the 'emergency roster' to cover for a hostess who was taken ill. Just my luck when I needed someone to talk to about my cancer... I mean, I was sure I had it.

After brooding for a while about operations, chemotherapy and everything that goes with it, I made some coffee, munched several chocolate biscuits and read one of Tania's 'goss' magazines. It was lunch time when I plucked up enough courage to phone Mum and ask if any of our family had ever had breast cancer.

'Not that I know of dear, why do you ask?'

'Because I may have it,' I replied as tears ran down my cheeks.

'Oh dear God, no,' she whispered.

'Fraid so, Mum.'

'Have you seen a Doctor?'

'Not yet...'

'Why not?' she interrupted.

'I've made an appointment but it is two days until he can see me.'

'Dear God... so how do you know you've got cancer?'

'Because Martin found a lump this morning,' I replied.

'Well I shouldn't worry about that dear, we've all got little lumps, especially as we get older,' she said in a reassuring tone.

'I'm sure... but Martin is a Doctor and he should know.'

'I suppose so... but come over and we can talk about it... I'll get some lunch for us.'

'Thanks, Mum... see you soon.'

Over lunch of beans on toast with an egg on top, I told Mum my fears, she assured me that there was never any hint of cancer in the family, with the exception of a distant aunt who had died from the disease years ago. Mum was not quite sure what type of cancer she had, but it made me worry all the same. I left Mum and drove home thinking and wondering what was going to happen next in my life. At last I'd found a wonderful man who I was beginning to have deep feelings for and now I was confronted with bloody cancer! God… it never rains but it pours! I was still battling in my mind with the dreadful disease when I arrived home, parked outside the flat and sat for a few moments before turning the engine off with a sigh. I was very confused to say the least… what if Martin was right? What if Mum was right? Only my GP would be able to shed some light on my lump, although I thought Martin might be right rather than Mum. Oh dear God help me! And I had to wait for two days before I could see my GP… however was I going to survive the wait? There's nothing worse than not knowing is there?

As I climbed out of the car and locked it a voice behind me said, 'hello, Samantha.' I knew instantly who it was and turned round to face Eric. He smiled and I thought, 'you're the very last person I want to see today!'

'And what do you want, Eric?' I asked angrily.

'Just to talk to you.'

'Well I'm not in a listening mood, so you'll have to go off and bother someone else!'

'It's not that simple…'

'It is for me, Eric,' I replied before I pushed passed him and made my way up to the entrance to the flat. He followed me to the door and I turned and said, 'you're not coming in, Eric!'

'Please just give me a few moments alone with you.'

'And why should I do that?'

'Because I know you are worried and I need to speak to you about your concerns,' he replied with a gentle captivating smile. I hesitated for a moment then gave in, saying, 'alright then, but you can't stay long,' and he nodded.

After we had sat down opposite each other, I asked, 'well?'

'You have a very difficult time ahead of you, Samantha, and…'

'Don't remind me… and how do you know?' I interrupted

angrily.

He smiled and replied, 'I know everything about you.'

'Well that doesn't suit me, Eric, so I think in future you best…'

'Just calm down will you and let me speak?' he interrupted… so I pulled a face and shut up.

'Good… now you have a period of uncertainty about your health which you will overcome in due course,' and as he spoke I thought, 'I don't like the sound of that… does he mean operations, chemotherapy and God knows what else before I am better?'

'… but you must face this ordeal with courage and reflect on your life,' he said with a smile.

'Reflect on my life? What is there to reflect on?' I asked.

'Everything, Samantha, just everything you have.'

'Like what?'

'You are beautiful, vivacious and lovely to be with…' and I thought, 'this is what I like to hear from a good looking man!'

'And you have parents who love you and a sister…' 'There, he just went and spoilt it for me!' so I pulled a face.

'And Martin, who loves you very much… love is the answer to everything and it is what makes the world go around.' I didn't know what to say to all that so asked, 'am I going to die?'

'Eventually,' he replied.

'But not yet?' I asked hopefully.

'That time is not in my hands.'

'Oh, dear God,' I whispered.

'You're quite right,' he said with a smile.

'Well you're not much help… I mean to say, I'm confused… will I die from this cancer or what?'

'I don't know…'

'And will I marry Martin before I die?' I interrupted.

'Probably…'

'So I am going to die then?'

'As I told you, eventually… everyone does.'

'Bugger everyone… I want to know about me!'

'Samantha, calm down a little… I am here to guide you, not predict your future…'

'Well it's as I always thought… you're no angel, but just a

crazy stalker!'

He sighed and said, 'you believe what you want to believe... but I can assure you that I do have your best interests at heart.'

'Well, I'm not so sure, Eric.'

'Then I had better leave you... but please think about what I said about reflections and love in your life.'

'I might,' I replied as he stood up and made for the door.

'I will always be close to guide you, Samantha.'

'I shouldn't worry too much about that,' I replied and he smiled before he strode out of the flat.

The next morning I phoned work and told Human Resources that I was very ill and had an appointment with my GP the following day. Tania didn't arrive home so I sat alone and brooded about my condition until I went to bed thoroughly fed up.

I arrived at the packed surgery just before ten and waited for what seemed an age before I was called to see Doctor Cooper.

'So what seems to be the trouble, Miss Harris?'

'I've a lump in my breast and my friend Doctor Palmer thinks you should examine it,' I replied.

'Does he now... well let's have a look... please go behind the curtain and slip off your blouse and bra while I call the nurse.' I did as he asked while he called for her and waited until she arrived. The curtain was pulled back and the Doctor looked at my boobs then gently held them as nurse peered at me with piteous eyes.

'Is this it?' he asked as he gently touched the lump.

'Yes.'

'Hmm... I think we'd better organise a Mammogram for you...just to make sure, Miss Harris.'

'So is it serious, Doctor?'

'Probably not... but we must make sure its nothing to worry about,' he replied with a smile and I thought, 'oh dear God... it's serious.'

After lots of questions about family history I eventually left the surgery feeling absolutely sure I had breast cancer. On the drive home I cried a little and swore at some idiot when he cut me up. I shouted at him, 'don't you realise I'm dying here from cancer?'

As I arrived outside the flat I saw Tania's little red car parked and my heart leapt. Thank God I had someone to talk to who would understand. Tania looked totally shocked when I told her and she started crying which set me off. We eventually managed to pull ourselves together and she made us a pot of strong coffee. I phoned Martin but he didn't answer his mobile so I left a message on his home phone.

It was in the evening that Martin called and asked how I was. I told him everything and he was pleased that Doctor Cooper had organised a Mammogram for me.

'That will show one way or another if there's anything to worry about, darling,' he said reassuringly.

'Hope so... when am I going to see you again?'

'How about tomorrow night?'

'Suits me.'

'Let's have dinner at my place... I can cook you know,' he said.

'Sounds great... what are we having?'

'That's a surprise... I'll pick you up at about eight.'

We said 'goodbye' with kisses down the phone and after hanging up I sighed and said, 'he's so lovely, Tania.'

'You're very lucky, Sam, to have someone who thinks you're the best thing on earth.'

'Yes I am,' I whispered and thought about what Eric had said to me.

The next evening Martin collected me at eight and drove me to his flat in his fabulous silver Aston. He cooked Scampi Provençal, which was divine, accompanied by two bottles of Burgundy... and I was absolutely 'squiffy' by the time he served fresh fruit salad with ice cream. We didn't bother with coffee but went straight to bed where he performed passionately... oh, but so lovingly.

Two days later I received a letter from the hospital telling me that my Mammogram was booked for the following Thursday at

10.00 am. I phoned Mum and told her the news and she insisted that I go over for lunch, I agreed and after phoning United and telling HR that I would not be coming back to work yet, I drove over. Mum was all sympathy and smiles when I told her what Doctor Cooper had said.

'Well I'm sure there's nothing for you to worry about, dear.'

'I hope not, Mum.'

'So let's not think about it... I'll get us some lunch... we'll feel better after we've had something to eat,' she said with a smile and I nodded.

We were in the middle of lunch when Kate walked in with a face like a black cloud.

Mum glanced up at her and said, 'Kate... I didn't know you were coming home for lunch.'

'I wasn't... but I've been feeling a bit funny this morning so my boss said I should go home,' she replied.

'Oh dear, what's wrong with you?'

'I don't know... is there any lunch left for me?'

'No, Kate... but I'll get something for you when we've finished,' replied Mum.

Kate sighed, walked out and slammed the door, which did not please me. She's such a miserable little cow sometimes and I glanced at Mum who raised her eyebrows and said, 'well she's not happy today.'

'No change there then.'

'It seems not,' replied Mum with a sigh.

'Have you told her about me?' I asked.

'About your lump you mean?'

'Yes.'

No, dear, I think it best she doesn't know for the moment... unless you want to tell her,' replied Mum. I shook my head and said, 'I'll only say something if she really gets on my tits,' and we both laughed.

I was about to leave for home when Kate started being silly about Martin saying that she hoped he dumped me so I would know what it was like. It only took a spark like that to set me off and so a blazing row followed and in the end I said, 'listen to me you stupid, jealous, miserable little cow... you've got everything to live for while I'm dying with bloody breast cancer!'

'Oh my God!' she whispered.

'And I tell you, Kate, it doesn't get any worse than this!' I screamed.

CHAPTER 11

SAMANTHA, WHY DO YOU ALWAYS HAVE TO SPOIL EVERYTHING?

As the days passed Tony and I became more wrapped with each other. At work he was constantly popping down from his lab to see me with colour patterns he wanted checked... and Roger became suspicious.

'Is that new chap after you, Kate?' he asked when Tony had left for the second time that morning.

'Probably,' I replied with a smirk.

'Well he's got a bloody cheek...'

'Why?'

'Don't you remember? He dropped you in it with that old fart Towns,' he replied.

'And what's that got to do with anything?'

'Well...' Roger hesitated and I suspected he was jealous of Tony.

'Go on.'

'Oh, nothing, Kate... it's all up to you,' he said before he shrugged his shoulders and wandered off to the other side of the lab.

Tony sat with me in the canteen every lunch time and chatted while Emma was distinctly put out... but never mind... she'll get over it. We saw each other most evenings and ended up in his flat over the showroom making passionate love before he drove me home. Now this affair was beginning to get very serious so I began to think how I really felt about Tony... he had asked me to marry him on two occasions after we had enjoyed a particularly long sweaty session, finishing with a breath taking climax and lay panting. I had not said 'yes' or 'no' to his proposals but made some lame excuse like, 'I don't think I'm ready yet.'

'So when will you be ready?'

'I'm not sure.'

'Well take your time, Kate, and be sure... I want our

marriage to be successful and not a nine month wonder,' he said.

'So have you been married before?' I asked anxiously.

'No, I haven't... but I know many people who have married for all the wrong reasons and it has always ended in disaster.'

'And what makes you think we won't be the same?'

'Because we have become best friends, Kate... that's the difference,' he replied before giving me a gentle kiss.

'Ah... you're so sweet... as well as being a bloody good bonk!' I said and we both laughed.

'I aim to please,' he giggled and he kissed me again.

After Tony drove me home that night I lay in bed for a long while thinking about him. He was right, we had become good friends and laughed a lot at the same things and that surely is a good foundation to a life long marriage. He certainly met all my needs in bed and was always very attentive, gentle and considerate. I decided he should meet Mother dear... unfortunately it was necessary... but I would keep him out of Satan's Sister's clutches... just in case! I wanted to meet his parents first so when I met him in the canteen the next day, before Emma arrived, I asked him.

'Oh Kate, they would be pleased to see you... I've told them all about you but I was anxious that you wouldn't want to meet them yet... well, at least not until you'd made your mind up about us.'

'Well I almost have,' I replied with a smile.

'And?' he asked and I just smiled.

'Oh come on Kate, please tell me and put me out of my misery,' he pleaded.

'Now should I tell you... or wait for a more romantic time...'

'I'll go mad if you don't tell me!' he interrupted and he looked serious about that.

I hesitated then replied, 'yes of course I'll marry you, my darling.'

'Fantastic!' he shouted before he leaned across and kissed me just as Emma arrived with her tray.

'What's all this?' she asked in surprise as she placed her tray on the table.

Tony glanced up at her and replied, 'we're going to get

married!'

Emma looked shocked and mumbled, 'oh, nice,' before she glared at me.

I wanted to say, 'it's not my fault,' but just smiled... I knew she was jealous but I couldn't help that.

Emma sat opposite me and said, 'well congratulations, Kate... when is the big day?'

'We haven't fixed a date yet,' I replied.

'Will I be a bridesmaid?'

'Of course,' I replied and she gave a little smile.

In the afternoon Tony came into the lab several times with colour patterns for checking and left silly little love notes stuck on the underside. I was reading the last one and giggling when suddenly Roger appeared at my desk and asked, 'what's that, Kate?'

'Oh, its nothing.'

'Are you sure?'

'Yes, quite sure,' I replied firmly.

Roger raised his eyebrows and said, 'I hope that new bloke is not bothering you.'

'No he's not... in fact we're going to get married,' I said with a smile before making my way over to the master colour panel rack and I thought I heard him gasp before he walked away.

Tony agreed that we wouldn't see each other that evening as he was going over to see his parents and I wanted some time alone to think about everything. Not that I was having second thoughts about marrying Tony but I just needed to try and make plans for the future. I arrived home and found Mother dear in quite a good mood so I decided that after dinner I would tell her about Tony.

As she busied herself about the kitchen she was all smiles and when I sat at the table she announced that George was coming over to take her out for the evening.

'Oh, that's nice... where's he taking you?' I asked, thinking my plan to tell her about Tony would have to wait.

'We're going to see a performance of 'The Gigolo Murders'...'

'What?' I interrupted.

'It's a new stage play adapted from a book by an unknown author,' she replied.

'Dear God, it sounds awful and no wonder the author is unknown!'

'Well George has seen it at rehearsals and says it is very good, so I am looking forward to it... now I've cooked us mushroom omelettes for a quick dinner.'

'That's fine.'

'And after we've eaten I must go and get ready, George will be here at seven and he's always on time,' she said with a smile.

After dishing up the omelettes and chips she sat opposite and I asked, 'are you and George getting serious?'

She blushed slightly and replied after finishing her mouthful, 'well, he is very nice and I do like him.'

'But are you serious about him?'

'Well, yes, I suppose I am.'

'And does he feel the same about you?'

'Well he doesn't say... but I think so.'

'That's nice... are you going to get married?'

'Good heavens, Kate... so many questions... what's brought this on?' she asked

'I don't know... I suppose I'm just in a happy mood at the moment.'

'Well that's good to know... and it makes a pleasant change.'

'Now, now, don't spoil it,' I said and she laughed.

George arrived spot on seven and luckily Mother dear was ready to go. He was all smiles and I could see that he did think a lot of her and to her credit she did look very presentable, all made up and wearing her little black dress. They said, 'goodbye' and I replied, 'I hope you have a nice time and enjoy the play.'

'Oh, I'm sure we will... it's very good you know,' said George with a smile. After they left the house I thought, 'he is a nice man... I do hope they get married as I think he'd be quite good as a Dad.'

I phoned Emma and we had a good long chat about Tony and my wedding plans, although I told her that I had not made up my mind about many things yet, as it had been so sudden. After about half an hour we said, 'goodbye,' and I decided to go for a walk in the park in the hope of seeing Eric. It was a lovely warm evening and I felt very happy and contented as I walked along. Somehow my life seemed to have turned a corner and I just hoped that Samantha would not cause me any problems with Tony or anything else for that matter. As I made my way into the park, I glanced over to where I had met Eric before and my heart skipped a beat when I saw him sitting on the bench under the tree. I hurried over to him and he smiled as I got close. He stood up and held out his arms and said, 'Kate,' before I surrendered to his warm embrace and said, 'it's so good to see you, Eric.' We hugged and he replied, 'you too, Kate... and I'm glad that you're happy now.'

'Yes, I am thank you.'

'Good... now let's sit and talk for a while,' he said, releasing me from his strong arms.

'Yes, why not.'

We sat and I waited for him to speak.

'I know that you are now on the right path for your future happiness, which is my concern, but you have one more set back that will change your mind about Samantha...'

'Oh please don't talk about her!' I interrupted.

'I must, Kate...'

'Well I don't want to hear it!' I said firmly.

He remained strangely quiet for a few moments and then said, 'as you wish,' before gazing into the distance.

'So you know about Tony?' I said brightly.

'I do... and you will be very happy together,' he replied and I thought, 'that's good to know because it means that the Devil's Handmaiden won't stick her bloody nose in!'

So I sighed and said with feeling, 'I'm sure we will... he's such a lovely man.'

'He is... and he will be good to you... now I must leave you as I have many things to attend to,' he said before he stood up.

'Will I ever see you again, Eric?'

'Yes... from time to time,' he replied and smiled then walked away towards the far trees and disappeared from view. I returned home in a happy mood but just wondered what he was going to tell me about Samantha... I must try to shut up and listen in future.

The next day at work was just dreadful. The only bright spot was when Tony came into the lab with panels for me to check and left his little love notes stuck on the back of each one for me to read later. I signed off the colour panels and gave them back to him with a smile.

'See you at lunchtime, honey bun... I've lots to tell you,' he said before he hurried away. After a few minutes I saw Nigel Towns arrive and go into Charlie's office. They seemed to be talking angrily and Charlie gave me an occasional glance so I guessed they were talking about me for some reason. I wondered what I might have done to upset the old fart Towns and I hoped it didn't involve Tony. I carried on with my work until Roger suddenly appeared at my desk and said, 'Charlie wants to see you in his office, Kate, I think Towns has been complaining about you.'

'Oh bloody hell,' I half whispered and thought, 'what now?' I was more than anxious when I knocked and went into Charlie's office.

'Sit down, Kate,' he said firmly and I did before glancing at Towns, who looked decidedly unhappy.

'Now Mr Towns has made a complaint about you...'

'Oh, what have I done now?' I interrupted.

'Apparently you are causing his department some problems...'

'For instance?' I asked and glared at Towns.

Charlie cleared his throat and replied, 'you're distracting Tony Simpson from his work and consequently he is not doing what Mr Towns is asking him to do...'

'And the situation is becoming very serious as we are now behind with checking the next batches of colour due to go to Land Rover and Vauxhall!' added Towns angrily.

'Well it's not my fault!'

'My whole department is affected by you, Miss Harris!' said Towns.

'I can't believe that!'

'Well I assure you it is!'

'So what do you want me to do?' I asked, looking at Charlie for an answer.

Before he could say anything Towns said, 'I've instructed Simpson not to come down here any more and in future Mr Talbot will be bringing colour panels for verification and I have asked Mr Butler to appoint someone else to do this work.'

I looked at Charlie and he shrugged his shoulders and I wanted to shout at the injustice of it all... life isn't fair and the old fart was blaming me for everything. I decided to tell them the truth, so I blurted out, 'Tony Simpson and I are engaged to be married and I am sorry if he has been coming to see me more often than you would like but that's how it is!' They both looked stunned and Towns jaw dropped while Charlie smiled and said, 'congratulations, Kate!'

'Thank you.'

Towns pulled himself together and said, 'nevertheless, what I have said still stands, Simpson will not come down in future, so that's an end to it!'

Charlie looked surprised and replied, 'as you wish, Nigel, but I think it's a bit harsh.'

'Think what you like Charlie, good morning,' he said before walking out of the office. Charlie looked at me, smiled and said, 'well perhaps it's all for the best Kate.'

'I hope so.'

'Now as they say, keep calm and carry on.'

'Yes, I will.'

'Good.'

I went back to my desk but as the time went on I became even more angry about what had happened until I began to feel quite unwell. I went to ask Charlie if I could go home, he smiled and said, 'yes, of course, Kate, I can see you're upset.' I thanked him, picked up my bag from under my desk and left work with tears in my eyes.

I arrived home and to my horror found Samantha there eating lunch with Mother dear. Obviously I was not expected but when I asked if there was any lunch for me, Mother dear told me I'd have to wait... and in the mood I was in that didn't go down well so I left them to it and went to my room. About half an hour later Mother dear came up to tell me she had prepared some lunch for me. I went down, sat at the kitchen table and ate while Samantha carried on talking to Mother about Martin, his super car, his flat and bloody well everything else until I could stand it no longer... so I erupted and told her that I hoped Martin dumped her so she would know what it was like! After I had said that, it seemed to spark her off and Satan's Sister went absolutely bloody mad! Her eyes blazed as she shouted, 'listen to me you stupid, jealous, miserable little cow... you've got everything to live for... while I'm dying from bloody breast cancer!'

I was totally shocked and could only whisper, 'oh my God.'

'And I tell you Kate, it doesn't get any worse than this!'

There was a stunned silence before the enormity of what she had told me sunk into my confused mind and I burst into tears, saying, 'oh my God, no... oh, my God, no!'

Samantha said in a quiet voice, 'oh, yes, I'm afraid,' before she burst into tears and sobbed. I immediately got up, went over to her and put my arms around her. She whispered in my ear, 'I'm dying Kate... and soon you'll be free of me for ever.' That made me sob uncontrollably and we held each other tightly while I whispered between sobs, 'I'm so sorry... so dreadfully sorry.'

'So am I, Kate... for all I've done to you... can you ever forgive me?'

'Of course... of course I can... please don't say any more, Sam.'

'Alright,' she whispered.

We held each other for a while and I suddenly realised how very lucky I was. I had lovely Tony and our future together, a reasonable job and my health. Everything Eric had told me was true and I had been blind not to see it... I was always so interested in me and never stopped to think of other people. Sam was right... I was a stupid, jealous, miserable little cow... and now I was desperately sorry.

Oh dear God, if only we could live our lives again and put right all our dreadful mistakes!

CHAPTER 12

I THINK I HAD BETTER FINISH THIS SAMANTHA.

After Samantha's revelation of her suspected breast cancer we waited anxiously for the results of her Mammogram. Mother dear was in pieces over it all and I really thought she wouldn't get through the waiting without some sort of nervous breakdown. I desperately regretted everything I had done and said about Samantha and I was sure my guilty feelings would stay with me forever... especially if she died. I told Mother about my true regrets and she just smiled in a knowing way but she was a worry and I decided that some good news might take her mind of whatever was to come... especially if it was bad. I talked to her about Tony and then announced one evening that we were engaged. She gave me a surprised look and asked, 'you're engaged?'

'Yes I am, and I would like you to meet him,' I replied.

'Oh, I don't think I'm really ready for that at the moment, Kate.'

'I think it would cheer you up.'

She sighed and said, 'I suppose it might do... take my mind off things.'

'I'm sure it will,' I said with a smile.

'Alright, invite him over for Sunday lunch,' and I did just that in the canteen the next day.

'Oh that would be good, honey bun,' Tony said with a smile.

'Lovely, then she can see what sort of man I'm going to marry,' I said.

'Well, your Mother may not be that impressed with my sort...'

'I'm sure she will,' I interrupted.

'I hope so... and will Samantha be there?' he asked.

'No, I don't think so.'

'Oh, that's a shame... you must be very worried about her at the moment.'

'We are... and Mother could do with some good news,' I replied.

'And am I the good news?'
'You certainly are.'
'That's nice to know,' he grinned.

As soon as I arrived home from work that evening, Mother announced that Samantha had phoned to say she would bring Martin over for lunch on Sunday.

'Well that's nice... it means Tony and I will meet him at last,' I said with a smile.

'Yes, and it'll be quite a family get together... because I've invited George as well,' she said with a smile.

'That's lovely, dear,' I replied.

'I think so... after all, we must make the best of any time we have left as a family,' she said as her voice faltered and tears streamed down her cheeks. I put my arms around her and said, 'yes of course, dear, but we don't know about Samantha's condition for sure.'

'I fear the worst, Kate, I really do.'

'I know you do... but we just don't know for certain if she's got cancer... do we?'

Mother shook her head and replied, 'I suppose not.'

'So let's wait and see.'

'Alright,' she said between sniffles and I did feel very sorry for her and my regrets surfaced once more. I wondered how we would get through this without both of us falling to bits, so I decided to go the park as often as I could in the hope of seeing Eric and getting some guidance. I think it is always helpful to have a guardian angel close by in times of personal tragedy... don't you?

After dinner that evening I went for a walk in the park and found Eric there... God bless him! I hurried over to the bench and he stood up to greet me with a smile.

'Hello, Kate.'

'Hello Eric, I'm so glad you're here for me.'

'I'm never far away, I promise you,' he replied and gave me a hug.

'That's good to know.'

'So tell me all about your concerns,' he said as we sat down.

'It's Samantha... she thinks she has cancer but we don't know for certain yet, my Mother is almost out of her mind with worry and I am full of regrets... especially if she really is ill... and dies,' I said as tears began to fill my eyes.

Eric put a comforting arm around me and said, 'you must face the uncertainties of this life with calmness knowing that what will be, will be... no matter how unpleasant.'

'Oh Eric... I just can't cope with this,' I whispered.

'I'm sure you will, Kate.'

'Well I'm glad that you think so.'

'I do.'

'So what should I do now?'

'Just give all the love and support you can to Samantha and your Mother during this uncertain time,' he replied with a gentle smile.

My lips quivered as I said, 'yes, I will, Eric.'

'That's good to hear, Kate.'

'Is there anything else that I should do for them?'

'No, just your love and support will be sufficient,' he replied.

I waited a moment before asking, 'is she going to die?'

'I'm afraid I can't tell you that.'

'Why not?' I asked but he just shook his head and gazed into the distance.

I became angry and said, 'we'll you're supposed to be my guardian angel... so why can't you tell me if my sister is going to die or not?'

'Because such things are beyond my knowledge or control,' he replied.

'For God's sake, Eric!'

'That is precisely it, Kate,' he said with a smile then stood up and walked away.

I sat for a while thinking about what he had said before I made my way home in an unhappy mood. I didn't feel like talking to Mother when I arrived and just said, 'goodnight,' to her while she watched the television and went up to my room. I phoned Emma and said 'hello.'

'Hi, Kate, have you been calling me?'

'No, why?'

'I've only just got in from work,' she replied.
'So where have you been?'
'Well it's a long story... but I am so happy now.'
'Good... so do tell.'
'Well after the accident...'
'Accident?' I interrupted.
'Yes, when I was driving home from work some old scrap metal lorry going the other way dropped a fridge or something on my car.'
'Oh my God!'
'And of course I had to stop quickly as my windscreen was smashed so I couldn't see out and I was scared of crashing into something... I was really frightened but managed to stop and get out.'
'Were you hurt, Em?'
'No, luckily... only a bit shaken up,' she replied.
'Then what happened?'
'Well, the old lorry stopped and the driver came back and said he was very sorry...'
'I should think so too!' I interrupted.
'I didn't know what to do then some other drivers stopped their cars and came to help me.'
'That's was good of them.'
'Yes it was... but just then a police car arrived... and I was very pleased to see it.'
'I bet.'
'The two policemen realised what had happened and came over... one started talking to me while the other one spoke to the lorry driver.'
'So what happened next?'
'Well... the policeman talking to me was absolutely gorgeous...'
'Never mind about him, Em... tell me what happened!'
'He asked me if I was hurt and what had happened... I told him, so he made a note and asked me for my licence and insurance... then he went back to his car to check my details.'
'Go on.'
'Well when he came back he said everything was in order and as my little car was undrivable he said he'd arranged for a

breakdown lorry to come and take it to a garage then he said he'd take me home while the other policeman stayed to examine the lorry.'

'How nice.'

'It was…and when we got to my house I asked him his name… and he said, 'are you going to report me?' and I said, 'I will if you don't come and see me!' he laughed and told me he was PC Mark Nelson and he would contact me in a few days for a full statement… isn't that wonderful?'

'Well that just proves that you never know what's round the corner,' I said with a chuckle.

'Oh, that's so true, Kate… now, as I haven't got my car, will you take me to work in the morning?'

'Of course I will, Em.'

'Thanks, Kate.'

Tony arrived for Sunday lunch before Samantha and Martin, which suited me as he was able to meet Mother without her being distracted by Sam and her dishy Doctor.

'So you're engaged,' Mother purred after I had introduced Tony.

'Yes we are, Mrs Harris,' replied my handsome fiancé.

'Oh, do please call me June,' said Mother with a broad smile so I guessed she approved of Tony… after all, it's not many men who get to call her June.

'I hope you approve, June,' said Tony with a smile.

'Well, I think it's too early to say just yet,' she replied and I thought, 'you misery!'

'Possibly,' he replied with a smile. I was just about to say something to her when the door bell rang and came to my rescue. Mother hurried away and I glanced at Tony who smiled and said in a whisper, 'I'll win her round if necessary.'

I sighed and replied, 'I hope so, but she's always been the bloody same about me,' as Mother came in followed by George. After introductions, Mother said, 'I'll make some coffee and we can chat until Samantha and Martin arrive.' Over coffee Tony and George were very relaxed and talked about the Army, cars and amateur dramatics. I was surprised when Tony said how he enjoyed the 'live' theatre and was full of praise for actors like George who spoke so well. They got on like a house on fire while Mother looked very happy, just listening and smiling when George complimented her on her acting... occasionally she blushed.

Samantha and Martin arrived just before midday and Sam introduced him to us all. When Martin said, 'hello,' to me, my knees went slightly weak as he was simply gorgeous and I could understand why Sam had gone for him in a big way. Mother was in a state of complete ecstasy at the sight of this dishy Doctor and her lips quivered with excitement each time before she spoke. While they were all talking, I looked at Samantha and felt deeply troubled about my jealous deceptions and regretted ever going to New York. My sister was probably suffering with cancer and she could easily die... oh, dear God, I hope not. I began to blame myself for everything and felt a bit depressed until Tony interrupted my thoughts by saying, 'Kate and I intend to get married as soon as it can be properly arranged.'

'That'll cost you!' said Martin with a smile.

'Possibly, but Kate's worth every penny of my parents money,' replied Tony and everyone laughed.

'So are they going to pay for everything?' asked Mother in a relieved tone.

'Yes, they intend to and Dad said it would be a pleasure... but only if you agree, June,' replied Tony. Mother opened her mouth in shock but was unable to say anything for a moment before she blurted out, 'well, yes... I mean... who am I to argue with your Father?'

'That's what my Mum always says,' Tony grinned, and we laughed.

'Well, we must be related because that's exactly what my Mother says to me,' said Martin and more laughter followed. Mother asked Sam and me to help dish up the lunch while leaving the men to carry on chatting. In the kitchen Mother said, 'they all seem to be getting on very well together.'

'They do, Mum,' replied Sam and I added, 'it's so nice.'

'Yes, and we seem to be more of a family once again,' said Mother.

'We do,' I replied as I looked at Samantha and she smiled at me.

'So, what do you think of Martin?' she asked.

Mother replied, 'he's absolutely wonderful, dear.'

'Yes I think so,' said Sam.

'And I do too,' I added.

'Oh, I'm pleased.'

'So when are you getting married?' asked Mother.

'As soon as I know for sure if I've got cancer because we may not have long together,' replied Samantha and I burst into tears. Within a few moments Sam started crying and put her arms around me before Mother came over and cuddled us both, whispering, 'my poor babies... my poor lovely babies.' I started to sob and the tears just streamed down my cheeks... I felt dreadful for being so jealous of Sam... what could I do to put things right between us for ever? Mother started to cry and said tearfully, 'perhaps you should have a double wedding, before its too late.' I stopped sobbing and said in a whisper, 'yes, why not?'

Sam nodded before replying, 'that's a good idea, Kate... I know Martin doesn't want to wait for a moment longer than he has too.'

'Neither does Tony,' I said with a smile as George came in, looked at us in surprise and asked,' whatever's wrong?' and before Mother could answer he added, 'don't tell me you've ruined the lunch, June!' That changed everything and we laughed before she explained to him that we were having a private 'girlie moment' and the roast beef was just ready, so if he would like to open the wine and get the boys to the table, we all could have lunch. George looked relieved, smiled and said, 'yes of course, dear.'

Over the roast beef Sam announced our plan for a double wedding and both fiancé's were absolutely delighted. Mother and George were all smiles and Mother started to ask questions about the arrangements but before we could answer, she gave her opinion. I looked at Samantha, raised my eyebrows, and thought, 'so, nothing new there then,' while Sam smiled at me in a knowing way. I only hoped we could have our weddings before Sam became too ill... it was a terrible thought and I would never forgive myself if that happened. Martin was very kind and gentle with Sam and I could see plainly that he deeply loved my sister. Tony was very positive and supportive with good ideas about how we should do things... he is a treasure. We talked all afternoon and became quite excited by the prospect of our marriages. The conversation turned to where we should go on honeymoon. Mother suggested we should go all together somewhere nice, but not too hot... but we said that the wedding was quite enough and both of us needed to be on our own with our new husbands... and George agreed, bless him. After some tea and a selection of Mother's cakes, Martin and Sam left as he had to be on call later. We said 'goodbye' and for the first time in years I kissed Sam on her cheek and I noticed the tears in her eyes.

'Take care, Sam,' I whispered, she just nodded and replied, 'I will, Kate... but I'll be glad when Thursday's over and I know the results.'

'I'm sure,' I replied thinking about her hospital appointment for a Mammogram. I just prayed at that moment it would be good news.

At work my mind was taken off Samantha's appointment by Emma talking incessantly about PC Mark Nelson. He came to see her on the Saturday morning to take her statement and asked her out for a drink that evening. Apparently they had a wonderful time and Emma was already making plans for their future... she is always so optimistic.

As soon as I arrived home from work on Thursday, Mother told me that Sam had phoned with the news.

'Well?' I asked eagerly.

'She has to wait for the report,' replied Mother.

'And how long will that be I wonder?'

'She was told that it usually takes a week or so.'

'This is torture.'

'It is, but we should soon know.'

I sighed and said, 'I do hope so.'

We waited anxiously for several days before Sam phoned to say that she had seen her Doctor who told her that the Mammogram had proved inconclusive and that she would now have to have a biopsy. I looked at Mother and asked, 'dear God, will this never end?' She shook her head, began to cry and whispered, 'I don't know, Kate, I really don't know.' I made some tea for us, thought about Samantha and wondered if our double wedding was now only becoming a remote possibility.

The following weekend Tony and Martin brought their parents to meet us and have a family get together to discuss the planned weddings. Tony's parents were lovely and so relaxed, while Martin's were just a little patronising at first, but soon came down to earth. Nothing was mentioned about Sam's condition but everyone knew that the weddings' should be as soon as possible. Saint Edmund's, our local church, would be the place we would be married and George said he would arrange that on our behalf with the Reverend Mitchell, whom he knew. The reception was planned to be held at the Windsor Hotel with no expense spared, which made Mother smile. All we had to do now was decide who we would invite to the wedding, our dresses, number of bridesmaids, the cake, our honeymoons, going away outfits and too many hundred and one other things to mention… so no pressure there then!

A week later Sam went into Hospital for her biopsy and we were all on tenterhooks once again. A few days later the results were known and her Doctor contacted her to say that the biopsy showed that the lump was not malignant and she was absolutely clear of any cancer. Mother and I cried with heartfelt relief and had to have several Scotch whisky's to steady ourselves. From that moment on we knew that we could look forward to a wonderful, happy future… and so it was.

We had a splendid double wedding two months later, which went off perfectly and would you believe that Eric appeared, standing at the back of all the guests. He smiled and gave us a little wave as we posed for the official photographs. I wanted to see him before we went off to the reception but he mysteriously disappeared. I asked Sam if she saw him when we were being photographed and she replied with a smile, 'yes, I did… and I wonder if we will ever see him again.'

'Somehow I'm sure we will.'

Tony took me to the West Indies for our honeymoon where we just lazed in the sun on the white coral beaches, swam in the clear blue water, made love most of every night and ate all the wonderful food at our luxury hotel… I was sorry when it was all over and we had to return home. Martin and Sam went to Florida for their honeymoon and had a wonderful time.

After we all arrived home Mother announced that she was going to marry George. We were delighted and the ceremony took place a month later at our local Registry Office in Bracknell. It was a quiet family affair, compared with our double wedding, with just us and a few guests from Am Dram but nevertheless it was a very a happy occasion.

Six months later I was expecting our first baby when Emma and Mark were married. It was a lovely affair and I was so pleased for my optimistic friend and her handsome Policeman, who went on up through the ranks to eventually become a Chief Inspector. They had two sons, David and Charles, who were a great credit to them. Emma always stayed close and we often laughed when we talked about our time with Delacor Paints.

Tony left Delacor Paints after a year and took up his management position in Bracknell Motors paint shop. Our first baby was a boy who we christened Geoffrey and a year later I was expecting once again. This time it was a beautiful little girl who we named Wendy. Tony expanded the business and we did very well, we moved from the flat over the showrooms to a comfortable detached house on the outskirts of the town where we stayed for many happy years. As time went on Samantha and I became very close and I was delighted when she had her first baby, a girl, they named Sophia, followed two years later by a boy, they christened Peter.

Sam often talked about Eric and we sometimes thought we saw

him just fleetingly at a distance and wondered if we would ever see him again... and of course we did. It was at Wendy's wedding when he next appeared standing at the back of the onlookers as my beautiful daughter and her handsome husband, Colin, stepped out of the church. I noticed him first and whispered to Sam that he was here before we looked at him and smiled. He gave a little wave as he smiled back at us... it was so comforting to know he was always close.

The years passed and Tony and I believed that we were very fortunate to be blessed with our children, grandchildren and elderly parents. Although my early life had been consumed with jealousy for Samantha it had all faded away into insignificance and I often thought about Eric's advice. I think we all have a wonderful guardian angel with us... although most of us never actually see them... if only we would listen to their guidance, life would be so much easier!

Follow Eric's next adventure with the attractive young widow...
it is very complicated!

THE FRENCH COLLECTION

AMUSING AND EROTIC TITLES FOR ADULTS

MARSEILLE TAXI by Peter Child

This is a tantalising revelation of the twilight existence of Michel Ronay, a Marseille taxi driver. Every moment of his life is crowded with incident. Compromised by the lecherous women of Marseille, chased by the Police, harassed by the underworld and encouraged by 'gays', his life is a non-stop roller coaster. Stay with him, in his Taxi and feel the heat of the Marseille streets, smell the odours; then have a bath with someone to cleanse your body and mind of the experience.

ISBN : 0-9540910-1-9

AUGUST IN GRAMBOIS by Peter Child

Michel Ronay, a taxi driver, leaves his tiring work driving through the hot, dusty streets of Marseille and heads for the cool tranquillity of his villa in Grambois, for the whole month of August. With his second wife, Monique, her mother, two aunts and Frederik, his stepson, Michel prepares to enjoy a holiday relaxing in the peace and quiet of Provence. So what could possibly disturb him in the ample bosom of his family? His many mistresses perhaps? Or Edward Salvator? Or Jacques and Antone? Or Gerrard? Or….

ISBN : 0-9540910-2-7

CHRISTMAS IN MARSEILLE by Peter Child

Follow Michel Ronay, a taxi driver, around the cold, bright sunlit streets of Marseille in the frantic run up to Christmas. Laugh with him when he discovers that all of his wife's family are coming to stay, cry with him when the Police involve him in undercover work that goes wrong, sympathise with him when his mistresses find out about one another. His life is just a frantic kaleidoscope of drink, sex and the fear of being found out. You will never get in a taxi again without thinking of Michel Ronay.

ISBN : 0-9540910-3-5

CATASTROPHE IN LE TOUQUET by Peter Child

Michel Ronay escapes from the hustle and bustle of Marseille to Le Touquet, where he plans to start a new and prosperous life with his fiancé, Josette. After making business arrangements with his cousin, Henri, everything is set for a relaxed and wonderful future, until he meets Madame Christiane. Monique, Michel's wife, Monsieur Robardes, a solicitor and Henri, are not at all amused by what happens in Le Touquet and Josette wonders if she should ever have bothered to leave Marseille in the first place.

ISBN : 0-9540910-5-1

RETURN TO MARSEILLE by Peter Child

Michel Ronay, a taxi driver, leaves Le Touquet after a failed attempt to start a business with his cousin, Henri. With his fiancé, Josette, he sets off on the long drive back to Marseille, where all his friends and family are waiting for his return. As he drives onto the autoroute heading south he relaxes, knowing that he is going home and nothing can possibly go wrong...

ISBN : 9780-9540910-7-1

Lightning Source UK Ltd.
Milton Keynes UK
UKOW05f0642230114

225083UK00001B/1/P